HERO

JOEL ROSENBERG

A ROC BOOK

For Eleanor Wood,
one of my heroes

ROC
Published by the Penguin Group
Penguin Books USA Inc., 375 Hudson Street,
New York, New York 10014, U.S.A.
Penguin Books Ltd, 27 Wrights Lane,
London W8 5TZ, England
Penguin Books Australia Ltd, Ringwood,
Victoria, Australia
Penguin Books Canada Ltd, 10 Alcorn Avenue,
Toronto, Ontario, Canada M4V 3B2
Penguin Books (N.Z.) Ltd, 182–190 Wairau Road,
Auckland 10, New Zealand

Penguin Books Ltd, Registered Offices:
Harmondsworth, Middlesex, England

First published by Roc, an imprint of New American Library,
a division of Penguin Books USA Inc. Previously published in
Roc hardcover and trade editions.

First Mass Market Printing, November, 1991
10 9 8 7 6 5 4 3 2 1

Printed in the United States of America

Acknowledgments

I'm grateful for the comments and other help I've gotten:

—from my *de jure* copyeditor and *de facto* editor, Mark J. McGarry, who, thankfully, hasn't mellowed with age;

—from my *de jure* and also *de facto* editor, John Silbersack;

—from the other members of the workshop: Bruce Bethke and Peg Kerr Ihinger;

—from David Dyer-Bennet, Beth Friedman and, particularly, Harry F. Leonard (2LT, Connecticut National Guard, Ret.), who helped with the glossary;

—and for the additional help I've gotten from Mickey Zucker Reichert, M.D., and, of course, Felicia.

Metzada, noun—

1. [Archaic] An ancient rock fortress in the Palestine satrapy of Great Persia, about twenty kilometers south of En Gedi. Scene, circa 72-73 A.D., of the final stand of the Jewish zealots against Rome; the defenders killed themselves rather than surrender.

2. The second planet of Epsilon Indi, inhabited primarily by descendants of Jewish refugees from the state of Israel and the North American Federation. Metzada's only significant commercial export is the sale of the services of the Metzadan Mercenary Corps.

3. [Colloq.] The Metzadan Mercenary Corps.

Nueva Terra, noun—

1. The third planet of Tau Ceti, inhabited primarily by descendants of colonists from La France, Deutschland, Greater Britain, Italia and Afrika Del Sud.

2. [Colloq.] Any particularly earthlike planet upon which unmodified terran flora and fauna can readily flourish. (e.g., "Dean's World is a real nueva terra.")

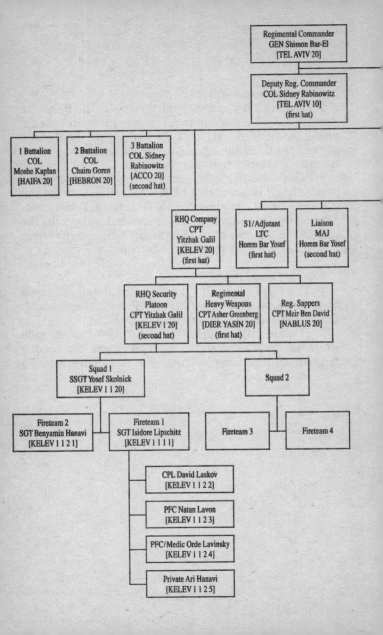

Regimental Commander
GEN Shimon Bar-El
[TEL AVIV 20]

Deputy Reg. Commander
COL Sidney Rabinowitz
[TEL AVIV 10]
(first hat)

1 Battalion
COL
Moshe Kaplan
[HAIFA 20]

2 Battalion
COL
Chaim Goren
[HEBRON 20]

3 Battalion
COL Sidney
Rabinowitz
[ACCO 20]
(second hat)

RHQ Company
CPT
Yitzhak Galil
[KELEV 20]
(first hat)

S1/Adjutant
LTC
Horem Bar Yosef
(first hat)

Liaison
MAJ
Horem Bar Yosef
(second hat)

RHQ Security
Platoon
CPT Yitzhak Galil
[KELEV 1 20]
(second hat)

Regimental
Heavy Weapons
CPT Asher Greenberg
[DIER YASIN 20]
(first hat)

Reg. Sappers
CPT Meir Ben David
[NABLUS 20]

Squad 1
SSGT Yosef Skolnick
[KELEV 1 1 20]

Squad 2

Fireteam 2
SGT Benyamin Hanavi
[KELEV 1 1 2 1]

Fireteam 1
SGT Isidore Lipschitz
[KELEV 1 1 1 1]

Fireteam 3

Fireteam 4

CPL David Laskov
[KELEV 1 1 2 2]

PFC Natan Lavon
[KELEV 1 1 2 3]

PFC/Medic Orde Lavinsky
[KELEV 1 1 2 4]

Private Ari Hanavi
[KELEV 1 1 2 5]

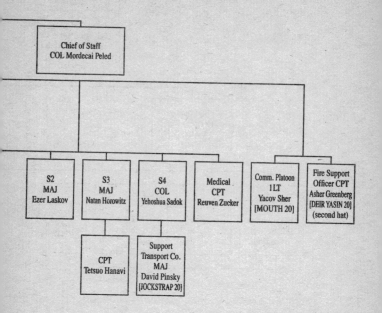

**Partial Table of Organization
30th Regiment Metzadan Mercenary Corps
(Operational)**

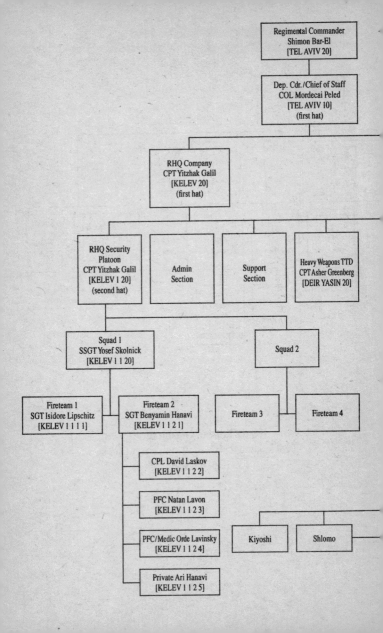

Regimental Commander
Shimon Bar-El
[TEL AVIV 20]

Dep. Cdr./Chief of Staff
COL Mordecai Peled
[TEL AVIV 10]
(first hat)

RHQ Company
CPT Yitzhak Galil
[KELEV 20]
(first hat)

RHQ Security
Platoon
CPT Yitzhak Galil
[KELEV 1 20]
(second hat)

Admin
Section

Support
Section

Heavy Weapons TTD
CPT Asher Greenberg
[DEIR YASIN 20]

Squad 1
SSGT Yosef Skolnick
[KELEV 1 1 20]

Squad 2

Fireteam 1
SGT Isidore Lipschitz
[KELEV 1 1 1 1]

Fireteam 2
SGT Benyamin Hanavi
[KELEV 1 1 2 1]

Fireteam 3

Fireteam 4

CPL David Laskov
[KELEV 1 1 2 2]

PFC Natan Lavon
[KELEV 1 1 2 3]

PFC/Medic Orde Lavinsky
[KELEV 1 1 2 4]

Private Ari Hanavi
[KELEV 1 1 2 5]

Kiyoshi

Shlomo

Partial Table of Organization
30th Regiment Metzadan Mercenary Corps
(Administrative)

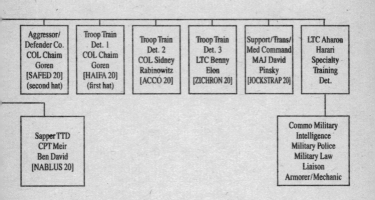

| Aggressor/ Defender Co. COL Chaim Goren [SAFED 20] (second hat) | Troop Train Det. 1 COL Chaim Goren [HAIFA 20] (first hat) | Troop Train Det. 2 COL Sidney Rabinowitz [ACCO 20] | Troop Train Det. 3 LTC Benny Elon [ZICHRON 20] | Support/Trans/ Med Command MAJ David Pinsky [JOCKSTRAP 20] | LTC Aharon Harari Specialty Training Det. |

Sapper TTD CPT Meir Ben David [NABLUS 20]

Commo Military Intelligence Military Police Military Law Liaison Armorer/Mechanic

Ezer Hanavi, His Wives, and Children

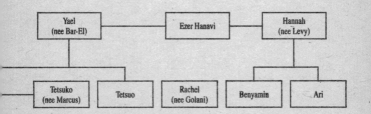

| Yael (nee Bar-El) | Ezer Hanavi | Hannah (nee Levy) |

| Tetsuko (nee Marcus) | Tetsuo | Rachel (nee Golani) | Benyamin | Ari |

PART ONE

AMBUSH

CHAPTER 1

Spare Parts

He was a spare part, newly machined and shoved into a place where he didn't quite fit, where he never would fit.

The cargo bay stank of plastics and oil and sweat and his own fear. Ari Hanavi tried to keep his trembling under control as the skipshuttle took another lurch. Gripping the arms of the acceleration frame helped, but only a little. He shifted a centimeter or so to his left, as though huddling up against the smoothly curving wall could offer some protection.

It couldn't. Not to him, and not to more than seven hundred other men crammed into two decks in the cargo bay of the skipshuttle, packed tightly into rows of acceleration frames divided by the same kind of steel that divided the lower deck from the upper, all divided from the screaming air outside by only a few thin layers of titanium aluminide.

Ari couldn't stop thinking about how thin those layers were.

Beyond Benyamin's acc frame, Yitzhak Slepak grumbled something. Ari didn't pay him much attention, although, packed in as tightly as they were, he probably could have made out his words despite the noise.

Slepak was only a couple of thousand hours older than Ari, but he tried to act like it was years. He was always grumbling about something, probably trying to sound like a man instead of a virgin.

Some of the men complained a lot. It helped, they said.

It wouldn't have helped Ari any. All it would have done was remind Benyamin and the other three that he wasn't experienced. He wasn't even a PFC. He was just a very green private, a seventeen-year-old virgin, and he didn't fit in, he'd never fit.

There was something that the rest of them didn't know, not yet: Ari Hanavi was a coward.

If they knew, everybody he loved would turn against him.

No, not if. *When* they knew. . . .

His brothers, both of his mothers, the Sergeant, even Miriam. If they found out. When they found out. *But maybe not yet. Please, not yet.*

The whine of the outside air got louder, now easily loud enough to drown out casual conversation. Ari tried to force himself to relax.

The Nueva Terra job was just going to be cadre, he told himself, the regiment configured for training, the platoon Ari was a very junior member of acting as a mainly token security element. It was likely he would spend most of his time standing guard duty at a Casalingpaesan training facility a thousand klicks from the war zone while the regiment turned Casa virgins into soldiers.

At best, he would have some time off on a new world while the senior staff took the trained and tuned Casa division into the field. At worst, the RHQ security platoon would accompany Division HQ into the field, and perhaps Ari would have to help his brother debrief a returning Casalingpaesan patrol or two. More likely, he would just help teach some Casalinguese to do it.

Easiest thing in the world. No courage needed, no warrior's reflex required.

Please.

Benyamin muttered something; Ari couldn't quite make it out. Ari's fingers were groping at the air under his chin where his mike should have been before he remembered that he wasn't wearing his headset. The captain of the skipshuttle didn't want any RF interference—much less the seemingly random spurts of packed and coded packets—from inside the skipshuttle: all their comm gear was stowed away in their chestpacks.

"Say again?"

"Relax," Benyamin said. "It'll be okay."

That was what his big brother was always saying, and when he wasn't saying it, he was making it so.

It wasn't just that Benyamin was fifteen years older than Ari, although that made a difference. It wasn't just his size: Benyamin was actually a centimeter shorter than Ari's 176 and only a bit thicker, massing about ninety-five kilograms to Ari's eighty-five—but Ari always thought of him as a giant of a man, even when he stood next to Dov.

Benyamin wasn't just his big brother, he was *the* big brother, forty days older than Kiyoshi had been. They all said that Ari looked like a younger version of Benyamin, but that was nonsense. There was a lot of nonsense that was passed around the family. Like the way that the other boys called Ari "the General," as if he'd be an officer some day.

It was all stupid. Ari didn't look anything like his big brother. Benyamin's jaw was firm, his head covered with tight curls of brown hair, his gaze level and even. Ari shook all the time. While Ari couldn't even move the tight grimace that his face had become, the smile that covered Benyamin's pleasantly ugly face was warm, even in the harsh green light of the overhead glows.

As Tetsuo always said, Benyamin's smile didn't have

anything to do with an emotion; that smile was a report. It said: I'll handle it, I'll take care of it. I've got it all under control, don't worry for a moment.

How can you take care of your little brother being a gutless coward?

There was no way out.

Ari shifted fractionally in his acc frame, held there more by the straps than by what little weight there was. He couldn't do more than twitch: there was no real back to what would have been a couch or chair in a civvy skipshuttle. What would have been the frame for a seat cushion was built differently, to hold his loosened buttpack; another steel frame, replacing the back of the seat, supported his backpack.

All of them were like that, held into their little niches like a set of specialized tools in a preformed case. Which was, in a sense, what they were.

Lots of them were spare parts, sometimes new, sometimes cannibalized from other units. Benyamin, Alon, Laskov, Lavon, Lavinsky had all been in the old Fifth Regiment, under Becker. The regiment had been cut to pieces on Kinshasakisasa, then cut to pieces after Kinshasakisasa, its colors retired, the survivors shuffled into other sections, platoons, companies, battalions and regiments.

The skipshuttle screamed as they descended, 750 men and virgins packed into a crowded, smelly space that would have been tight for half that many.

Some were taking the ride a lot more casually than Ari was; the soldier in the acc frame directly above him was patiently drumming his bootheels against the footrests. By the TO, it should have been Pinhas Gevat, Kelev One Two Four Five, Ari's equivalent in Section Two and one of the other five Kelev virgins—but half the time you didn't get the right spot. Ari's fireteam had been split up; he and Benyamin were two rows away from Laskov, Lavon and Lavinsky.

He pumped first his right leg, then his left, trying to

keep from getting cramps. Ari had good Metzadan circulation, but his blood tended to pool in his chest and head in zero gee. Like the low-gee acne speckling his face, the cramps were a common complaint. He had learned in school and in training that both would go away after he was down—the cramps within a day or two; the acne within a week or so.

He rubbed at his face. Nothing to be done about the acne. A brisk sprint on a running ring would prevent the cramps—that was what he had done on the troopship—but there wasn't room in the skipshuttle even to swing a knife.

His rifle was clamped across his lap, holding it and him in place. His hands fell to the clamps, fingers resting lightly on the cold aluminum. It would only take two quick pulls to release it, and he had never liked being held down. Back when he was a boy, wrestling with his brothers, that had been the way they could always make him furious: just pin him down and hold him. If he didn't concentrate he would panic, he would lose control and—

No. Stop it. He forced himself to breathe slower, to at least simulate relaxing. There was nowhere to go. What could he do? Rattle around between Benyamin and the wall, or bounce up and down between his acc frame and the one above him?

His right hand, as though of its own volition, came up to his backpack's release, right over the sternum, just under the swell of his chestpack, while his left fell to the release of his buttpack. Two quick pulls and he would be free.

It would be good to be free.

Benyamin caught the movement and his smile broadened. "Really," he shouted over the almost deafening roar. "Everything will be fine."

He was right, of course. If anything went wrong, there was nothing they could do. Which was why they were all clamped in tight and were supposed to just sit still. It only stood to reason.

If only his palms would listen to reason; the grips of his acc frame were sweat-slick.

"Hey, come *on*." Benyamin smiled. "Would you rather be here in the first shuttle, or waiting up in zero gee with the other two loads?"

Ari shrugged. He really didn't mind zero gee.

"Relax," Benyamin, said. "If something were to happen," he shouted, "at, say, Mach 5—I said, if we take a glancing hit from some local artillery—we'd be dead, spread over the sky, before we even felt it."

That was supposed to reassure Ari. Benyamin was like that. Ari had more than a sneaking suspicion that despite Ari's supposedly better training, Benyamin's six campaigns had taught him that the possibility of sudden death was reassuring. Or maybe it was the series of four puckered scars that ran from his fused right wrist and up that arm, almost to the elbow. Benyamin had never told him how he got those. The only thing he would say was that there was nothing that Ari could learn from it because not being a damn fool is something you had to learn for yourself. He—

The lights went out.

A few rows behind him somebody screamed, and the scream became a chorus of hoarse shouts.

Ari Hanavi clamped his hands around the stock of his Barak assault rifle, shut his eyes tightly and waited to die.

"Tel Aviv Ten. Ease *up*, all of you." Colonel Peled's crisp, cold voice, broadcast over the wall speaker high above Ari's head, cut through the shouts and the cries. "It's just the fucking *lights*."

Even in cadre regiments, Metzada generally tries to get the most out of its senior field grade officers, and Shimon Bar-El worked that tradition hard: Peled was the regimental chief of staff and deputy commander, mainly responsible for running the company-sized Support/Transport/Medical Command. He had been with Uncle Shimon even longer than Galil had, although not as long as Dov and Avram.

Nobody had been with Shimon as long as Dov and Avram.

"There's no need to be loud, Mordecai." Shimon Bar-El's voice was dry and distant over the speakers, its lazy calmness reassuring. "After all, there were no shouts just now. I am not going to believe that Metzadan soldiers are afraid of the dark. And the Casas aren't paying us for screams," he said.

"Not ours," Captain Yitzhak Galil said with a boyish laugh. "Shit, if I got paid for every time I screamed, I'd have retired ten years ago."

"Fifteen-year-olds don't retire," Bar-El said.

The other two laughed, joining in on the weak joke. The general, his chief of staff and the commander of the regimental HQ company were a well-polished comedy act, and their routines had been refined by frequent use. Or overuse.

The noisy whine of the outside air intensified even further as their weight started to press them down.

The lights flickered on for a moment, then dimmed.

"Just what we need," Benyamin said. "A funny RHQ company commander."

In front of Ari, Tzvi Hirshfield leaned his head back against the mesh to talk to Benyamin. "Hey, remember the time on Rand? Back when he'd just made sergeant in the Fifth?"

"With the jecty and the goat? Yeah. Asshole."

Hirshfield shrugged. "Well, *I* thought it was funny."

"You would."

The lights went out again, then came back on. This time there were no shouts, only the scream of the air outside.

Ari leaned toward Benyamin. "I thought you said Galil's good."

"When there're shots going off, he's supposed to be pretty good." His brother shrugged. "But I can get real tired of this shit in garrison."

Which is where they were going to be for the foreseeable future. Cadre work is, by definition and in practice, garrison work.

"Now, martinets aren't too bad," Benyamin went on, warming to the subject. "I can take a martinet; they're predictable and—"

"You can take a martinet? Bull*shit*." Hirshfield grunted. "Tell that to Simchoni."

"Simchoni? A bit strict, maybe, but I wouldn't call him a martinet."

"Not Ezra. Sol."

"That shithead." Benyamin scowled, then shrugged. "Rest in peace."

A passenger skipshuttle would have had an accelerometer mounted high on the forward bulkhead for the convenience and relief of passengers, so they could see that their weight was only returning, not growing and growing. . . .

Watching the accelerometer was supposed to control the sense of panic you get when your stomach tells you that you're getting more weight than you're supposed to. Then again, a passenger skipshuttle probably wouldn't have hit even two gees for a Nueva Terra landing. Ari was sure they were hitting four—better than three times the grav on Metzada. Like having three of his brothers sitting on his shoulders and chest.

Benyamin's chuckle sounded forced as the lights flickered and then came back on, while their weight began to ease. "Told you it was nothing," he said.

Beyond him, Yitzhak Slepak grunted. "Wonder if that was the pilot having a bit of fun with us," he said. "I might look him up later."

"Shut up," Benyamin said, strangely without heat.

If Ari had mouthed off like that, Benyamin would have been jumping up and down on him, perhaps literally, but ever since the regiment had boarded the skipshuttle on Rand, he had noticed that the men treated Yitzhak and a few other boys more gently than most of the virgins.

Didn't make any sense, but Ari didn't ask about it and they didn't talk about it. One of the first things they taught you was that you'd usually be told what you need to know, and when you needed to know it. Questions weren't really discouraged—but they had better be pertinent.

Benyamin bit his lip, considering, as the roar of the skipshuttle started to lessen. "Final approach; the grav feels about right."

"You sure?"

Benyamin didn't smile. "No. I don't have that kind of feel. Dov would know. Want me to get up and ask him?"

Ari didn't answer. Dov Ginsberg frightened him, a lot, and he was sure he had only heard some of the stories.

"Tel Aviv Ten. We are *three* minutes from touchdown." Peled's voice, businesslike as always, came over the speaker. Peled couldn't talk over a comm system without coming down hard on at least one word every sentence; Ari could never quite figure which word it would be. "Estimate of *fif*teen minutes rollout and cooldown before they unlock us—and for those of you who have forgotten, that means the heat shields will still be *hot*. You section leaders will keep your people the hell *away* from the skin. Support/Transport Command will deploy administrative, repeat administrative—and keep *cool*, people. In case anybody's memory is slipping or their fingers are getting itchy, this is not, repeat *not*, a hot LZ, and we will not have any accidents."

"Exactly right." Uncle Shimon's voice came on in quiet counterpoint. "Headquarters is administrative;

all of Regimental HQ Company is operational—not just Kelev."

Ari didn't understand the reason for that, although he didn't mind. It meant that the headquarters security force, call sign Kelev, would get priority for getting off the bus to Camp Ramorino and would be the last ones on.

"Additionally," Shimon went on, "Heavy Weapons Troop Training Detachment and Sapper TTD deploy operational."

"Tel Aviv Ten." Peled, again, "That means that Nablus and Deir Yasin will monitor the RHQ company freak. What was that? Hang *on*. Louder, Meir; I can't hear you."

There was a pause.

"It's a fair question," Shimon Bar-El said. "Repeat it."

Ari looked to Benyamin. "Which Meir?"

Benyamin shrugged. "Probably Meir Ben David, Nablus Twenty himself."

"Tel Aviv *Ten*. Yes, sir. Nablus Twenty wants to know what good it's going to do to put a sapper platoon—"

"Accurately, please," Bar-El said, gently correcting.

"—what fucking good it's going to do to put a fucking *sapper* platoon and a fucking heavy mortars platoon fucking operational until they've fucking gotten their fucking groceries and fucking *tubes*. I think I missed a 'fucking' in there."

"From what I hear, that'd be the first time, Mordecai. And it's a fair question," Shimon Bar-El said. "Two answers. First, you're operational because I want you off the buses first when we get there—your equipment should be already at Camp Ramorino, and I want your I&I before we turn in for the night. Secondly, you're operational because the way it works is that I'm the general and I get to decide how we do things."

A laugh echoed in the crowded bay.

"But relax, people. This is the easy part."

The last moments took forever. Automatically, Ari had tapped his right thumbnail against his left when Peled announced the time to touchdown—it was no warrior's reflex, but it was a trained one. His primary noncombatant assignment was as assistant to the RHQ company clerk, and one thing they taught clerks early and well is that timing is everything.

So he knew it was three minutes, but it was a long three minutes until the pilot pulled the nose up and set the craft down gently, like it was a passenger skipshuttle or something. Ari decided that a hard landing would have been as tough on the pilot as on the cargo.

The skipshuttle's wheels screamed. "We're down," Galil said.

"Like we can't hear," Benyamin said. He really didn't like Galil.

"Phones on," Shimon said.

Ari took his helmet off, set it down on his lap, on top of his rifle, and pulled his phone out from his chestpack, slipping the cup over his right ear, tightening the headband with one quick pull, spinning the sound louvers fully open with his right hand as he brought the mike down in front of his lips with his left hand. He gave five quick puffs into the mike to bring it into test mode; it gave a friendly quintuple chirp in his right ear. He slipped his helmet back on, snapped the faceplate down to make sure that it locked into place, then unlocked it and pushed it back up and into the crown of the helmet.

"Bar-El on All Hands One," Shimon said. "Test mode, all hands." He wasn't the only Bar-El in the Thirtieth Regiment—most of the Thirtieth was of the clan, and maybe five percent was of the family—but his idea of comm discipline, for himself, didn't require him to identify himself properly. It's called a double standard; Shimon Bar-El was a lot like that.

Ari puffed; his phone chirped.

They all started repeating "Testing, testing," a babel of voices in his ears.

"Tel Aviv Ten to all hands." Peled's call sign cut through the sound. "Sound off."

Ari quickly puffed for the fireteam freak.

"Everybody on?" Benyamin asked.

"Kelev One One Two Five," Ari said, blushing when Orde Lavinsky, the team medic, came on with an informal, "Orde here."

"Natan," Lavon said.

"Laskov," David Laskov said.

"Okay; everybody on to Platoon."

Ari puffed for the platoon freak. The first fireteam, Lipschitz's, was sounding off. Ari waited until he heard "Kelev One One One One; team freak nominal."

"Kelev One One Two Five," Ari said. Number five in the second team of the first platoon of the RHQ company, call sign Kelev. The others were *supposed* to use that, even in private conversation on the team freak.

"Kelev One One Two Four," Orde said, and the call was passed down the line.

Ari took his time puffing back to the company freak in time to hear the TTD commanders sound off.

"Deir Yasin Twenty; we're nominal," said Asher Greenberg, the commander of the heavy mortar training detachment.

"Nablus Twenty," Meir Ben David grunted, for the sappers. "I've got two fucking sets out. I'll have the fucking spares up in five minutes. Otherwise it's fucking nominal."

"I don't understand him." Benyamin bent his head close to Ari's, their helmets almost touching. "The man can set charges to cut a tree—any tree, any world— off at the base, flip it up into the air and set it down across a road, neat as you please, but he can't keep on the air to save his life."

"Kelev One Twenty and Kelev Twenty," Galil said,

reporting both as First Platoon's leader, Kelev One Twenty, and as Kelev Twenty, the company commander. For administrative purposes while traveling, the two training detachments were considered part of the security element and configured as grossly oversized platoons under RHQ company. It wouldn't be the way Shimon Bar-El would take them into combat, but it was a handy means of organizing them while they loaded people on and off buses. "Nablus has two sets down," Galil said, reporting. "Otherwise, communications nominal. ET five minutes to nominal."

"Kelev Eleven Thirty-One," a dry voice said. "Hey, Kelev Twenty, that was real interesting and all, but maybe you should try that on a channel where the general is likely to hear it? You just reported that the company's okay on the Company freak. We kind of already knew that, sort of."

"Shit. And blush," Galil said. "I screwed up; I had both freaks open. Sorry, people."

"No problem, Yitzhak."

"That's easy for *you* to say, David," Galil said. There was a click.

By the time they were done testing, the skipshuttle had rolled to a stop. Distant machinery kachunked against the skin. With a whirr and a hiss and a clank, the forward hatch eased open.

Ari's ears popped. Forward and above his head, sunlight splashed into the dark of the crowded cabin.

"Tel Aviv Ten to all hands," Peled said. "Let's *move* it, people. By the numbers, we *will* unload, and smartly. You *will* use full grips and lanyards; pass the wrenches to the sides."

Unloading a full troop skipshuttle was supposed to take a solid hour—the men were packed in tightly, and after the top tier unloaded themselves it generally took the port loaders too long to unbolt and remove the top tier.

Administrative or operational, Shimon never liked

having his people locked in, waiting on the pleasure or in the sights of others. Wrenches, tied to short lanyards, were ritualistically passed down to those of them up against the hull. Benyamin smacked one into the palm of Ari's hand.

Eager to get out, Ari let discipline slip for a moment; he started to rise, but Benyamin shook his head. "No. Tie it down."

He clipped the lanyard to a free ring on the front of his shirt, and waited while the upper tiers cleared themselves out.

"Eighth row, second tier, prepare to unbolt."

The soldiers two rows in front of them started moving. Ari released himself from his seat, passed his rifle over to Benyamin—dropping the wrench in the process; it was just as well it was tied to him or it might have dropped through the mesh and hit somebody on the bottom tier—and tightened the strap of his buttpack as he rose.

He unbolted the rack. Eager hands above grabbed it and stacked it; he traded the wrench for his rifle.

"Eighth row, *go*." They scrambled up to the narrow walkway and filed out of the dark.

And then the light hit him.

It hit him hard, like a physical shock. Which was understandable, he decided. He grew up in Metzada's underground corridors, under the glows of home. But Metzada is a dull world, of grays and browns, and the glows are a harsh, actinic light.

The regiment had just come off training exercises on DelAqua's Continent on Rand, but the northern part of DelAqua is a horrible joke on the watery name: it's a desert, and not the gentle rolling sand dunes in the southern part of Eretz Israel, but dry, cracked ground, broken only by squat, jagged mountains. All dark reds and browns and grays, sometimes eerily pretty at dawn or sunset, but mainly ugly under the dirty brown sky.

He had seen the holos in school, of course, but

when you're really there, it's different. He knew that an analytical illumeter would say that the hue of the holos isn't an angstrom off that of reality, that the saturation is accurate to a thousandth of a percent, that the luminance doesn't vary by a decilambert, but he didn't care what an instrument said: it looks different when you're there.

Portocielo Grossi was a gray island rising out of a sea of color. Off to the north, the rolling hills were covered with an intricate blanket of luxurious blue-green, interwoven with red and yellow threads and slashed by weaving roads. To the west, a field of golden grain rippled gently, lovingly, in the wind. To the south, a shining lake of an impossibly deep blue beckoned invitingly.

The west wind brought smells of something delicate and floral, mixed with the warm brown smells of grasses baking in the sun, and a hint of a distant, acrid odor that would have been overpowering if it were any stronger.

It was all so beautiful he almost could have cried.

Benyamin touched his arm. "Down the stairs," he said, gruffly. "Something, isn't it?" he added, his voice soft.

"Move it, people, *move* it," Peled shouted, not bothering to use a mike when his bullhorn voice could serve. "We have ground transportation due here in just *one* minute. We *will* not keep them waiting."

They assembled on the concrete below; at a gesture from Galil, RHQ company shuffled off to one side.

"What I want to know," Lavon said, "is how we all can be locked up in the same shuttle for the same time, in the same size seats, and I come out looking and feeling like I've been hung in a meat locker and Galil looks like he just stepped out of a training holo."

Lavinsky chuckled. "You got a point. Complete to the rifle stuck up his ass."

Ari looked over at the captain. Yitzhak Galil stood

too stiffly on the tarmac, his face and khakis unwrinkled. His short hair was slicked down and neatly parted, his beard and mustache closely trimmed. The only note out of harmony were his sleeves, rolled up to reveal arms thickly covered with black hair. Even so, the sleeves were rolled up neatly.

"What do you bet he combs his forearms?" Benyamin asked.

"All Kelev units," Galil called out, "check your weapons." He was unslinging his own assault rifle as he spoke.

Benyamin gathered his squad around him. "Lock and load," he said, unfolding his Barak's metal stock.

It was mechanical, something Ari had done a hundred thousand times: flick the selector all the way forward to full automatic with the right thumb, then pull it back through five-shot, three-shot, single-shot to safe; check to see that the rear sight was obscured by the brown shutter that indicated the weapon was on safe; then brace the butt of the weapon against his belly, under his chestpack, while he reached up and took a magazine from his pack—the ammo on his web belt was to be used last, not first; the chestpack could be disposed of when empty—and slammed it into the receiver with a satisfying, rippling click.

His hand fell to the charging bolt, but he caught himself and let the rifle hang from its patrol sling.

"Hey, Orde?" Benyamin raised an eyebrow. "You special?"

Lavinsky, the medic, hadn't unfolded the stock or used his patrol sling; he had loaded his rifle, then hung it on the right side of his H-belt, balancing the load of his medical kit on the left. "It's easier this way," he said.

"Tell you what," Benyamin said. "I'll get you a nice medic's brassard—Christian cross and all—and we can make you a real good target."

Lavinsky laughed as he tugged at his scraggly black

beard. "Okay, adoni, okay." He took his Barak from his belt, unfolded the stock and rigged the rifle patrol style, the strap running over one shoulder, across the back of his neck, leaving the rifle hanging in front, just above his waist. "Not to worry, eh?" He bounced experimentally on the balls of his feet. "Feels good to be back, eh?"

Benyamin shrugged. "My first time here. I was in the 101st RCT when the Fifth was on Nueva. The 101st was broken up five years ago, not six."

"Not in '26?"

"Honest. It was in '27. I was there. Trust me."

It was Lavinsky's turn to shrug. "Shit. All blurs together after a while. 'See strange new worlds, experience exciting cultures and meet strange and interesting creatures—' "

" '—and kill them,' " Benyamin finished. "That joke was old when I was young."

"Hey, to an old man like me, you're still young." The medic was the oldest member of the squad, well into his forties. Probably getting ready for retirement, Ari decided. For a private soldier—even one with a medic's warrant—it would be either retirement at forty-five or back to school to get a medician's caduceus, or both. Medicians could make a decent living on Metzada, although not as good as combat pay or even cadre pay allowed. But Orde Lavinsky only had one wife, and both of their children were grown; he might not mind moving to a smaller flat.

Ari took a moment to look around the landing field. Civilian, not military: Thousand Worlds Commerce Department type. Facilities above ground, tall buildings of concrete, glass and steel poking hundreds of meters into the sky, protected by evenly spaced skywatches at the perimeter. Laser launcher near the south wall, the twin mushrooms of its power plant sending white puffs of steam into the afternoon air.

A gleaming tractor, looking more like an oversized

child's toy than anything else, clanked toward the skip-shuttle, dragging a long, thick power cable across the hot tarmac.

"HQ, spread out," Peled said, gesturing them all away. "We're operational, remember?"

"Nah," Shimon Bar-El said. "Bunch up and save them the trouble."

They spread out.

Shimon Bar-El wasn't much to look at, as he stood on the hot tarmac, considering the horizon between puffs on his tabstick. He was a decidedly average-looking man in his late forties, a bit less stocky and broad-shouldered than was usual for somebody raised under Metzada's one point two standard gees, his close-cropped hair more a faded blond than gray, his nicotine-stained stubby fingers always wrapped around a stylo or near the keys of a typer, when they weren't playing with a lit tabstick.

He smiled very rarely and very little.

His rumpled khakis were usually caked white with salt under the sweat-stained armpits, although he wore no field pack, carried no heavy gear at all—just a durlyn briefcase, which he handed to Avram Stein as he turned to confer with Galil.

A holster hung from the web belt pulled tightly around his gut, but it always carried tabsticks, not a pistol. He was famous for being a terrible shot—he was even worse than Ari, and that was pretty bad. Bar-El didn't carry any sidearm except a knife—a line infantryman's utility knife, not a skirmisher's Fairbairn dagger.

Shimon Bar-El dipped two fingers into his holster and pulled out a tabstick, puffing it to life as his eyes took in the field.

His eyes were special. Not just because he had the epicanthic folds that some Metzadans had inherited from the few Nipponese who had been exiled along with the children of Israel. That wasn't uncommon.

The eyes were special because they could see anything.

That's what they all said. Shimon Bar-El's eyes came to rest on Ari's for a moment. Ari was sure that the general could see that he was a coward, that he was going to disgrace his family, his clan, his world, his people.

But then the eyes turned away to two men standing next to him, Avram Stein and Dov Ginsberg, and Shimon's expression softened faintly.

Dov was a head taller than Shimon and almost twice as broad across the shoulders. Dov's hairline came to within a centimeter of his heavy brows as he stood squinting in the bright sunlight. He was an ugly man, but not pleasantly so, like Benyamin; the proportions were all wrong. His arms were too long, as was his torso. His legs would have looked normal on a shorter man, but they looked almost comical on him, although nobody laughed at Dov.

Avram was skinny, too skinny for a Metzadan. And he wasn't Metzadan, not by birth. Neither was Dov; they were both survivors of the Bienfaisant affair, of Shimon's Children's Crusade, halfway around this planet and a quarter of a century ago.

Ari had heard about it, but he wasn't sure he would have believed that it was possible even for Shimon Bar-El to have carved his way through enemy lines with nothing more than a couple hundred child-soldiers . . . except that there were six survivors—seven, if you included Shimon—who had lived to tell the tale. Not that they talked about it much.

Peled's rifle barrel must have come a degree too close to pointing at Shimon; Dov batted it away with the butt of his shotgun. Peled started to complain, then grimaced and shrugged apologetically.

"Dov, be still," Avram said.

Dov ignored him. He wasn't open to reason about people pointing guns at Shimon.

Dov lightly, reverently, like a rabbi lifting the silver pointer to read a spread Torah scroll, tapped Shimon on the shoulder, then pointed when Shimon looked up.

"Thanks, Dov. Transportation's almost here," Shimon said, raising his voice. "I was wondering if we were going to have to stand in the hot sun until the other groups were down." That would be several hours away, at least; there were two other full shuttles still skyside, in the TW troop transport, and they needed the same window that the first skipshuttle had used to bring down HQ, the Support/Transport/Medical Company, and the Sapper and Heavy Weapons troop training detachments.

Four buses hissed over the tarmac, the blast from their plenum chambers sending sand and grit whipping into the air, then one by one settled down onto their rubberized skirts. They were wide, squat vehicles, windowed all the way along their length, windows covered with a drab green mesh.

A slim man—a Casa light colonel if Ari was correctly reading the broken golden stripes on the collar of his tailored fatigues—got out of the nearest bus and was guided over to Shimon. At Shimon's nod, Avram pointed a microphone at him. When in doubt, fill the troopies in.

Ari puffed for All Hands Two, the selectable all hands channel.

"Tenente Colonello Sergio Chiabrera, senior aide-de-camp to Generale DiCorpo d'Armata Massimo Colletta," the Casa said, drawing himself to attention, and saluting crisply.

Lavon snorted. "He does that real nice."

"Shut up," Benyamin said, without heat.

"Generale Shimon Bar-El? Very good, Excellency. My orders," Chiabrera said, producing a sheaf of flimsies. "We can have your men at camp in about an hour. Generale DiCorpo d'Armata Colletta sends word that he would like the pleasure of your company at table tonight—as soon as your men are settled in, of course. We dine at the twentieth hour, local time."

"I'll be there," Bar-El said. Some of the Metzadans had started to drift over toward the bus. "Mordecai," he said.

"Tel Aviv *Ten*. As you *were*, people," Peled snapped out. "Let's pretend we're all soldiers, shall we?"

Shimon jerked his chin toward Galil. "Check it out."

Galil picked out Benyamin and two other fireteam leaders by eye. Ari followed his brother up the ramp and into the darkness of the second bus. It wasn't anything special, he decided; just a converted civvy vehicle, turned into military transportation by the addition of mesh grenade screens to the windows.

Benyamin rapped a ring against the nearest window. "Glass. Shit."

"Kelev One One Two Two," Laskov said. He was all the way in the back. "Somebody's idea of cleaning out this thing was to shove a bunch of old bottles and tools under the back benches."

"We'll clean it out, then move out," Shimon Bar-El's distant voice said.

"My apologies, of course, Generale, but I'm afraid I don't understand the problem."

"No big deal, Colonel," Peled said. "But you have to keep gear stowed away. If the bus hits a mine, the bang turns every loose bottle or piece of metal into shrapnel. Pretty mean shrapnel," he said, idly rubbing the edge of his thumb against an old scar on the bridge of his nose. "Never knew no nice shrapnel, and that's a fact."

"But we are 200 kilometers from the front, and the front is quiet."

"His fucking point pre-fucking-cisely." For a moment, Ari thought that it was one of the soldiers near the colonel who had said that, then he realized it was Meir Ben David, the sapper captain, on All Hands One.

"Shut up, Meir," Shimon Bar-El said quietly. He turned to Peled. "Mordecai, send a detail to police the buses."

"Tel Aviv Ten. Yes, Shimon."

"We have to—" A helo roared by loudly overhead, sending some hands to the grips of their weapons, everybody desisting when Shimon came back on All Hands One. "Easy, people, easy. Few of us are operational, and none of us are engaged."

"Not at the moment we aren't," Benyamin said as they walked out into the daylight. "Not fucking yet."

CHAPTER 2

Dov Ginsberg:
A Simple Man

Avram's chatter irritated Dov. Avram always chattered. This time it was something about maps and overlays and coordinate systems.

Who cared? Avram always had to make things complicated, Dov Ginsberg decided, not for the first time.

For Dov, it was simple. He would handle his own job and leave the rest to Uncle Shimon. That was the way it had always been. That was the way it was supposed to be. That was enough; he was content.

Dov Ginsberg smiled. One hand wrapped around the anodized barrel of his shotgun, he leaned back, not quite letting his head rest against the seatback as he looked across Avram, out the window.

The road to Camp Ramorino cut gingerly across the rolling hills above the valley, as though it were too weak to cut deep and hard. Perhaps one klick below and ten to the south, a river twisted slowly through the greens and reds of the valley. Kind of pretty, really.

"The river is the Dora della Maestra," Avram said, tapping a map. He had taken off his field jacket and rolled it up so it could prop the clipboard on his lap. "Ag report says that they've got the salmon cycle going all by itself, now, or had it going before the war, at least." He pointed to a spot on the map. "There's a hydropower dam just beyond that bend, with a salmon ladder and all."

Officially, Captain Avram Stein was Shimon's aide-de-camp while Dov was his bodyguard and driver; the TO called for a captain to watch over the general's needs.

In practice, Avram was more of a junior chief of staff than simply an aide, and what with the demands on his time, Dov and he had always split the dogrobber duties. They never had a problem deciding who ought to do what; it was always obvious, which seemed to bother Avram. Dov liked it that way. Keeping track of maps, having the right map instantly available, was obviously Avram's responsibility, not Dov's.

"But only on the western arm of the Dora; eastern arm's the Dora di Goro," Avram went on. He sounded excited, as though it mattered. "We had it in Geography, remember? Way back when?"

"No." Dov didn't like remembering. Not that part, not that far back.

"At the orphanage?"

"No." Dov didn't remember much about the more important things that had happened in the orphanage, and he didn't want to. This might matter to Avram, but not to him; Dov wouldn't have cared if the river was called the Big Creek.

But things like this were important to Avram, and Shimon liked it that way, and Shimon wanted the two of them to get along, so Dov forced a smile for a moment, just as if he cared.

You had to decide what to care about, and what to let go. If it weren't that Shimon said otherwise, Avram and all his piddling little details wouldn't matter at all.

Salmon and fishing and rivers didn't matter. The details that mattered involved guns and knives. Dov hadn't liked the way the others, all of whom had guns and knives, had milled around Shimon as they boarded the bus.

It was good that they were all Metzadans, and better that they were all in Shimon's regiment, but that didn't mean Dov could relax.

Shimon wouldn't tell him to relax. Kick that aside, Dov; move this vehicle; just get me in there; do your exercises; start my bath, Dov; eat this food; fire this weapon; make my bed; kill them all, Dov; open that door; get my lunch; ignore the pain, Dov; gut this bastard like a trout for me, Dov; be very strong for me; Dov.

Dov had done all that, and all that was fine. All that was the way it was supposed to be.

Relax—no.

Turning like a turret, he looked around the crowded compartment.

In the seats behind him and Avram, Shimon and Yacov Sher were engaged in a discussion about some flimsies, punctuated by an occasional peremptory tap of Shimon's finger against the sheets. The aisles were crammed with buttpacks and backpacks, weapons of the operationals, either held or lashed in place. The rest of the gear, along with the administratives' weapons, was stowed below, in the ring of baggage carriers above the buses' rubberized skirts.

And, as usual, the virgins watched the scenery wide-eyed, while most of the veterans slept. It was a conditioned reflex: a seasoned soldier sleeps when and where he can. It didn't matter that this was a cadre job. A reflex isn't a reasoned judgment.

At the thought of sleep, Dov almost yawned. But he decided that he wasn't tired and didn't need to yawn, so he didn't. He had gotten enough sleep on the way down, and he never needed much. There wouldn't be much he'd have to do here, but at least there was some point in staying alert.

Reflexively, he licked his knuckles to be sure they weren't gritty—they weren't—and then rubbed at his eyes.

He looked past Avram, through the mesh, out the window again. Not a military road, or at least not a good one. The brush wasn't cleared more than two meters on each side of the ditch running along the bare dirt road.

Not bad, though, for a civvy wheel road, although it was hard to see a lot of it, what with the fans kicking up dust.

A military road should have been more direct, carving its way more urgently through the countryside. Ditch-edged roads were okay for fans, although you'd have to be careful riding a tracked vehicle down one if you wanted some speed.

Not bad for buses or merkavas, but it would be dangerous for the tracked vehicles: they could get themselves stuck too easily. If the bus slipped over into the ditch, it would just slide to the bottom, perhaps riding a bit higher on its air cushion as it rattled from side to side. No problem, there, but a wheeled vehicle would likely break an axle, and a tank would surely throw a track. A tank with a bad track was like an infantryman with a broken leg: too often you had to leave it behind.

It wasn't a bad road, but it wasn't really a fan road: the curves were unbanked; the bus had to slow at each turn for fear of going over the high side.

Again, the bus slowed and swung gently through another bend.

"Mountains there are the Rosso Magginines; most of the fighting's on the Plano Amiata, just beyond." Avram bit his lip for a moment. "If I was Generalleutnant Müller, I'd be thinking a lot about how the Casas have to get a hundred kilos per man up and through the Rosso Magginine passes every day."

"Eh?"

"I was just saying that I don't like those numbers," Avram said, pursing his lips judiciously. "Two of their fat divisions are about forty thousand men, total. Figure four thousand tons per day. Local trucks can haul about, what? Twenty tons, maybe? That's two hundred trucks up, each day. Three hundred, once they bring the new division online."

Dov grunted, as though he followed. Or cared. Numbers weren't his responsibility. They were too complicated. Leave it for logisticians like Avram. Worrying wasn't his department, not about this. It was good to worry about the right things, but a waste of energy to worry about the wrong things. So Dov would leave all the worrying to Uncle Shimon.

All Dov had to do was take care of what Shimon told him to. It had worked that way for twenty-five years, and not a day had passed in that time that Dov hadn't marveled at how perfectly it worked.

Just do what Uncle Shimon said and the rest of the universe fell neatly, quietly, elegantly into place, like a body slumping into the grave.

He was still angry about Peled. Peled should have known better than to let his rifle get too near Shimon. It didn't matter that the safety had been on, it didn't matter that his trigger finger wasn't even on the trigger housing. It was simple: people didn't point guns at Uncle Shimon.

Keep things simple, that was the trick. Don't worry about who is the friend, who is the enemy. That can get too complicated when you stand next to Uncle Shimon because sometimes friends wear funny foreign uniforms and sometimes enemies wore good Metzadan khaki.

Protect Uncle Shimon, and do what Uncle Shimon says.

Nothing else mattered.

Avram shifted nervously in the seat next to him, his attention split between his clipboard and the view outside. Avram was the organizer. He had been, ever since Shimon Bar-El's magic had touched him and the little boy who wasn't yet Dov. Shimon had touched all of them; and of the six who survived Shimon's Children's Crusade, all were different.

Poor Avram, always made things complicated. He liked it complicated, now. It hadn't always been that way. Things had been very complicated once, for the both of them, back when their names hadn't been either Dov or Avram, neither Ginsberg nor Stein, back when they were children in Bienfaisant, half this world away.

Dov didn't remember much about that; he'd lost most of those memories over the years.

It was only the end that he remembered at all clearly, and that only in flashes, because that was complicated. Little Annette running into the boy's dormitory, clutching scraps of her dress to herself, blood trickling down her skinny thighs; the men in the black uniforms kicking in the door and laughing at her, then pinning her down while they took turns with her; two of the men in black uniforms hacking Ton-ton to bits, and not because the poor spaniel had tried to attack them—it had just cowered under the porch. They had just done it for fun.

The men had used up the girls too quickly; they started in on the boys.

Two of them had grabbed Etienne and bent him over a table; a third pulled his pants down.

He didn't let himself remember much about that, only the end, with all the bodies scattered over the rough wood of the dormitory floor, some of them in the gray shirts and trousers of the orphanage, some of them in the black uniforms of the soldiers, and the thick man in torn khaki with the funny slanted eyes kneeling over him, gripping little Etienne's shoulder with surprising gentleness and saying, "You're the biggest one still living—well, still ambulatory, anyway— and I need you. Can you hear me?"

He remembered nodding, the movement sending

pain shooting through his broken teeth. "What's your name?" the man asked.

Little Etienne, the complicated little fool, he couldn't say anything, not through the pain and the tears. It hurt so *much*.

And the man with the funny slanted eyes said, "Well, then, I will call you Dov, because that means 'bear' in my language, and you're a big boy—you remind me of a bear. Hmm, you don't know what a bear is? That's fine, don't worry about it. I'll do the knowing for both of us. You're Dov—and you can call me Uncle Shimon. Can you remember that? Uncle Shimon."

Then he said the words that Dov would never forget, could never forget, the words that changed Dov's life, right then and there.

They were beautiful words:

"You must be very strong for me, Dov."

It was so simple. *You must be very strong for me, Dov.*

It was the most natural thing in the world, the easiest thing anybody had ever done, even through the pain and the tears and shattered teeth and the blood, for Dov to say, "Oh, yes, Uncle Shimon. I will be very strong."

He would be very strong, and he *was* very strong. Uncle Shimon wanted it that way.

Dov gripped the seatback in front of him and squeezed, hard, exercising his hands, not quite tearing the upholstery. It was important to Uncle Shimon that he be strong, and to be strong you had to get enough rest, you had to eat enough of the right kinds of things, and you had to train your body and your will at being strong and staying strong.

But that was all there was to it. Everything was always so simple.

And when the bus slowed to negotiate another sharp turn on the road, and the men in the brush beyond the ditch opened fire, two rising to their feet, each with a launching tube on his shoulder, it didn't matter that they were all wearing the mottled Casa fatigues, it didn't matter that there wasn't supposed to be any trouble, not on this job.

No. That would have been complicated. That would have called for decisions and caring and thought. None of it mattered.

It didn't matter when the stream of bullets stitching across the windows caught Avram in the head, spraying Dov's face with his oldest friend's blood and brains, the air filled with flying glass and gore and shouts.

It was utterly unimportant, because the bullets missed Uncle Shimon, and while splinters of glass dug deep into Dov's cheek and forehead, they missed his eyes.

The spray of blood and brains only filled and blinded and pained his left eye, and that didn't matter because one eye was all Dov needed. It was simple, it was so easy for Dov to spit out the warm salty gobbets and then snap his faceplate down with one hand while his other hand brought up his shotgun, thumb brushing away the safety.

Dov snatched up Avram's field jacket and used it to shield his hand as he punched out the remaining splinters of glass, then tried to push out the mesh over the window.

It didn't give, and, encumbered by his seat straps, he couldn't quite reach far enough to put enough pressure on it. He punched the release and the straps fell away.

You must be very strong for me, Dov, Uncle Shimon had said. And Dov was strong.

Oh, yes, Uncle Shimon. I am very strong.

Dov wound Avram's jacket tight around his left fist. Rising to kneel on Avram's corpse, Dov leaned forward and punched hard, metal squealing, feeling the distinct snap as small finger bones broke.

But they were just bones, they didn't matter, and the pain didn't matter as he threw the field jacket aside. He shoved the muzzle of his shotgun out through the mesh while he turned sideways to grab Shimon.

He didn't need to see where Uncle Shimon was in order to grip his shoulder; Dov always knew were Shimon was.

It was simple: Uncle Shimon had to be pushed out of danger and the man trying to kill Uncle Shimon had to die. The rest of the universe could fuck itself up the ass.

Dov squeezed the trigger gently with one hand while his other hand, his broken hand, gripped Shimon Bar-El's shoulder and forced him down, hard enough to move him but not to hurt him. Nothing was allowed to hurt Uncle Shimon; that was the rule.

The shotgun kicked gently against Dov's right hand while Shimon went limp against his left, letting Dov push him down, and the world was simple and beautiful.

Dov released Shimon and nudged Avram's body out of the way. He pumped, fired, pumped and fired again, ignoring the shouts and the sounds of explosions and gunfire.

The shotgun kicked against his good hand with gratifying firmness; the first rocketeer dropped his launcher and grabbed at his belly.

Pump, fire, pump, fire.

This time Dov's first shot missed, but his second blast smashed the other rocketeer's face to bloody pulp and the rocket launched straight up, riding a pillar of smoke and fire into the sky.

Pump, fire, pump.

Another of the enemy leaped for a rocket launcher but Dov led him just enough, firing instinctively, sending the bastard screaming off into a neatly timed stutter from a Barak.

Dov's shotgun locked open, empty. The first two fingers of his left hand were bent at impossible angles. Clumsy, broken fingers refusing to obey properly, Dov awkwardly reloaded as the crack of Baraks echoed through the cabin, and more shots from outside starred the window to his right.

But he finally was reloaded, and there were shapes in the bushes, and they were targets, and that was enough.

Fire, pump, fire, pump, fire.

It took a strong man to keep the barrel so level, so steady, but Dov was a *very* strong man.

The only sad part was that Shimon, too busy barking out orders, didn't have time to give Dov a quick "Good boy."

But the rest of it was pure simplicity.

It was beautiful.

CHAPTER 3

Warrior's Reflex

It was one of the reasons that they were valuable, that other worlds paid them, and it was something a Metzadan was supposed to carry with him, inside him. Ari had always known he didn't have it.

His Uncle Tzvi had explained it best, years ago, one night when Ari was guesting at his table. Ari had said something stupid—he didn't remember what—and the Sergeant had just smiled.

"Lesson time," Tzvi Hanavi had said. He was a constant, the Sergeant was: he was always a big man, even after Ari had reached his full growth, always freshly shaven, his cheeks lightly dusted with talc. Always patient when Ari didn't understand. He leaned forward, resting his elbows on the table, tenting stubby fingers in front of his thick lips. His eyes went vague and distant.

"See," he said, slowly, carefully, "when it all hits the fan, most soldiers take cover. Instinct; built-in. Ninety-seven percent of green offworlders are useless as a bucket of warm piss in the first minute of a firefight, and only about ten percent get better in the first five minutes. Some of them don't use their guns at all, some fire blindly. Some freeze in place; most take cover and cower. A few take cover, then get hold of themselves, and *then* aim, but they're in the minority.

"Blooded troops are better, but not much. Figure fifty percent of their riflemen return fire with any effectiveness—tops. It's instinct.

"Which is why the real firepower from the opposition'll come from their autoguns and mortars. The crew-manned weapons, not their rifles—and for shit's sake, not the officers' pistols. You been taught about priority of fire?"

Ari had nodded.

"Right. The reason you go for their autoguns first isn't that they fire faster or have more ammo than the rifles—it's because the autogunners will usually aim and fire, so that's where their real firepower is.

"We're different. From age eight you've been taught—what? Bap. Bap. Bap. Bap. What do you do, first thing when you're fired on? Quickly, now: Bap—"

"Warrior's reflex: I return fire until—"

"Bap."

"—the weapon is cleared, while—"

"Bap."

"—seeking cover forward, reload and—"

"Bap."

"—empty the second magazine," Ari had said quickly.

"Good boy. Damn straight you do."

The drills and the training routines had driven in the words and the feel of it: of the lock-load-charge-auto-aim-fire if the weapon was unloaded, of the charge-auto-aim-fire if it was loaded, of diving to the ground, the slam of the rifle butt into the ground to break the fall, rolling over onto his side for cover while reloading, finding hasty targets while he emptied his second magazine. Each step had been analyzed, each step had been practiced thousands and thousands of times until it was the most natural thing in the world. And there had been more: the drugs and hypno sessions that he could only dimly recall, all to make the warrior's reflex as automatic and involuntary as the gag reflex.

"It just might keep you alive," the Sergeant had said. "Sure to keep some of your cousins and brothers alive who'd be dead otherwise. Works in a lot of situations, not just charging an ambush. Indirect fire, too. Most of the time—"

"Tzvi—*enough*. Let the boy eat," Aunt Tabe'in, the Sergeant's new wife, had interrupted. She was a small, dark woman from clan Aroni, mainly of Beta Yisroel stock. With a quick flick of her hand she tried to wave the discussion away.

The Sergeant took her hand, gently but firmly, and put it in her lap. "No," he had said, speaking as patiently but adamantly as he had lectured Ari. "There's nothing more important than Warrior's Reflex."

The bus banked to the right and the whole world skewed as it slipped into the ditch, its hull ringing dully as the bus slammed into the far side of the ditch, bounced once and crashed down hard, slamming Ari against his safety straps.

Hundreds, thousands, millions of guns were going off, most of them in his ears.

"Make it stop, please make it stop," Yitzhak Slepak shrilled.

Ari sagged forward against the straps, unable to move. All he could do was huddle there while the others emptied their weapons, some reloading, some kicking open the emergency exits on the far side of the bus.

The shots were quieter than they should have been, each bang in the stream somehow more distinct than it ought to have been, than it ever had been in practice.

His fingers, white against the stock of his rifle, couldn't move. It was supposed to be: click the fire selector to full auto, his thumb pushing hard on the selector's sharp checkering, then pull the stubby charging bolt back, aim and fire, the muzzle blast putting what was almost a beam of light on the target, but all he could do was huddle there, a dampness at his crotch.

"Okay, everybody," Benyamin's voice said over his headset, calm and level, "out the far side."

"The kid fr—"

"Shut up. Help me with him." Two pairs of rough hands clutched at the shoulders of Ari's tunic, more carrying him than pushing him toward the window.

"All even numbers: I need a quick spray to starboard. Do it now and reload." Shimon Bar-El's voice cut through the gunshots and the smoke and the decreasing whine of the bus's fans. "Everyone: as you exit, spray the bushes and stay down, in the ditch. There'll be claymores on the starboard side and we've got nowhere to run."

Laskov and Lavon half-carried Ari to a window and half-threw him through it.

Now, trained reflexes didn't betray him: when he hit the ground, he let his knees give, falling forward, breaking the fall with the butt of his Barak.

"Where's Orde?" Benyamin asked.

Laskov grunted. "Caught one in the eye."

Ari crouched in the dirt, his rifle still clutched tightly in his hands, with nothing but his chestpack.

That should be enough. It held his ammo and a spare knife and—

"Shit, people, where the fuck are they?"

It was all smoke and fire and sound. From off in the smoke, Baraks stuttered and the wounded screamed.

Ari tried to bring his rifle up. But where should he aim? He couldn't just fire randomly.

As if of its own volition, Ari's rifle jerked and shook, sending lead and flame into the leaves overhead.

Into the ditch, that was what Shimon had said.

But everything was silent on the squad freak; he puffed for the company freak.

Benyamin was talking. "—lev One One Two One. No claymores to the east. Can't be," he said, almost too calmly, too casually.

"Kelev Twenty. You sure?" Galil sounded more placid than Benyamin, if that was possible.

"Kelev One One Two Two," Laskov rasped. "We're all alive, aren't we, asshole?"

"Twenty. It's—"

"He's right, Yitzhak," Shimon Bar-El's quiet voice cut through the shouting, accompanied by a high-pitched hum that announced he was talking in override mode.

"There's no claymores and too many of us are alive—it's a hasty ambush, by no more than a platoon. Kelev One is going to have to take it; the rest aren't operational, won't be for five, ten minutes."

It would be more than that, Ari thought; they'd have to retrieve their weapons from the cargo bays of the buses and somehow arrange themselves into squads.

Bar-El's voice was seething with calm. "Take it, Yitzhak; it's yours," he said quietly, the judge passing a death sentence on God only knew whom.

"*Kelev,*" Galil came back, sharply. "Got it. Nablus Twenty—"

"Nablus. We go north with our fucking handguns, while you cross south?"

"Kelev. Do it, Meir. Grazing fire to keep their heads down—but stay in the ditch, this side. Don't cross; they'll cut you to pieces."

"Nablus."

"Deir Yasin Twenty," Greenberg said. "Autoguns will be up in a minute, maybe less. I've got the two rockets heating up, if you can get me a target."

Thank God that the heavy mortar training detachment traveled with a half dozen autoguns and as many of air-suppression rockets when operational. Their tubes couldn't possibly to do any good, even if they could be brought on line: the enemy, whoever it was, was too close.

"Kelev," Galil said, "negative on a target. I—"

"Tel Aviv *Ten*. I will spot for the rockets," Peled said, his shout automatically damped.

"Kelev. Do it."

Ari Hanavi huddled in the ditch, trying to press himself into the ground, breathing shallowly to keep his back low.

"—One One Five. Second bus is burning. Gonna blow any minute."

"Listen, I've got one, would you fucking listen—"

"Identify yourself, dammit," Galil snapped.

"—bearing perp to the road, listen to me, perp to the road and right a quarter, one hundred meters, base of big tree, at least two of them, probably more. And I'm, shit, I'm TTD Two One Fifteen, Chaim Goell, and—"

Shimon Bar-El's voice cut through, again override mode. "I spotted what looked like a hiking trail. Crosses the road out beyond the bend, about half a klick back. You might want to try that."

"Kelev. We'll do that, Shimon. Tel Aviv Ten, I'm taking Kelev One around and behind. You form up the rest, and lay down a cover from here."

"Tel Aviv Ten," Peled said. "*Got* it."

"Kelev Twenty. Okay, Kelev, One to the south; follow me."

"Two prisoners," Shimon Bar-El said.

"Kelev Twenty. Yes, Shimon."

"Ari, come on." It took him a moment to realize that Benyamin was shouting in his ear, not over his 'phones. Benyamin pulled him to his feet.

"He's not worth shit." Lavon had his weapon loaded again and braced against his hip. "Leave him."

Benyamin nodded. "Okay. Ari: you took a blow to the head. Stay here. That's an order."

He couldn't remember taking a blow to the head, and they were all running away, all abandoning him.

He couldn't stop crying, but Ari forced himself to his feet and staggered after them. At least they were running away from the shooting.

CHAPTER 4

Yitzhak Galil: Moving the Pieces

"Follow me," Yitzhak Galil said, charging across the wide dirt road, his rifle held chest-high, smashing through the brush on the other side.

Two dozen men followed him at a dead run, although when he glanced behind him to check his quick count, he could see Ari Hanavi, staggering down off the road, slipping, falling far behind.

Forget him, Galil decided. Save it for later. On the chessboard or in the field, it was all the same: pieces don't do a lot of good until they're developed, deployed. Shimon and the rest of the company were castled across the road. Galil moved his men out.

As always, it was the little things that tripped you up. The dominant vegetation in the forest was a ten-meter-tall dull green plant, its bifurcated trunk smooth, topped with an explosion of long strings of leaves that never came within a man-height of the ground.

Those were spaced widely enough not to be a problem. It was their younger versions that littered the floor of the forest, clawing at Galil, smashing at his faceplate as he pushed on.

The ground was covered with humus and a plant called melfoglia—slimy gray leaves, ranging in from a

42

few centimeters to half a meter across—interspersed with cadapommidor—vaguely cubical white fungi the size of a man's head. It looked like bleached cheese and smelled like death when you kicked it open. Galil had to fight to keep on his feet.

Radio discipline on the multi-person channels was always among the first things to go to hell, particularly when everyone hadn't smelled real gunsmoke for awhile; the company freak quickly became a buzz of noise.

He puffed for the private line to his first section leader. "Yosef. Drop off a fireteam on this side of the road. One that's already got casualties—I only need two or three effectives."

"Will do."

He wasn't about to waste a complete team on guarding their rear, but he wasn't going to run through the woods with both his flank and his ass hanging out, either.

Keep pieces protecting other pieces, that was the idea. It was just another chess game, but it was always a chess game in the fog, played by a crazy drunkard: you never really knew the value of the pieces, and never knew for sure which ones you were risking.

He should have had his exec and top sergeant at his side, but both were down, probably dead. Had to move the pieces around the board by himself.

So be it.

He puffed back to the company freak.

"—can't see any of them," somebody said, "there's got to be a hundred of them, a hundred—"

"Shut the fuck up, Isenstein."

"Shit, shit, they're all around us."

"Oh, God, Mother, I'm hit."

He puffed for override mode. "Kelev Twenty," he said. "Tighten up, chaverim." His voice felt tight and squeaky in his throat, but it sounded almost too calm in his ears. "Company freak and platoon freak is for orders down to all and for information everybody needs going up. Keep the bullshit and the chatter on your squad freaks, or better yet, shut the fuck up."

Damn, but that sounded good. It sounded like he knew what he was doing.

He hoped the feeling was contagious—he might catch it.

He was out of shape, he decided, as he paused in the lee of a huge tree. He squatted, trying to catch his breath while he got himself oriented.

They were about a hundred meters down the road from the ambush, and maybe fifty beyond the road. Time to organize things.

He puffed for his private line to the general. "Kelev Twenty here; I need a sitrep."

"Stable, but shitty. Hang on." Shimon Bar-El was back in a moment. "Colonel Chiabrera's on the line to Division Ops; they had two flights of helos on the pad; getting them up. Estimate five minutes over target. You want any help?" he asked drily.

"Fuck, no. Keep them clear." The last thing he needed was a bunch of locals overhead firing down at God-knew-what. "Get them opconned to us quick, eh?"

"I'll try."

As the old saying goes: Friendly fire isn't.

He had to get this company organized fast or there were going to be a lot of his people dying—because Yitzhak Galil hadn't done his job. Unacceptable.

He stood and puffed his mike off. "Okay, everybody," he shouted, "over here. Take a bearing on me. Move it, move it," he said, raising his rifle over his head.

Kelev One carried twenty-four men on the books; he counted eighteen, including himself, and at least a half dozen of them were men from Support/Transport/Medical who had picked up fallen men's weapons.

Not too pretty for an elite security and assault platoon of the best military force in the Thousand Worlds, but everything was always a mess. You practice and you train and you plan, and you learn to do it by the numbers, and then you find yourself improvising your way across a wooded ridgeline, never quite knowing what the hell to do next, your scrotum so tight your balls hurt.

But never mind that; just move the pieces.

The piece with the three bars on its shoulder was to be in front, with its fireteam, but most of his HQ fireteam—his platoon sergeant, the mechanic and one of his driver/gunners—were out of it. That left him and Moshe Bar-El, the driver/gunner/medic. It could be worse.

Two of the squads were mostly intact; he'd move them out and fill in with the remnants of the others.

He pointed at Skolnick. "We move out in a wedge. You take the left flank," he said. "Improvise another squad."

He turned to solid, rooklike Benyamin Hanavi. Lipschitz's fireteam was intact, but Hanavi was saltier. Shit, though, it looked like he was down to himself and two others.

"You got two down?"

Hanavi hesitated, then nodded. "Lavinksy's dead; Ari took a knock on the head."

"Then why—save it." It didn't matter that he didn't like Benyamin Hanavi a whole lot, and Hanavi liked him even less. The chessmaster needed a rook, not a hug. "Your squad's on the left—your fireteam and these five," Galil said, gesturing at five more men. "You're designated Red section. Rest of you with me, you're Green section, arrowhead to my left flank—Moshe and I are the spur. Let's go, quick and quiet. Moving overwatch—twenty-meter interval. We don't have time for run-and-cover."

They moved quickly, boots crashing through the slimeleaf plants littering the floor of the forest.

"Autogun one is up," Shimon reported over their

private line, his voice drowned out by a crash. "But the second bus just blew, and I don't think these people are running out of ammo." His voice was distant, dreamy. "Any chance you can hurry things up?"

"On my way." Galil didn't alter his pace. Yes, you hurry. But you don't hurry things so much that you blunder blindly into a rain of bullets.

Rifle fire beyond the next knoll caused him to stop for a moment. He puffed for the platoon freak.

"Kelev Twenty to all Kelev One units. Green section hold in place; cover my advance."

Near the base of a tree, his foot slipped on something and he almost fell headfirst into one of the corpse-white fungi.

"Shit." Which is what it was. Human shit. It had to be. While terrestrial fauna had long been turned loose successfully on Nueva, it was small stuff. Galil didn't think that was the end product of a rabbit. This didn't make any sense, not at all. The ambusher *had* to have been hit by an elite assault group, but basic field sanitation was something that elite field soldiers would long have gotten down pat.

He was trying to figure out the implications of all that when two rifles to his left opened up.

"Got 'em. Two men in Casa utilities. The fucking Casas—"

"Shit, David, don't be an asshole—he was shouting in German. They're fucking Freiheimers in Casa uniforms."

Galil grinned tightly. The rules of the game were very specific about what you could do to pieces caught in a war zone while showing false colors: anything. They'd be captives of war, not civil detainees, prisoners, prisoners of war or criminal detainees—not even capital criminals awaiting execution.

Captives of war had no rights. None.

He puffed for Shimon. "Kelev Twenty. We're about

two points south of west of you, three hundred meters out. Moving in for—"

A helo roared overhead. What the fuck?

Gunfire rained down through the leaves. Pain lanced through his right leg, knocking him to the ground.

"Go, go, go," he shouted. Sometimes if you shout, you can manage not to scream. "Two prisoners. *Do it.*" He waved the rest on.

Half blind in pain, he pulled an injector of valda oil out of his belt pouch. His fingers trembled and shook as he scrabbled uselessly at the release tab, then swore and bit the package open, slid the injector out and jammed it into his leg, just above the knee.

A warm wave of dull distant pain washed away the agony, and then dissolved itself. He puffed for his private line to the general. "Shimon, we're taking fire from above."

"How many hit?"

Galil had just caught the edge of the rain of bullets; Moshe Bar-El had been stitched diagonally across the chest. He sprawled on the ground, almost cut in half, fat, broken, yellow worms of intestine peeking out through the crimson mess of his midsection.

Two men beyond him lay broken and bloody, and for the life of him Yitzhak Galil couldn't put names to the broken pieces.

"Three dead; I'm dinged." Keep the pain distant.

"Do I need to replace you?"

Galil took a quick inventory. His leg was still bleeding, the blood running down his khakis and into his boot, but it didn't look like much; probably only cut through the muscle. No spurting—venous, rather than arterial blood.

The piece with the triple bars of a captain on its shoulder was only injured, not out of it.

Besides, he could monitor and control things from here. No. You had to leave decisions for those who were going to have to live with them. "No, Shimon.

I'm passing it along." He puffed for Skolnick. "Kelev Twenty—you've got the assault commando; I'm auto-patching you through to the General."

"No need; it's okay, Captain. Got three of them knocked down. Others are retreating toward the road. Estimate a total of fifteen. What do you want me to do?"

You can't pass control of an operation over to some-body who's asking you what to do; the piece named Galil would just have to function as chessmaster a few minutes more.

"That was a Casa helo overhead, possibly circling for another pass," Shimon said. "Chiabrera says an-other one from the same flight'll be overhead any second; two more in two minutes. They say they can patch me through for direct control in one minute. Peled's got both Hunters ready, busy acquiring. Call it."

The pain was a distant thing—*no*, it was nothing. A chessmaster didn't feel any pain when one of the pieces was endangered. All he had to do was call the right move.

He puffed for the regimental freak, override mode. "Kelev Twenty to Tel Aviv Ten. Target Casa helo. Perp to the road, eleven o'clock. Green light."

A minute? A minute was an eternity. The autoguns on a Casa attack helo fire upwards of five thousand rounds a minute. Maybe they were supposed to be a friendly force, but there were three men dead on the ground because the assholes hadn't held their fire as told.

And that had nothing to do with it. Not a damn thing. It was just data. A chessmaster didn't have any affection for his pieces; he just had to evaluate the danger and react.

"Tel Aviv Ten. *Say again*. Request confirmation."

"I said green light, Colonel Peled. *You get that*

fucking piece off my board." He leaned hard against the tree. "Burn the bastard down," he added. But his microphone wasn't on.

"Tel Aviv Ten, roger. Acquired." Peled's voice was crisp and flat. "Rocket *away*." High overhead, the world exploded into flame and noise that didn't quite drown out Peled's quiet mutter of "*Got* him," before the colonel shut off his mike.

Good: the enemy was on the run; the friendly forces weren't overhead shooting up his pieces.

Galil puffed for Skolnick. "Kelev Twenty—who'd you leave on flank?"

"Litvak. And it's clear there. We got one whole prisoner, one injured. Leg and wrist wound. Both secured."

"Keep the injured one alive; Shimon needs two."

"Understood. They're pinned down in the ditch across from the burning bus. You want to try for more captures?"

"No. Finish it."

"Will do."

The firing intensified, then started to taper off, punctuated with a triple bang of grenades.

"I think we got all of them," Skolnick said.

The chessmaster named Galil leaned back hard against the smooth bole of the tree. His bad leg couldn't support him and his good leg was getting all distant and vague, like the clumsy fingers that couldn't hold the assault rifle any longer.

He slipped down onto the slimyleaves, the world starting to swim in front of his eyes. He closed them. Just play it blindfold, that was it.

You didn't have to look to see the pieces.

He listened to the babble of voices in his headphones for a few seconds.

"Kelev Twelve Thirty-One. I see three down, none moving."

"Kelev Eleven Eleven." That was Lipschitz. "Burning helo on the ground north of the bend, maybe four hundred meters. No sign of life."

"Kelev One Two Three Three. What are we going to do about Slepak? He—"

"Save it, Twelve Thirty-three."

"—motherfucker froze—"

"This is Kelev One Two Three One. I said, *save it*."

It looked like it was settling down; it was time to move to cleanup. Galil puffed for All Hands, and found that he still had override mode. "Kelev Twenty to all units. We're. . . ." The world started to go black around him, but he forced it back to gray. "We are staying operational, but it looks like it's almost over. Don't waste ammo. Everybody except fireteam leaders switch to single shot. Designated sharpshooters only are to fire insurance rounds; everybody else to fire only on active targets. Fireteam leaders, use your judgment, but keep it clustered. Medics and medicians to medical duty."

"I've got operational control of the helo overhead," Shimon said. "What do you want from him?"

"We're on cleanup; you take it. I suggest you land him just ahead of the first bus and use him for medevac. You'd better get me a medic, and find somebody else to take over the mopping up."

"Fair enough. I'll take over, now?"

"It's yours, General."

"I've got it. Good job, Yitzhak."

Galil started to say something, but the distant world at the end of the dark tunnel, the dim world surrounding the piece with the triple bars of a captain, the gray world was going black. Maybe he had lost too much blood after all.

Damn.

CHAPTER 5

Mordecai Peled: Cleaning Up

Mordecai Peled kicked through the smoking remains of the roughly square piece of composite. Part of the outer wall of the cabin, maybe, although it was hard to tell. The whole damn thing stank of burning petrochemicals and scorched meat. A scorched fragment of bone stuck up through the wreckage. He nudged it with his toe, but couldn't decide whether it was part of an arm or leg.

He eyed it coldly. That was just something that had happened to get in his way, and he'd knocked it down. That didn't matter at all.

Hey, Casa mamas, teach your boys not to point guns at my boys.

There's some things you have to give up on. Teaching morality, for one.

You can't teach them that it's wrong to run through the streets of Berlin smashing your people's windows and burning their shops. You can't teach them it's evil to herd your people into the Umshlagplatz and load them into cattle cars to be hauled away and boiled down for soap. You can't teach them that it's unjust to wrap your revered teachers in the Torah scroll and burn them alive. You can't teach them it's immoral to wait on an overpass and then, shouting, "Arafat will fuck your sister," throw firebombs at an auto on a Jerusalem road and boil a baby in his mother's womb.

You can, however, teach them that it's *unsafe* to raise their hand to you and yours.

That was good enough for Mordecai Peled.

The bodies, some still in Casa uniforms—had to save something for the Thousand Worlds observers—scattered across the lightly wooded slope were something else, though: they had him irritated. The bastards had *tried* to get in his way, and he didn't like that much. But the dozen or so bodies didn't seem a fair trade for what was shaping up to be at least thirty dead Metzadans and five times that many wounded.

There weren't enough Freiheimer bodies in the universe to trade for the least of his people.

But that was personal, not professional. His professional judgment was that the Thirtieth had been fucking lucky.

Seven hundred and fifty men, all except one stripped company organized into a support/transport/medical command and two specialized training detachments, the lot of them ambushed by fifteen well-armed infantrymen, would be expected to take upwards of fifty percent casualties. Well upwards.

Looking at it the other way: if Peled had staged an ambush like this, he would have expected to knock out more than half the buses and kill well over half the men.

Buses. He shook his head. Buses. Not even APC's, although he didn't think much of APCs, not in a combat zone.

He was an old infantryman, and he took the old infantryman's view: the worse place to be in a firefight was a pillbox—but being inside a vee-hicle was almost as bad. If you need a foxhole, you dig one; you don't build it above ground. Putting tracks, wheels or fans underneath it doesn't make it better. Still an above-ground foxhole.

Well, they weren't organized into two fucking training detachments and a transport/support/medical command now: they were now the First Battalion, call sign Haifa, operational in a combat zone.

Peled didn't necessarily like that, but he understood it.

His earphone hissed. "Haifa A One Twenty, err, Haifa A Twenty," Avigdor Cohen said, correcting himself. "That is, Haifa A Twenty for Haifa Twenty. Clear at the streambed."

"Haifa Twenty," Peled said, acknowledging as battalion commander. "Post guards to cover your sector, then move up to the CP, double time." The command post was the spot near the first bus where Shimon was interrogating the prisoners. Not much of a CP, but when in doubt, the command post was where the commander was.

"Haifa A Twenty, you got it," Cohen said, identifying himself yet again as the commander of A Company, First Battalion.

Senior Captain Avigdor Cohen had been on the books as an armor and ordnance repair specialist, not a trainer—Cohen was a lousy teacher, but he was good at getting local arty back online faster and running better than anybody thought possible. Cohen was commanding the hastily improvised A Company now, what there was of it: it was more of a platoon than anything else. Resnick, who would have been Peled's first choice for a combat company commander, was dead in the first bus, along with too many of the support people.

Still, putting Cohen in charge of the company might have been a mistake. Normally, Peled would have preferred Adelberg; Stu had more infantry experience. But Avi Cohen was senior, and he'd handled himself well toward the end of the firefight. Damned if

Mordecai Peled was going to jump somebody over his head—not in front of the Casas, particularly not in front of the perverted IG corps they called the Il Distacamento de la Fedeltà, the Loyalty Detachment.

Fucking DFs.

As Peled and his team worked the clearing, a pair of the DFs—one male, short and skinny; one female, fat and dumpy—kept them under observation. Idiots. What did the DFs think they were going to do, run off with the bodies?

Peled didn't mind things being done wrong—war is the domain of mistakes—but he didn't like things being done stupid. Command and authority are supposed to flow up and down, not be shoved in from the side by a bunch of official kibitzers who didn't have to live or die with their mistakes.

He sighed. He was getting too old for this, wool-gathering when there was work to do. The area was secured; fine. The captives had been pulled out and were up at the road under the control of Shimon and Galil—no, Shimon and Skolnick. The sharp-eyed sergeant was running Kelev for the time being; he'd be glad to be rid of that once Galil was back on his feet.

Peled still had to figure out what to do about staff.

The officer complement of a Metzadan infantry battalion headquarters was supposed to consist of six: a battalion commander, either a colonel or light colonel; an exec, generally a major, who doubled as S3, the ops officer; the deputy S3, generally a captain; and S1, S2, and S4, all lieutenants or captains. Usually there was a senior medician in the rank of a captain, but he was out of the chain of command, in general practice although not in theory. For the time being, Reuven Zucker was very much in the chain of command: he was running Company C, which was busy handling field aid and triage up on the road.

The officer complement of First Bat HQ was supposed to be six; right now, it was Mordecai Peled.

Period. First Bat was operational in theory, and it would fire back if fired upon, but it was headless.

Except for me, he thought, *and God knows that I can't carry Bat HQ in my hat.*

Peled needed a good battalion staff, and quick. It didn't matter that they would probably reconfigure themselves as a training regiment again tomorrow; right now, right this fucking minute, they were a goddamn infantry battalion, and that's how he had to run it.

In other armies, the senior NCOs, the men who really ran a battalion, could manage about as well without officers as with—sometimes better. But Metzada didn't do things that way, and this was supposed to be a cadre job. While the enlisted complement of the improvised Bat HQ weren't virgins, they weren't ready to run things, not if things got sticky.

Which they already had. Assuming they were going to stay configured this way for even a day or two, Shimon was going to ask Peled for some recommendation on what do about personnel, and Peled hadn't the slightest idea what to tell him.

SOP was to promote from below—and that would be fine for S4, any damn fool could run supply—but who would he get for S3? Peled was acutely conscious that he was good at carrying out someone else's plan, not drafting his own, and he needed a good S3 and deputy S3 or the battalion would be stepping on its dick the next time guns started going off all around them.

At least they were all operational now. Fuck this administrative shit.

Possibly he could raid the Goren's training detachments for some officers. Maybe; he'd have to think about it.

He didn't know what to do about the personnel problem, but Mordecai Peled had always gone by the simple rule of if you didn't know what to do next, figure out what to do now.

Establishing and clearing a defensive perimeter was easy and clean, and besides, Cohen could use the practice of moving a company, even a platoon-sized company, through the slimy woods. There was every indication that that would come in handy.

This was supposed to be a simple cadre and command job: finish the training of a division made of green recruits and recycled officers and noncoms—mostly misfits who had burned out in the line. The senior staff—battalion-level staff and up—would take that division into the field for ten days of combat and then turn it all over to their Casa deputies.

It still could be a cadre and command job, but Peled had a suspicion about that. He hadn't liked the look in Shimon's eye. Shimon didn't keep Mordecai Peled around as chief of staff because he needed a buffer between himself and his top officers; Shimon wanted a spare combat commander handy, somebody whose mind as well as his reflexes could function when it all hit the fan.

And, maybe, who could supervise the cleanup afterward.

Mordecai Peled sighed, then returned to work, under the watchful gaze of the two Distacamento Fedeltà onlookers.

The next body was clearly dead; the right foot was blown clear off, and it had bled out. He chalked an x on it and moved on.

One of the unchalked Freiheimer bodies wasn't visibly injured enough, although it was lying face down and it had soiled itself. Probably dead—the only thing more amazing than how much punishment a human body could take without dying was how little damage could kill—but nobody under Peled's command had ever been killed by a supposedly dead man. Seeing to that wasn't a particularly ugly job, not compared with what you sometimes had to do, but it was disagreeable enough that Peled didn't want to delegate it, not when he could do it himself.

He thumbed his Barak back to single-shot and mechanically raised it to his shoulder. The front sight ring had broken loose during the fight, but the body was only two meters away; even without working sights, he should be able to put a bullet in a spine at that distance.

"Haifa Twenty to All Hands," he said on All Hands One, override mode. "Barak rifle, firing one."

He squeezed the trigger, and was rewarded by a jerk, a bang and a gout of flying flesh and gore. But just to the right of the spine, dammit.

You're getting old, old man. Couldn't even kill a dead man right.

Still, while the hole was bloody, it wasn't bleeding. There was no heart pumping; Peled had just killed another dead man.

He thumbed his rifle back to safe and handed it to his clerk/driver/bodyguard, who slung it over his own shoulder. He was still able to work his stylo and notebook, although he did look a bit hunched over.

Peled pulled on his blood-spattered field gloves as he knelt at the corpse's side. He drew his knife. "White male, brown-haired, apparently," he said, slashing down at a hunk of hair, then examining the roots carefully as he laid the scalp open to white bone. "True dark." One of the others had had dyed hair.

He slashed off the uniform shirt and stuffed it into the sample bag at the left side of his waist. The shirt looked like a real Casa uniform blouse. Maybe it was, and maybe it wasn't. Ditto for the undershirt. It was a normal Casa tee.

He chalked the corpse.

Ezer Laskov, the regimental S2, hadn't been on the commo net before, but he wasn't among the RHQ casualties, far as Peled knew. Maybe he was back on. Peled flipped the identity switch at his belt—making him Tel Aviv Ten, the regimental chief of staff again, and not Haifa Twenty, the First Battalion commander—and bulled into the RHQ freak.

"—and that's ten, repeat ten—"

"Tel Aviv Ten for Tel Aviv Two Twenty."

"Laskov. What is it, Mordecai?"

"Tel Aviv Ten. What's the standard issue Freiheim undershirt?" Most Metzadan Intelligence officers had eidetic memories, although Laskov's was only close.

"Err, that'll be A-shirts for three-season wear—ten- or fifteen-weight—long shirts for winter. Polysil for officers, cotton for the enlisted."

"Tel Aviv Ten. Casa?"

"Cotton tees. I don't have manufacturer data."

"Tel Aviv Ten. Get it. I'll have some samples for you to compare."

"Fine. Now can I get—"

"Tel Aviv Ten. You *will* follow comm discipline, Two Twenty."

"Tel Aviv Two Twenty to Tel Aviv Ten. Aye, aye, roger and will cooperate on that, sir," Laskov said, his intonation carrying not a whiff of insubordinate irony.

"Tel Aviv Ten out."

Peled flicked his identity switch back to Battalion, and called up the company commanders. Everything was quiet. He slashed the shirt off and bagged it, too. Just as he thought. Real Casa shit. He—

Shimon's voice cut through the thought. "Ebi's on RHQ One for you. Too busy?"

It was a reprimand; Peled should have delegated somebody to monitor regimental freaks while he was doing battalion commander things. His own deputy would normally have done that for him, and while he hadn't picked out a deputy yet, that didn't excuse the lapse.

"Tel Aviv Ten. I'll get it."

There was a crackling in his phone. "Hebron Twenty for Tel Aviv Ten."

"Tel Aviv Ten."

"Hebron here." Chaim Goren—called "Ebi" by everyone, in a not-particularly-funny bilingual joke; he was barely one hundred sixty-five centimeters tall—sounded tense. But Ebi was always tense. "We're down; next shuttle is due in one-two-five minutes. Orders?"

Hebron was the administrative designation of the second group of men down—the Aggressor/Defender Company, the Special Training Group, and the third Troop Training Detachment.

It had been just an administrative designation, until now.

"Tel Aviv Ten," Peled said. "Hebron—you are now Second Battalion; go operational now, and when we're done, call up Bar Yosef and Laskov for briefings."

"Hebron. Got it. Hang on." There was a click, but Goren was back in about five seconds, less time by at least ten minutes than it would have taken Peled to issue even the preliminary orders to turn an odd collection of units into a hastily operational battalion. Who was his deputy? Natan Horowitz? Was he *that* good? "Hebron Twenty. We're operational in five-zero minutes, but I've got one company up now."

"Your Ag/Def detachment?"

"Yeah. You need relief?"

"Tel Aviv Ten. Negative." But exactly the right question; this was the sort of thing Goren was good at, and Ebi wouldn't need more than a hint. "Yossi Bernstein is taking care of your transport; he's going to arrange a full escort—and you ride in APCs, not buses. Have Laskov fill you in on the situation, then call up Bernstein. It won't be there for a few hours, at least, but in any case you wait until Third Bat's down, and you—that's both battalions—stay operational for the trip to Camp Ramorino. You're senior; you take command."

"Hebron. Understood. Any idea of how soon we can expect to move?"

"Tel Aviv Ten. I told you, we're working on it." What the hell did Goren expect? A bus schedule?

"Hebron. I don't like things so up in the air; what say I assume we're going to throw up a quick biv just this side of the fence and you come get us in the morning?"

The Commerce Department busies wouldn't like that, but they weren't likely to make a big fuss about it; there was room on the reservation for a dozen battalions to camp.

Peled pulled his maps out of his chestpack and found the one covering the TW reservation. "Tel Aviv Ten. Tentatively, sounds good; I'll check with Shimon. Coordinate with the local CD Inspector's office; Map Gimel One, Hex Oh Eight Two Three. I'll see about getting rats out to you. Anything more?"

"Not to worry—I'll send Meyer Kaplan out to the Commerce Department company store. I've got some tweecie vouchers."

"Tel Aviv Ten. Fine. Out?"

"Out."

That would do, for a start. Maybe it was locking the barn after the horse was stolen, sure, but damned if Mordecai Peled was going to let any more of his brothers and cousins die administrative, not here. Maybe the locals didn't like foreign troops going operational this far behind the front lines, and maybe that was in the contract, but Peled would be perfectly happy to explain to even a TW observer why he should overlook the violation: he'd stick the observer's ass in the front seat of a bus going from the port to Camp Ramorino.

"Mordecai," Shimon said over their private channel. "If you're done playing soldier, I've got some work for you. Minor problem of prisoner custody. Need a light touch."

Not too fucking light. He clapped his hands together to get the attention of the soldiers in the clearing. An improvised five-squad commando was about right. He pointed out five squad leaders one by one, spread and closed his fingers, then pumped his arm up and down.

By squads, form on me, it said.

He reclaimed his rifle from his clerk and led his commando back up the slope, the butt of his rifle braced against his hip, like a trapshooter out for a few clay pigeons. His finger was away from the trigger, but the safety was off.

Shimon was supervising the final loading of the last of the wounded under the watchful eye of the rest of the Casa DF squad.

A platoon of Casa regulars stood watch a couple of hundred meters down the road at either end of what had been an ambush, but was now a roadblock.

There were a lot of white knuckles among the neatly uniformed Casas, as they looked over the somewhat scraggly Metzadans.

Hey, c'mon, boys, haven't you seen combat soldiers before? Actually, it was possible that they hadn't, not soldiers with fresh blood on their hands. They all made Peled's hands itch—the Casas were wearing the same kind, the same shade of uniforms as the Freiheimer attackers had.

The line of halted trucks and buses was up to about half a dozen on either side, watched over by twin merkavot riding low on their air cushions. Despite their Hebrew name, the merkavot were of local manufacture from local plans—the name had caught on here, too—but each of the lightly armed air-cushion vehicles had a Metzadan gunner in the lefthand seat.

"Tel Aviv Ten for Haifa C Twenty," he said into his microphone, even though Reuven Zucker was only thirty or so meters away. "You're sure that this is it?"

"Haifa C Twenty. Affirmative. Last of the criticals." Zucker didn't waste words as he and a junior medician helped Private Yonaton Shapir onto the helo. Shapir didn't look too bad—his left eye and right hand were heavily bandaged, but he held onto his own assault rifle and ammo kit, and accepted help with his pack reluctantly.

Either the local medical teams understood triage, or Zucker had managed to have Metzadans run the evacuation, Peled decided with satisfaction.

Accompanied by the whine of the engine, the slowly turning rotor picked up speed. Peled snapped down his faceplate and turned away as the helo lifted into the air.

There were only two helos left, and it was getting to be time to clear out.

But first, there were the Casas to deal with. And the fucking Commerce Department observer.

He—well, it could be a she, but most of them were male—looked silly, standing off to the side in the red, bulky, all-over body armor that the Thousand Worlds Commerce Department provided for wear in the field. It was important to the CD that their representatives be both visible—and the bright, day-glo crimson was that—and protected. The armor, a product of offworld technology that even Metzada couldn't duplicate, and certainly wouldn't be permitted to import, could protect the TW observer from a stray round or even burst, or a near miss of a grenade. Additional protection for the observer was provided by an overhead CD helo and a squad of Peacemakers, each in shiny black reticulated armor, looking for all the worlds like a half dozen oversized insects.

The armor and bodyguards wouldn't do any good, not outside the fringes of a real battle, and it was a certainty that the observer knew that. The TW might be run by a bunch of assholes, but that didn't make them cowards.

Under the eye of the silent observer, Shimon Bar-El squared off against the fedeltists.

Il Distacamento de la Fedeltà, the Casalingpaesesercito Loyalty Detachment, dressed its officers and enlisted differently than the plain olive drab or speckled camo of the Casa regulars: their uniforms were black tunics over scarlet trousers, the three officers' tunics trimmed in gold and silver, their six enlisted bodyguards' in yellow and white. They were all in garrison uniforms, not field gear, despite the businesslike rifles the bodyguards were carrying. Each of the officers had a shiny chromed pistol in an open holster. Ridiculous, for a combat zone.

Peled never liked garritroopers. Standing next to rumpled, dirty Colonello Sergio Chiabrera, who held a borrowed Barak in two clenched fists, they looked like toy soldiers.

But if an apparently harmless writing stylo could kill—and Peled knew that it could; he had done it—so could a shiny chromed pistol, completely unsuited for a combat zone.

Chiabrera pursed his lips and nodded a greeting at Peled.

Shimon, Dov looming next to him, had squared off with the Casas. That put them squarely between where the Casas and Sergio eyed the captives—

No. Peled caught himself. Shimon and Dov stood *between* the Casas, *including* Sergio Chiabrera, and the Freiheimer captives, each hand- and leg-cuffed, each controlled by two husky Metzadan PFCs, rifles and knives rigged properly, well out of the prisoners' reach.

"—you really must turn the prisoners over to us. We'll find out the truth, never fear, General," said the senior fedeltist, a major. He was a short, stocky man with a too-easy grin, his cheeks and chin covered in a manifestly affected combat soldier's three-day beard. "We'll find out the truth." He spoke Basic with the fluid melody of a native speaker of Italiano.

Shimon shook his head. "Negative on that, Maggiore Zuchelli. Once I turn them over to you, they're saboteurs. Caught out of uniform, local rules apply. We caught them in *your* uniforms. If they're Casalingpaesan—"

"Please."

"—if they're Casas, dammit, then you're in violation of our contract: deliberate assault on friendly forces."

"And our helo? What was that?"

Bar-El's lips whitened. "My men, dammit, came under fire from the Casa helo, *after* it was warned off. You want to make something of it?"

"Three of his men were killed by that helo, Maggiore," Chiabrera said quietly.

"*No.* That's not the way I play the game, Colonel Chiabrera. Irrelevant," Shimon Bar-El said. "We didn't down the helo because it killed some of my men; I ordered it down because it posed a threat to my regiment. *Claro?*"

Next to him, Dov stiffened, desisting at Bar-El's microscopic headshake.

The fedeltist didn't catch it. "These sorts of things happen, Generale, as well you know. 'Friendly fire is not,' eh?"

Bar-El looked the DF officer over long and hard. Then he shrugged. "Fine. And as to these, if they're not Casas, then they've dressed as Casas in order to provoke an apparent violation, and that puts them outside the rules. They stay under my control. Your local rules are more restrictive, but at the moment they're captives of war—no rights."

The fedeltist opened his mouth as though to say something, but closed it. He smiled broadly, then spread his arms, wordlessly announcing that he wouldn't be bothered by issues of rights in his questioning of the prisoners.

It was half-clever, and Zuchelli almost strutted his pleasure. The TW observer was behind him, and wouldn't have been able to see the smile. From the point of view of the Thousand Worlder, the fedeltist had thrown up his hands in frustration at the Metzadan's intransigence. On Shimon's head be it.

Bureaucrat. Peled turned his back to the fedeltist and puffed for his private line to Bar-El. "He's just playing for the observer, Shimon," Peled whispered into his microphone. "I don't think he really wants them; he just wants to make it clear that he's not responsible for what we do to them."

He turned back in time to see Shimon Bar-El shake his head, as though to say, "Don't bother me with the obvious."

The elder of the two Freiheimers straightened fractionally; a Metzadan hand whipped out and clutched the back of his head. "I am Horst Fleiss, stabsunteroffizier, Der Freiheimdemokratischrepublik. Upon proper request, I will give you my vater's name and my service number; I will tell you nothing more." He squinted hard against the daylight, and didn't appear to be focusing properly. Metzadan doctrine for controlling prisoners in the field called for a few drops of carbachol sprayed into each eye.

Shimon didn't seem to hear him. He looked at the other Freiheimer. This one was younger, probably about eighteen standard years, wide-eyed. There was a trickle of fresh blood at the right side of his mouth.

Shimon looked at Dov and raised an eyebrow.

"Not me, Uncle Shimon."

"I didn't like the looks of one of his molars," Sergeant David Elon said, brandishing his medician's scanner.

"Poison pill?"

Elon grinned, then shook his head. "Just a lousy

crown," he said, digging two fingers into a chest pocket, pulling out a bloodied white tooth. "I guessed wrong." He shrugged. "Not all that elite, eh? Exit-pill was in his pocket," he said, rattling a small glassine vial.

"Name?" Shimon asked.

The younger Freiheimer didn't answer.

"You will not make him talk, either." Fleiss drew himself up proudly.

Bar-El puffed out his cheeks and sighed in irritation. "I don't have a lot of time for this, but let's give it a try, anyway. You were caught in Casa uniforms; by local rules, that makes you saboteurs. Death sentence, but the Geneva protections apply.

"But we're not under Casa authority, not at the moment. We're technically allied, not subordinate. That means that you've attacked us in allied uniforms. By my reading of the codes, that puts you outside the rules, and makes you captives of war. No rights. I can't turn you over to the Casas, 'cause all they can do is kill you or interrogate you under Geneva rules. And if they don't execute you as saboteurs, they'll prisoner-trade you.

"I'm not going to have that. Once we're out of my area of operations—and, shit, this is only technically my AO because you jumped us in it—they'll have the authority to ask for you, and they will, unless I've got some results out of you.

"I can't turn you over to my interrogation team for a sharp needle and a quick chat, because they're still skyside." Bar-El shrugged. "Comments?"

"It sounds like you have a problem, Herr General Bar-El." The stabsunteroffizier's voice dripped with sarcasm.

"Dov. *No.*"

The big man had shifted marginally; he froze in place.

Shimon Bar-El sighed as he looked over at Peled. "You've got your battalion staff put together?"

"Not really. Not yet." *Dammit, Shimon, you know I'm not an organizer.*

"Fine. I'll take care of it," the general said, turning back to the prisoners. "Well, then, we'd better end this now," he said, more to himself than to anybody. "Observer," he called out. "Over here, if you please."

Stiff-legged in his armor, the Thousand Worlder walked over, a brace of Peacemakers at each elbow.

Peled's boys, their weapons held almost mechanically at port arms, looked over the Peacemakers carefully.

"That is a *red* light on the assholes in the black armor, people," Peled whispered on All Hands One. "Big red light."

Without even trying, Peled could remember a dozen times he would have liked to have blown away one of the Thousand of alone Worlders, but the TW assholes controlled the Gate system, and without the Gate system, Metzada would be isolated from the rest of the universe, and you couldn't have that.

"Can we get a ruling on the status of the Freiheimers?" Shimon asked.

"No." The observer's voice was mechanically distorted; Peled couldn't guess the observer's age, or even gender. "I am here to observe and report, not to judge."

"Then observe this." Shimon jerked his head; guards dragged the two Freiheimers over to the side of the road and secured them, neck, wrist and ankles, to two trees.

The guards moved away.

"Dov. Aim."

Dov slowly brought his shotgun out and lined it up on one of the Casas. The younger one, the silent one.

"Start with the feet, Dov. Time's up, Fleiss. Last chance. I want some truth, and I want it now."

Peled puffed for All Hands One. "Tel Aviv Ten. Shotgun, firing many."

Behind him there was a hoarse whisper. "Nobody flinches. Nobody."

"Dov," Shimon Bar-El said. "Now."

Dov fired into the scream.

He fired again, into the screams and the whimpers, and a third time, into the whimpers and the silence.

And again, until the seven-shot clip was empty.

"Somebody reload for Dov," Shimon said.

They cleared out in an hour, taking with them a babbling Freiheimer stabsunteroffizier, leaving behind the Distacamento Fedeltà to deal with the bloody mess that had been a tree with a war captive tied to it, and the Peacemakers to see to the security of a gagging Thousand Worlds observer who was now out of the protection suit that couldn't get rid of a few ounces of sour vomitus.

That was the first time that Mordecai Peled laughed all morning.

CHAPTER 6

Questions

Ari slammed the helo's door shut and then quickly
backed away, ducking reflexively as the whirring blades
sped up. The rush of air pushed him down, the dust
raised by the wind beat hard against his faceplate as he
stepped back, half bent over, a peasant leaving the
presence of a king.

At best.

He wiped his hands on his khakis. He stank of
blood and piss and shit, but none of the blood was his;
you could get awfully dirty loading injured men and
pieces of men into helos for the trip to the nearest
hospital.

The Casa helo lifted off its skids, rising only a couple of meters before it dropped its nose and moved
off, building speed quickly, gaining altitude only
slowly.

Ari reslung his rifle patrol-style, then squatted and
wiped his hands on his knees. They were about the
cleanest part of his khakis. There was blood on his
hands, and he couldn't get it off.

What would Miriam say if she saw him now? What
would his mothers say? And his—

"Easy, easy, with the hands." Benyamin said from

behind him. Ari hadn't heard him move up. "That's the last one."

"Good." Ari kept wiping his hands.

"Stop fidgeting," Benyamin said. He pulled an envelope out of his breast pocket and tore it open, handing Ari the stericloth. The cloth was wet and cool against his skin, and it cleaned the grime and gore from Ari's hands, but it didn't make him feel clean.

There was always something special, if strained, about Ari's relationship with Benyamin. It wasn't that they shared a birth mother. Both of their father's wives had always treated all the boys the same, as far as Ari could tell, except that Yael—Tetsuo and Shlomo's mother—seemed to go out of her way a bit more for Benyamin than anyone else, watching out for him, just as Benyamin watched over Ari.

"Just take it easy," Benyamin said. "It'll all be over in a while. For a while. It's true what they try to teach you in school: relax while you can." He beckoned Ari over to the side of a road and leaned against a tree, loosening his own pack straps. Benyamin had had the squad reclaim their gear from the wreckage of the bus; their bus hadn't burned, so while the packs had been scattered, it was all intact.

Benyamin muttered something into his mike, then dug into his buttpack, coming out with a dull black canteen. He took a short drink, then passed it to Ari. "Take a swig."

The water was warm and brackish, but it was good.

"Look," Benyamin said, his face grim as death. "There's no point in pretending. You're in deep shit. You and Slepak. You both froze, first time out. I'll see what I can do, but this isn't good. Just remember that you caught the fringe of a blast. You don't remember much after that."

"Benyamin, I—"

"You shut up." Benyamin's grip on his sleeve was numbing. "You just shut up, shithead. Your way didn't work out, so you do it my way. There's no other options. The big three don't count. You can't claim battle shock," he said, extending a finger, "not on your first time out. You can't claim that you weren't ready—" another finger "—because Kelev was operational. You can't claim a gross physical injury, because you don't have one. You don't have a defense, so you just do it my way. Understood?"

"Yes."

"Very good." Benyamin smiled. It was a report. "So, I'll fix it, best as I can. Zucker owes me—he'll remember that you had a dilated pupil when he examined you. You don't remember much—just that you're a bit confused about what happened. Tetsuo'll be down later today, and I'll talk to him first thing tomorrow, have him square things with Galil."

"I didn't know they were friends."

"They're not. But Galil knows that Shimon respects him. So does Peled." Benyamin looked like he was about to say more on the subject, but he shook his head. There was a lot about Tetsuo that nobody spoke of.

Benyamin pulled a foodstick from his pack, unwrapped the end, and bit in. "Shit, I wish we had the Sergeant here—Uncle Tzvi's better at handling things than anybody else I know. You're stuck with me—but I think I can pull it off. Shimon may or may not buy the story, but there won't be a lot of time to think about that, not right now. He's not going to overrule Galil, Peled and Tetsuo, not unless he's damn sure—which he won't be. Not with me, Laskov and Lavon vouching for you.

"So you just keep low and stay in the middle of the pack—you don't come in first or last in the morning run, you don't go to the head or the foot of the mess line. You turn invisible and blend in. My guess is that you'll have another chance to prove yourself within a few days. Figure we settle in at Camp Ramorino to-

night, the rest of the regiment gets in tomorrow or the
day after, and—"

"Eh?"

Benyamin shrugged. "Think about it. We got hit by
some deep-cover Freiheimer saboteurs, folks who've
probably been making life miserable behind the lines.
Interesting that we never got a briefing on that, eh?

"Now, granted, they didn't have enough men, didn't
have enough equipment, didn't have enough warning
to do the job: a dozen more Freiheimers, half a dozen
rocketeers and ten minutes more of getting ready, and
we'd all be dead.

"I'll bet that there's another couple of squads of
sabs within a couple hours of here. Probably in hiding
now. For now. Ready to hit the whole regiment, which
they would have if we'd waited for the other two
groups to get down before moving out of the port."

Benyamin nodded toward the forest. "They're out
there somewhere, and somebody's leaking information. Shimon doesn't like stabs in the back. Like Uncle Tzvi says: Lesson time. What do you think he's
going to do—what would you do, General?"

Ari thought it over for a moment. "I'd commandeer
helo transport for the other training detachments—I
mean, the battalions—and not have them take a direct
route. If we can't get enough helos—"

"Which we can. The Al*ba*tro," he said, pronouncing the foreign word with careful correctness, "can
carry thirty. A Casa division is supposed to have twenty
of them integral. Figure we'll have the rest of the
regiment at Camp Ramorino by sundown tomorrow.
Which gives you a short while to get your head out of
your ass and into business, General." Benyamin's eyes
went all distant and vague, just like the Sergeant's
would when he was lecturing. "This was some sort of
ratfuck, and the old man doesn't like ratfucks. Which
means he's going to try to get some of our own back.

"It's not a matter of revenge, although maybe there's

a bit of that, too. But it's pretty clear that the Freiheimers just spent a whole squad of deep-cover saboteurs trying to kill some of us." His voice, in contrast to his words, was tired and flat, almost uninflected. "They must have thought that was worth the price, and Shimon's going to prove them right, one way or another. Just business, mind, nothing at all personal: the rule is that you don't fuck with Metzada." There was no smile on Benyamin's face, and none in his eyes. "Get your shit together, little brother. Two weeks, and we're back in it; you get another chance to prove yourself. If you're lucky."

"And if I'm not?" He didn't mean that. He meant, *And if I can't?*

Benyamin looked him in the eye and answered the unvoiced question. "Then you're no son of my father, brother."

CHAPTER 7

Yitzhak Galil: Staff Meeting

A Casa private held the door as Skolnick wheeled Galil into the back of the conference room, behind the last line of tables.

Outside, a triphammer pounded like a well-drilled mortar team: *Wham. Wham. Wham.* A long pause. Then: *Wham. Wham. Wham.* The sound was somehow reassuring.

Galil's right leg throbbed redly, painfully with every pulsebeat, which didn't worry him: Local trauma techniques were good, although Casa cosmetic surgery was for shit.

A fair deal: a week to ten days, maybe, until Galil would be back on his feet, and he would have two more puckered scars to add to his collection. The right leg seemed to attract fire for some reason or other. That and his left arm. Why was that? Some sort of cosmic coincidence. Nah. If it had been his head that attracted fire, it would only have happened once.

The aftermath of a night in the hospital was like a medium hangover: his teeth tasted of slime and ashes, a headache sawed at his skull, his stomach would rebel at anything except the blandest food, and an irregular, painful twinge had taken up residence in the back of his neck.

But he was alive, and that was what counted.

"I guess we should have come in the other way," Skolnick said. The other early arrivals were at the bottom of the banked conference room.

Too far away—the room was large enough to be a refectory, back home. Wasteful for a staff meeting.

No, it wasn't. This wasn't Metzada; space wasn't at such a premium.

Galil started to lever himself out of the wheelchair, preparatory to hopping down the stairs, but desisted at Skolnick's grunt.

"Sit tight, Yitzhak." Skolnick took the rifle off Galil's lap and slung it across his back, then picked up one side of the wheelchair while Meir Gevat took the other.

The two of them carried him down three landings to the bottom level, Support/Transport/Medical Command's David Pinsky pulling out a chair so they could slide his wheelchair up to the edge of a table.

"Ever think of going on a diet? You're fucking heavy, Captain," Gevat said as he lowered the wheelchair to the tile floor, although the full-breathed ease with which he spoke proclaimed his words a lie.

Imposing on them didn't bother Galil; it wasn't much of an imposition. Nueva's point ninety-one standard gee was only seventy-six percent of Metzada's one point two; with the two of them splitting the load, Gevat and Skolnick were barely carrying more total weight here than they did at home, stark naked.

While Gevat took his seat next to Asher Greenberg of Regimental Heavy Weapons, Skolnick flipped Galil's rifle to safe, popped the magazine out, then opened the bolt, showing Galil that it was empty.

All the other early arrivals were armed, too, although nothing had been said about that in the meeting announcement. The regiment had made up its collective mind that all of Casalingpaesa—or perhaps all of Nueva Terra—was a war zone.

Skolnick slammed the bolt home, then inserted the magazine and laid the weapon across Galil's lap. "Loaded; chamber clear," he said, as though Galil hadn't been watching.

"I have eyes."

"Shit, Captain, don't try that on me. I been around for awhile." Skolnick chuckled. "If I hadn't reported, you know damn well you'd have complained about my weapons discipline."

"Who ever said life was fair?"

"Not me." Skolnick tapped at his earphone, then brought his thumb up to his lips, miming puffing for a freak.

Galil nodded; he would call when the meeting was over. Skolnick left, bounding lightly up the steps.

Across the aisle from Galil, Meir Ben David sat stropping his Fairbairn dagger. He was unshaved, but he looked rested.

At his glance, Ben David set down his honing leather and rubbed a thumb against his stubbled cheek. It sounded like sandpaper. "Well," the sapper said, picking up the leather again, "the choice was another ten fucking minutes of sleep, or a shower and shave. I'm happy with the choice." He considered the edge of the dagger. "Nice call yesterday, by the way."

"The helo?" Galil asked.

"Yeah."

"Thanks."

"Your people did pretty good, too."

"True enough," Galil said.

Kelev One was shaping up nicely, Galil decided, and the platoon seemed to think that Galil was doing acceptably. You couldn't tell—and it didn't matter—whether or not the troopies liked the CO, but it was easy to know when they thought he was good at his job. There was an informal network that got Galil's bed made, took care of his laundry and meals, and now made sure that he didn't have to push himself anywhere.

But that wasn't an expression of affection, any more than was Ben David's careful treatment of his Fairbairn knife. It was respect for a piece that did its job: a knight that always jumped one down and two across; a rook that moved squarely along the ranks and files. The consensus was that Galil had better things to do with his time than worry about making his bed and doing his laundry.

A bit of a compliment. A suggestion that he was doing his job well.

Which, with some reservations, Galil decided he was. Better than he'd done in Third Platoon of A Company in the Sixth, Galil thought, shaking his head. It was five years ago, but a day didn't go by without him remembering how badly he had screwed that one up.

Not this time, though. He'd played the last game fine; best to figure out what the next game was.

The conference room held ten tiers of three tables each, a theater apparently intended to hold a battalion comfortably, although Galil had never seen any need for a lot of battalion meetings. A commander couldn't micromanage anything even the size of a company, much less a battalion, and while green platoon leaders and company commanders usually kept their fingers in too many kettles, no good battalion commander was stupid enough to try. Metzada didn't give battalions to anybody who hadn't outgrown a psychological need to bog himself down in detail, the sort of idiot who would busy himself with minutiae instead of looking at the big picture.

But, of course, this conference room hadn't been built to a Metzadan design. The locals were fuckups, as usual, and from the foundations up.

Galil snorted. Then again, if the locals weren't al-

ways fuckups, they could fight their own damn wars by
their own damn selves, and Yitzhak Galil's children
would have to learn how to eat rock.

Others wandered in and took their seats: Peled and
most of his instant battalion staff; Lieutenant Colonel
Horem Bar Yosef, the adjutant and liaison officer;
wiry, rawboned Ezer Laskov, the S2; Colonel Yehoshua
Sadok, who held the senior spot in S4, along with his
long-time assistant, Senior Master Sergeant Yossi Bernstein. They were a funny pair: Sadok short and pudgy,
thin hair slicked back over his balding head, Bernstein
a head taller, his curly brown hair always uncombed
and unruly.

Doc Zucker was conspicuous by his absence, but the
chief medician had been up until 0500, supervising the
care of the wounded.

The delegation from Third Battalion arrived en masse,
and quietly seated themselves along the wall, Colonel
Rabinowitz coming over to exchange a few quick words
with Peled and the adjutant.

Sidney Rabinowitz, now, he looked like something
out of an advertising brochure: he was tall and muscu-
lar, but not overmuscled, size 40 Long khakis fitting
him as though they had been tailored. His nose and
chin could have been carved from stone, and he wore
the triple oak leaves of a full colonel like the kings of
old must have worn their crowns.

The only trouble with Rabinowitz was that he was
always complaining, and Shimon couldn't dismiss his
complaints because they were always to the point.
Right now, he was probably fussing about the size of
his instant battalion: it was under-strength, built out of
one training detachment and some spare specialists
from Harari's special training group.

No sense of proportion, that was the problem with
Sidney. In another few minutes they'd be reconfiguring
for cadre. Why bother?

It was easy to tell who hadn't been involved in the

firefight yesterday: they were all in clean, crisp khakis, none of them displaying the bandages and chalky complexions of the wounded.

Ebi Goren strutted in, half a dozen officers from Second Battalion following closely on his heels. The trim little man nodded a curt greeting to all, then joined Peled, Rabinowitz and the adjutant over to one side of the room while the rest of the Second Bat delegation took seats.

There was a certain something to the officers Goren had with him. All were junior for their jobs—there wasn't even a lieutenant colonel among them—and that probably meant that Ebi Goren, with one reasonably well-organized aggressor/defender company and two 250-man training detachments, had skimmed off some of the young studs from Ag/Def for his command staff, even though that meant some captains and majors would be taking direction from junior officers.

Captain Yitzhak Galil strongly approved, although he wondered how strongly he would have approved if he were wearing oak leaves instead of bars.

As the others from Second Bat took their seats, one detached himself from the group and came over to Galil.

Galil had never liked Tetsuo Hanavi. For one thing, Tetsuo was too damned pretty: tall, his blond hair curled tight against his head, his chin too sharply chiseled. For another thing, he was a Hanavi of the Bar-Els, a member of the leading families of Metzada, destined—if he proved competent, granted; Galil tried to be fair—for at least the triple oak leaves of a full colonel, possibly even for stars on his shoulders.

"Yitzhak," Hanavi said. "How's the leg?"

"It'll do," Galil said. He pointed his chin to where Goren was still deep in conversation with Peled and the others. "What's Ebi got you doing?"

"Err, I'm not working for Ebi." Tetsuo Hanavi

smiled. "As of this morning, I'm assistant S3, regimental, working for Natan."

S3? Plans and Operations? Galil tried to keep his disgust off his face. Of the four Hanavi brothers, there was one asshole, one competent line soldier, one green coward—and what to do about Ari Hanavi was something that Galil didn't consider settled, not by any means—and Tetsuo.

But while he'd apparently been a decent enlisted striker—his Uncle Tzvi wouldn't have put him in for OCS if he hadn't been—he'd never commanded a company, or even a platoon. Each of the triple bars on his shoulder had been earned as a staff officer.

Galil didn't have anything against staff officers; shit, some of the most able logisticians couldn't command with smoke in their eyes and bullets whizzing around their ears. Galil was sure Tetsuo would have been fine where he was originally slotted, as an instructor in Military Law. But . . . Tetsuo Hanavi as assistant S3 for the whole regiment? Operations was too important, far too critical, to be left to somebody who didn't have the experience of command.

That was what bothered him. The fact that everybody knew that Tetsuo Hanavi was fucking his brother Shlømo's wife had nothing to do with it.

Galil would talk to Shimon about it. He—no. No, it didn't matter.

Galil chuckled to himself. Shit, he had just mentally chided Rabinowitz for doing what he was doing right now. This reconfiguration as a combat regiment was just temporary. This wasn't yesterday. Right now it was more of an exercise than anything else. They'd be back to cadre in a while.

Besides, Natan Horowitz was an operations wizard; an assistant ops officer's main job would be staying out of his way and keeping the coffee and tabsticks coming.

Leave it be.

"Congratulations," Galil finally said. "Good slot."

Tetsuo Hanavi shrugged. "It'll do." His grin threatened to split his face open. "You sure your leg's okay?" he asked, throwing his hip over the corner of the table. Hanavi pulled a pack of tabsticks out of his blouse pocket and offered Galil one; Galil shook his head.

"I told you: it's fine." *And how's your brother's wife?*

"If you want to switch slots until you're better, it can be arranged. I've already talked to Natan, and to the adjutant. No problem with either of them if it's okay with Shimon, and with you."

Galil snorted at the transparency of that maneuver. "Thanks. I'm happy where I am." Yitzhak Galil wouldn't give up a real command even for a permanent staff job, much less a temporary one. Not voluntarily, and he would put up one hell of a fight before submitting to any involuntary reassignment.

"As you like." Hanavi stuck a slim tabstick between his lips and puffed it to life, then held it and considered the coal for a moment. "I heard there was a . . . problem with my little brother yesterday."

"A problem." Galil kept his voice low. "Right. He froze in combat."

Hanavi was silent for a long moment. "Are you very sure about that?"

"Yeah. Ask Benyamin. *He* did good yesterday; I've put him in for his first class warrant."

"Good for you. And I already asked him. Now I'm asking you, Yitzhak," Tetsuo Hanavi's voice was low and even, no trace of threat in it.

"We had two troopers from Kelev freeze, both virgins—Ari and that other asshole, Slepak."

Tetsuo blew a ring of smoke into the air, watched it pull apart and drift away. "Benyamin thinks Ari may've caught the edge of a blast. Doc Zucker will second it. It makes sense to me that we give him the benefit of the doubt."

"We?" Galil shrugged noncommittally.

"I want you on board on this."

Galil shrugged again. "Leave it. Maybe we can talk about it later."

Hanavi refused to drop it. "What does the old man have to say about it?"

"Why don't you *ask* him, Tetsuo?"

"I just might, Captain."

"Go ahead, Captain."

"Captain—"

"Stop it," Dov Ginsberg said from just behind them.

Galil turned in his chair.

Dov Ginsberg looked like shit. Beneath the crooked bandage on his forehead, his eyes were red from lack of sleep and his face was pale, except where a shadow of beard darkened his chin and cheeks. His khakis were torn in several places, and stained in more; the damp patches under his armpits were white around the edges from caked salt.

The only thing that didn't look worn was the bright white cast wrapping his left hand and arm almost to the elbow, leaving only thumb and part of the forefinger exposed.

Galil was of above average height and Tetsuo Hanavi was tall, but Dov Ginsberg loomed darkly over them like a tank. Galil felt like a child being supervised by a strange adult.

"Shimon says no arguing." Dov turned to Tetsuo. "He also says for you to leave Galil alone."

Tetsuo Hanavi smiled thinly. "He thought it all out, did he?"

Dov didn't smile, and he didn't answer. "He says for you to leave Galil alone."

"I hear you. Perhaps we'll talk later, Yitzhak," Tetsuo Hanavi said, moving away.

Dov Ginsberg watched Tetsuo Hanavi, his broad face impassive, expressionless.

"You don't like him much, do you?" Galil asked.

Dov thought it over for a moment, then shook his head. "He isn't loyal to Shimon, not the way I am," he said, his gaze never leaving Hanavi. "Then again, nobody is." Dov pursed his lips and hefted his shotgun. "Sir, I need some help. I can't pump this thing worth shit, not with this cast on. Shimon said you had some sort of quick rig for when your left hand was broken, on Thuringia."

"Sure. Not with a shotgun, but with a Barak. Should work the same way."

Ginsberg didn't take that as an agreement. "So would you fix it for me?"

"Sure, Dov." Galil shrugged. "It's pretty simple— take about ten minutes. Meet me after the staff meeting. You just drill right through the charging handle —well, it's the pump grip here—and then you run a loop of cable or tubing through. One-centimeter siphon hose is fine, if you can get it. When you need to pump it, you just slip your hand in the loop and pump away. No need to grip, and I'll make the loop large enough that you can still hit the magazine release with your left thumb."

Normally, Kelev used the Aggressor/Defender Company's armorer, but with the reshuffling going on, it would be better to leave poor Shimshon Nakamura alone. The tools he needed ought to be in the local Casa armory. Hmm . . . what was the easiest way to get access to it?

Leave it to Bar Yosef, Galil decided; that's what the liaison officer is for, particularly if he's also the adjutant.

Galil caught Bar Yosef's eye and raised a finger; Bar Yosef mouthed a quick "Later?" and returned Galil's nod of agreement.

"I'll handle it for you," Galil said.

"Thank you." Dov nodded, then walked away, eyeing everybody in the room levelly as he took a seat near the front of the auditorium.

"Good morning, all." Shimon Bar-El was at the top of the stairs, briefcase tucked under one arm. His hair was slicked back against his scalp, damp from a shower. "Settle down, please. We have a lot to go over and not enough time." He bounded down the stairs, unsnapping the closures on his briefcase as he did.

He stopped at Galil's elbow. "Doc Zucker claims he's got a therapy that can get you healed quickly, if painfully—he says he'll have you ambulatory in a few days. Want to try it?"

"Of course." He couldn't run Kelev from a chair, not for long, and with Tetsuo sniffing after his job there wasn't a choice.

"Good man." Shimon trotted down the rest of the steps and took the center seat at the table on the raised podium. "Listen up. Agenda is as follows. After-action critique on yesterday, followed by status reports—Liaison, Regimental S1, S2, S4, Special Staff, Medical —mmm, I'll handle Medical. No S3 for now; Natan's off with his nose in some papers." He held up a hand. "Just hang on. I'll take questions in a minute.

"Then, battalion reports: bat commanders, bat S1, S4. We'll have to make it quick, because at ten hundred hours, we've got a briefing from Divisione"—he pronounced it with just the right accent—"Intel, and then we have a greeting from Generale DiCorpo d'Armata Massimo Colletta, followed by briefings from the rest of Divisione staff.

"Afternoon today, and all day tomorrow, is research. Sidney, I'll need your evaluation of the Araldo Model V, and your recommendation as to whether we get more firepower out of liaison with a salted—both senses—Casa tank company, or a quick—and I do mean quick—transition of some of your people. Chiabrera's laid on an eleven-tank company for you to play with."

"I can tell you right now."

"Bullshit. I'm not interested in your prejudices against

locals." Bar-El was visibly irritated. "I've fought with the Casas before. Some of them are real good, and most of the rest aren't as bad as you think they are. If they were, the Boche would have overrun them months ago. Manning the tanks ourselves would cost us more than forty men; if we put a liaison trooper into each platoon as loader or driver, that only costs us three men. And these are good tankers. Ezer?"

Ezer Laskov stood, leafing through the sheaf of flimsies on the clipboard clutched in a bony hand. "I've checked out their files. They're orphans from broken-up outfits, not apparent misfits. The least-qualified Casa tank commander has something like three hundred logged hours in the Araldo V." He looked up at Shimon. "If it's close support, though, we're better off with gunners aboard, not drivers. The fire-control system is just a copy of the Stadia Z, and there is a ranging machine-gun-mounted coax."

"Hmm. Possibly; save it for later." Bar-El turned back to Rabinowitz. "The point is, they've had hundreds of hours in their tanks, and we'd be lucky to get you fifty in the next week. So I want thought-out answers, none of this reflexive we're-better-than-they-are bullshit. And save your questions—well, what is it, Ebi?"

Colonel Chaim Goren, commander of the First Battalion, scowled as he rose. "Meaning not more than average offense, Shimon, what is all the rush about?" He sounded every bit as irritated as he looked. "I did a walk-around today and the training division has at least another two, three weeks to go on their introductory cycle. They don't need us now, and they've got security in hand here. I don't see that we need to reconfigure for combat, not to avoid another problem like you had yesterday."

"Well, you're right about that," Shimon Bar-El said. "There's been a change of plans. At oh-six-thirty this morning, the Commerce Department rammed a cease-fire down the throats of both sides, effective thirty days from tomorrow." He paused for a moment. "Which means that Generale Colletta has no need of a cadre to train a new division for him, and which also means, gentlemen: welcome to the Thirtieth Regiment, Operational."

Galil didn't look hard for the thin smile on Bar-El's face; he knew it was there.

Sidney Rabinowitz didn't like it. "We've been planning for cadre, not for strike. I've been training for cadre, not strike. We're manned for cadre, not for strike."

"Yeah. Well, I didn't know. If I had any reason to believe that the Thousand Worlds was going to pull this, I would have mentioned it, honest." Bar-El shrugged. "We'd have made some personnel changes at home—a lot more young PFCs than we have, a lot fewer career NCOs."

"Right." Ebi Goren's tone was just a hair short of insolence. "Dutch brevets all over the place." Goren was one of the more vocal critics of negative brevets, the practice of temporarily demoting soldiers to fit them into the table of organization.

"French brevets, as well. Real brevets, too," Shimon said, ignoring the tone, rubbing it in. "We're going to have enough trouble putting the right man into the right job to worry about whether he already has the right number of bars or leaves on his shoulder." He lit a tabstick and puffed on it for a moment. "Look, I know you all know me, and you know how I feel about the *Freiheimers,*" he said, pronouncing the word like a curse, "and I don't feel any better about them since yesterday. But it's just a job. We do what we're paid for and then we go home. Period. So let's get to it. Any urgent questions?"

"I've got one, Shimon," said Lieutenant Colonel Horem Bar Yosef, the adjutant. "Hell, I've got a hundred."

"I don't have time for a hundred. Can they wait?"

"No, sir. Well, most of 'em can, but one can't. Chiabrera's got me, Sadok and Yossi Bernstein meeting with Divisione G4 while the rest of you are getting yourself greeted. Divisione G4 is a full colonel, and you know how these folks are about NCOs."

Shimon shrugged. "Yossi?"

The Supply and Logistics sergeant was already reaching into his pocket; he extracted a set of lieutenant colonel's leaves, and switched them with the senior master sergeant's stripes clipped to his collar. "Any chance I can get lieutenant colonel's *pay*?" he asked, dryly. "Or even a major's?"

"No. This is just a French brevet, not a real one."

That was proper, Galil decided. Bernstein wasn't being asked to do anything beyond his normal responsibilities; the purpose of the added rank was only to make it easier for him to deal with the locals.

Bar-El turned back to Bar Yosef. "Will that do it?"

"Not quite. I'd better be a full colonel."

"Be my guest. Now, we'd better get to the after-action critique. Oh, what *is* it, Tetsuo?"

Tetsuo Hanavi waited until the room quieted around him. "General, if everything we've been planning is suddenly going into the dumper, then it would seem to me that we could put off an after-action critique."

Shimon Bar-El sighed. "No, we can't. Understood?"

"Well, no."

Shimon Bar-El's eyes closed, then opened. "Fine. I'll make it real clear for you, for all of you. We lost—*I* lost thirty-two men yesterday, and I've got one hundred ninety-three in hospital, shot up, chopped up, burned." His nostrils flared momentarily, but that was the only sign of emotion. When he spoke again, his voice was flat, almost too casual. "I will not have that be for nothing. I will not." He sighed. "Now, Yitzhak Galil, Regimental Headquarters Company, we'll begin with you. How did you fuck up yesterday?"

Galil had been waiting for this. He sat back in his chair, and folded his hands across his lap. "I don't think I did too badly, except in preparation. If all of the RHQ Company was going to go operational—even if it was more for admin purposes than any other—I should have insisted that we wait until the tubes and sapper gear were down."

"You did suggest that."

"I should have convinced you."

"Oh, get off it." Ebi Goren shook his head. "I know that a certain amount of breast-beating is supposed to be part of an after-action critique, but let's pretend we're all sober. Forgetting for a moment that putting Deir Yasin and Nablus under RHQ company is really just an administrative convenience, sappers and tubes aren't going to do you any good in an ambush—not if you're on the receiving end. If there was reason to worry about an ambush, then it's Shimon's fault for accepting unsecure transport."

"Bull*shit*, Ebi." Ezer Laskov, regimental S2, spoke up. "Anybody see anything in the Intel data to suggest that? I went over the folders last night—"

"When you should have been sleeping," Shimon Bar-El said.

"—and Shimon, I didn't see any hint of it. Minor, maybe annoying, industrial sabotage, sure. Maybe that cavitation problem they were having with their HE shells wasn't just quality control, and I'm damn sure that the premies they've been seeing with the pocket rockets are sabotage. But I've seen *nothing* to suggest an armed force like this. My evaluation—"

"Save it. You were saying, Yitzhak?"

"Other than that, I've no great criticism of me. I didn't try to overplan, or overmanage the firefight. I led from the front until I got shot, and I made the right call on the helo. I did okay."

"Yes, you did. Now, Deputy Regimental Commander and Chief of Staff," Shimon Bar-El said, as he turned to Mordecai Peled. "Are you happy about stalling on the knockdown?"

Peled's lined face reddened. "No, I'm not."

"Neither am I." Bar-El eyed the audience as a whole. "When you've got a green light, you shoot. End of discussion. Ezer, back on your feet. You have the report on the status of the knockdown."

Laskov stood. "There's not going to be any difficulty on that. The pravda is that it was done by the Freiheimers. Fleiss confessed to that."

Somebody snickered.

"And the Casas bought it?" Asher Greenberg asked.

"No." Laskov shrugged. "Or I don't know. But they're pretending to. The Distacamento de la Fedeltà doesn't have any authority over us, since we're technically allied, not subordinate—but if it was determined that a helo and crew was lost because somebody didn't listen to Chiabrera's request that they stay out of it, somebody would hang. Literally."

"Assholes." Rabinowitz shook his head. "Asinine to require hypocrisy."

"Yeah." Bar-El smiled. "We get enough of that anyway. Ezer, did you get anything else out of Fleiss?"

"Some data, but not much." Laskov shook his head. "He was ready to confess to the murder of Abel, and every crime since. I didn't see any point in keeping him around any more." He held his fists out in front of his chest and mimed wringing a neck.

"Fine," Shimon Bar-El said. "And may he rot in hell. Next—Meir, how did you mess up on the grazing fire?"

"Shit. Well, maybe I didn't do too bad, although I probably ought to be fucking shot for not having had a pistol drill for the past two thousand hours. We lost Pinhas Cohen when he tried firing over a fallen tree when there was plenty of room under it."

"He should have remembered that from Basic. Assume we're going into action in a week—how do you want to spend your time? Small arms work?"

"With what? You giving me a 260-man sapper team to take into the field?"

Bar-El scowled. "Don't ask silly questions. Two ten-man squads per battalion—integral to battalion. You put them together, you train them, but you don't own them. You get a sapper section attached to Regiment. The rest of your training detachment gets to be infantrymen—and we'll have too many three-man fireteams as it is. Now, you going to spend the next week at the Known Distance Range?"

Meir Ben David didn't pick up on it. "Fuck, no. One week, eh? Okay—twenty hours of classroom; forty or fifty of field time, half of that with the locals—"

"—and on the seventh day they rested," Ebi Goren said dryly.

"—and if we're going to have to depend on them for logistical support and replacement groceries, we'd sure as shit better be up on local methods and equipment. I'm real suspicious of some of the handling characteristics of that Ciottoloso plastique they like so much. I think it might—"

"Later." Shimon cut him off with a wave of the hand. "What you're telling me is that you really don't think that you need that much pistol training."

"You want my fucking recommendation, you've got it."

Shimon Bar-El smiled. "So I do. Recommendation accepted." He turned to Peled. "Still got to finish the critique, but put gambling next on the agenda. Minor thing, but I don't want it getting away from us.

"Now, on to the cleanup part of the operation. . ."

It was a long morning.

PART TWO

RECON

CHAPTER 8

Night Life

Ari was lying on his bunk when his brothers came into the barracks, each in turn snapping the rain from his slicker with a practiced flip of the wrist before hanging it up. Tetsuo didn't seem to see the poker game, while Benyamin stopped for a moment to exchange a few words with the players at the north end of the barracks.

They were both in khakis, wearing the short, plain field jacket over their uniform shirts. Tetsuo had one of his swords stuck crosswise in the nonstandard leather pistol belt that he wore tight across his hips, but at least it was only the short stabbing sword instead of the whole daisho. Ari had always thought it was just one of his brother's affectations, although Tetsuo claimed that he only carried them because the Nagamitsu blades were a thousand years old. He had the certificates to prove it, and he was always able to get them onplanet—a thousand-year-old sword couldn't be kept out on a Proscribed Tech regulation.

The x-shaped barracks was quiet, mostly empty. Down at the south end, salted troopers slept soundly under their blankets, oblivious to the overhead lights, while the never-ending barracks poker game was going on down at the opposite end. Ari's bunk was near the center of the x, just meters from the central arms locker; he knew that if he got up off his bed and peeked around the corner, he would see Galil and some clerks, at the far end eastern arm of the x, going over some paperwork.

"Officers work too much," Benyamin said, fingering the checkering of the striped insignia at his collar point. He unslung his Barak, tapped on the already-positioned safety, and then dropped it on a bunk, seating himself next to it.

"Some do," Tetsuo said. He didn't sit, and he wasn't smiling. "That why you never put in for a commission?"

Benyamin shook his head. "Nope. Mmm . . . maybe, just a little. Truth to tell, I don't *like* shouting 'Follow me' all the time, and dashing first into God knows what. I do enough of that as is." He touched his fused right wrist. "Plenty of officers in the family, God knows. Shlomo the Asshole, you, both Zayda Bar-Els— figured we didn't need another, what with the General here coming online shortly." He patted his hip. "And since Galil just put me up for my first class senior's warrant, the pay's just fine."

"He got you your warrant?"

"Yeah." Benyamin smiled. "I was thinking about sitting around the barracks and sewing on new stripes tonight." He shrugged out of his field jacket. Beneath, his khaki shirt was unadorned, except for the chain-circled Shield of David on the left breast. That was common, among both officers and men, although Benyamin generally went for sewed-on stripes.

"Pin them on, instead." Tetsuo dropped a pair of first class senior's collar pins to the bed. They looked just like the three chevron-and-double-rocker insignia Benyamin was wearing, except that the white and black checkering was finer, more squares to the centimeter. That only showed close up; they would still look like a gray blob in a sniper's scope. "I'm thirsty."

"Oh. Fair enough." Benyamin held the pins in the

palm of his hand and considered them for a moment. "How'd you know?"

"Galil and I had a little chat. He mentioned it."

"He mention anything else?"

Tetsuo looked long at Ari. "Yeah."

Benyamin exchanged his second class senior's pins for the new ones. He turned to Ari. "Tet and I are going into town, Ari; I think we need a few drinks—celebrate my new warrant. You're coming along. Tet, you want a Barak?"

Tetsuo shook his head. "I'm fine." He patted the pistol holster on the right side of his belt reluctantly before resting his hand on the butt of his sword. Tetsuo didn't like guns.

"Kiyoshi never wore swords."

"Ki couldn't cut worth anything," Tetsuo said. "Good hand with a phut gun, though."

It all felt less like a discussion and more like a performance for his benefit, and Ari wondered what the purpose of it was.

"Hang on a sec," Benyamin said, walking over to the arms locker, coming back with a holster, a pistol and two spare magazines. He dropped it on the bed next to Ari. "Put it on," Benyamin told Ari.

Benyamin picked up his assault rifle and expelled the magazine. He checked to see that it was loaded, the chamber empty, then slammed the clip home with a solid chunk. A quick manipulation and the stock was folded in; he secured it to the right side of his web belt, as though it were an oversized pistol.

"Put it on?" Ari asked. "Eh? What is it?"

"This is what we professional soldier types call a semiautomatic pistol—Belge copy of an old IMI Desert Eagle, the one that originally had the idiot safety. This leather thing is called a holster. What you do is you put the pistol into the holster, and then you put your arms through the straps there, and then tighten it up. Wear your fatigue jacket over it."

"I know what it's called."

"Good." Tetsuo gripped his hand, and pulled Ari upright. "You're carrying a pistol tonight."

"Why?" Ari shook his head. Whatever they had in mind, he didn't want any part of it.

"Trade secret," Tetsuo said, without the hint of a smile. "Something they don't teach you in Soldiering 105."

"I . . . I'd just as soon stay here."

"Look, maybe we shoot people for a living, but there are some bennies," Benyamin said. "Me, I like to travel to strange worlds, see strange sights—"

"—drink strange drinks, et cetera. I like et cetera particularly," Tetsuo said. And then there was a smile for just a moment. "There's a section of Gonfiarsi they call 'La Inguine'—I like it a lot."

Benyamin pursed his lips. "You would." He turned back to Ari. "We're going into Gonfiarsi. Orders are to travel in groups, armed always. And stay in touch." He unclipped his headset from his belt and set it on his head.

"Two is a group, if you feel like arguing. I don't, so we're going to be three." Tetsuo's hand dropped to Ari's shoulder. "You're three."

Ari started to shake his head, but Benyamin's smile broadened.

Tetsuo didn't let go of his shoulder. "Come on."

"No. I don't feel like it."

"Oh, you don't feel like it? Too bad." Benyamin's face was grim. "Until things clear up around here, we don't want you just hanging around. Somebody might say the wrong thing to you, or you might say the wrong thing, or not say the right thing."

"Besides," Tetsuo said, "there's parts of your education that need some remedying. So, little brother, let's go into town." His grip tightened until it hurt. "Now."

Ari's smile felt weak. "Sounds good to me."
Benyamin tossed Ari a slicker.

The rain was easing as they left the barracks and
walked the two klicks toward the distant front gate,
past rows of low, squat buildings barely illuminated by
the light poles. The sidewalk was chopped up; it looked
as though it had been idly chewed, sampled by some
passing behemoth that had nibbled at it and then
moved on. They stuck to the side of the tarmac lane
that ran parallel to the dirt tank road.

Underneath the skullcap of their radar domes, a
squad of skywatches kept guard on the night, the
quadruple snouts of their wireguns shifting position
with a crisp suddenness that made Ari jump.

Benyamin laughed.

Off in the darkness, rows of circled tank platoons
huddled in the night, one trio of the big steel monsters
lit with painful whiteness by portable field lights while
a team of Casa mechs in greasy coveralls worked and
swore and grunted, changing a set of treads on a big
Araldo V, tools squealing against steel and clicking
against ceramic.

The huge tank looked oddly vulnerable, its tread
spread across the tarmac, one side of the hull tilted up
on a set of field jacks, its main gun depressed the full
ten degrees. The steel monsters were silent and immo-
bile, the silence interrupted by only the chick-chick-
chick of the field generator, the click and creak and
whir of tools, and the occasional muttered instruction
or curse.

One of the work crew didn't have a tool in his
hands; he threw a sketchy salute in their direction,
Tetsuo and Benyamin returning it.

"Why'd you do that?" Ari asked Benyamin. "He
wasn't saluting us, just Tet."

"He didn't know that." Benyamin smiled. " 'When

in doubt, salute it' works on a lot of worlds. Not my idea of—"

"Heads up," Tetsuo said, stepping off the tarmac, snapping down his faceplate. Ari and Benyamin did the same.

Wind and water whipped against their slickers and faceplates as a battery of 200mm howitzers approached, then hissed past, the three big guns riding on their aircushion carriers, their tubes strapped down and pointed rearward.

"Glad of the rain," Benyamin said, wiping his faceplate, then raising it.

"Yeah. The grit would've cut us to shit if it'd been clear."

Buses left every five minutes from the front gate, rising into the air and hissing off into the night. The outbound one was half full.

The rain eased; they climbed aboard.

The smell of garlic and grilling fish drew them to a vendor, a red-faced man who took a mouthful from a wine bottle and swallowed half of it before leaning over the grill to spray the rest across the curled pieces of fish. Steam hissed out into the night.

"Clearprawns," he shouted over the din of the trumpets blaring from the bright end of the dark alleyways.

They bought three flat breads—sort of like matzot, but limp—wrapped around a crunchy, garlicky, meaty something.

"You like?" Benyamin grinned.

Ari nodded.

"Local breed of shrimp," Tetsuo said, echoing their big brother's grin. "Shellfish. Tref. Not kosher."

Ari stopped in mid-bite.

"But the law doesn't apply off Metzada, and we, little brother, are off Metzada," Tetsuo said, taking another big bite of his sandwich. "When in Nova Roma, eat what the Nova Romans eat, eh?"

"But we're in Gonfiarsi, not Nova Roma."

"Same principle."

They walked on.

In the sticky darkness and light of La Inguine, it was hard to think of Gonfiarsi as a city at war; it looked more like a city at play.

There was a sprinkling of uniforms among the men, maybe about twenty percent. The rest wore a variety of clothes, from the stained coveralls of the dockworkers, to the tailcoats and trousers of the officeworkers, to the elegant satin tunics and leggings of the grandees.

It all looked strange to Ari as they walked down the Via Giovale, eyeing the flashing lights, listening to the blare of music spewing from the narrow alleyways, from the bars' open doors. All of the clothes were different, but the men didn't seem to feel themselves awkwardly dressed. How did they know what to wear? He shook his head.

Among the young women, the uniform of the day seemed to be a tube dress in pastel, leaving them indecently uncovered from the tops of their heads almost to their nipples, from mid-thigh to their ankles.

Some of them were almost incredibly beautiful, although how they could walk on the ten-centimeter stilt heels—or why they wanted to—escaped him. But it did make their legs look longer, and somehow better. He liked the exotically short hair—hair cut short, not the pinned-up hair of a married woman—framing a variety of faces, none of which looked like they were related to others.

Very strange.

They pushed their way through the crowd into a dark bar, where two bartenders, one skinny, almost emaciated, the other beefy and red-faced, kept pitchers of red wine and golden beer coming. The tables were crammed with enlisted Casas and women with too much makeup keeping pace with them, all of them drinking and pounding in time to the heady beat of the six-piece combo at the far end of the bar.

"Check out the trumpeter," Benyamin said. Ari looked; it was Pinhas Shalvi, until today an S2 instructor, now an S2 sergeant for Second Bat. His eyes closed in concentration as he spurted out an improvised phrase, then opened when the fila player picked up the theme. He spotted the three of them and waved idly before putting the trumpet back to his lips.

A pair of paras and their women vacated a table; Benyamin grabbed the three chairs, beckoning at Tetsuo and Ari to get the drinks.

"Tends to be noisier in the enlisted places," he said when they returned, Ari carrying three glasses, Tetsuo with a pitcher of red. Benyamin poured each of them a glass and sipped. "Not too bad."

"Eh?" Benyamin had missed that last.

"I said, 'Not too bad, and it tends to be noisier.' " He turned back to Ari. "On the other hand, it tends to be a lot cheaper. Fair trade."

The broad-faced, balding sergeant at the table next to them had turned to eye them, then dismissed them with a shrug, but now he turned back and glared.

Ari looked away and sipped at his glass. He wasn't an expert on wine or anything, but it tasted good—fruity, without being sweet.

"You're wearing your bars, Tet," Benyamin said.

Tetsuo looked down at the triple bars of a Metzadan captain that decorated his collar points. He slipped them into a pocket with a friendly smile and a shrug at the Casa.

"Got any enlisted stripes on you?" Benyamin asked.

"Nah. Just—well, you know."

"Try these," Benyamin said, handing his old stripes to Tetsuo. Tetsuo put them on.

"Now," he said with a smile, "we're just three enlisted men out drinking. Drink up."

They listened to the music for a few minutes, a hot,

syncopated theme that the fila player hammered out, then passed around to the guitarist, the keyboard man, then back to the trumpet.

"Tet, you think he's ever going to retire?" Benyamin asked.

Tetsuo shook his head. "Hell, no. Two things Pinhas likes: shooting people—up close and personal—and playing trumpet with real good musicians. You think he'll get a chance to do either in the rock?"

"Not that he's done a lot of shooting lately."

Tetsuo shrugged. "Cadre work sometimes gives you a chance." He smiled. "Case in point."

"Nah," Benyamin elbowed Ari. "Hey, you dead or something? What this is, see, is a conversation. What that means is that I talk some and Tetsuo talks some and you talk some, too."

"Nice of you to explain things to me."

Benyamin pursed his lips. "Shit, kid, don't make too much of it. Things didn't happen the way they were supposed to, but then nothing went right—I mean *nothing*. They don't tell you this in school, but usually, the first time out, we give you something easy to do and help you through. Gets easier after that." He looked at the bottom of his glass. "Usually."

Tetsuo drained his wine and poured himself another glass. "You, little brother, were fucked by the flying fickle finger of fate."

"Yup. You got dorked by the dangling dong of destiny," Benyamin echoed. "Pounded by the pulsating piston of perversity."

"Raped by the reaming rod of randomness," Tetsuo said. "So, you be a good little private, and keep your privates ready to haul out of here, and Benyamin will fix you up with something. Get yourself blooded on something easier than being ambushed. Shit, there's nothing—and I'm including amphibious assault—that's harder to get right than being on the wrong side of an ambush."

Ari didn't answer.

"Seems there were two generals, standing on a hill-top, overlooking a battle," Benyamin said. "An occasional stray shot whizzes by, but nothing much happens. All of a sudden, one of the generals takes a ding—just a flesh wound in the shoulder.

"Says to his aide, 'Lieutenant, bring me my red jacket.' His aide trots off.

"The other general says, 'Hey, why'd you do that?'

"First general says, 'I don't want the men to see that their general is injured; it'll ruin their morale.'

"Second general says, 'Fair enough.'

"Few minutes later, a shell comes close, right between them, so close they can feel the wind as it whips by.

"Second general turns to *his* aide, and says, 'Lieutenant, bring me my brown pants.' "

Tetsuo laughed. Ari didn't. His knuckles grew white around the glass, and he could feel his cheeks burning.

"Okay, little brother, maybe you're not cut out to be an infantryman. So what? You think there's not other things that need doing?"

What could he say?

The Sergeant, his uncle, had once said something about how when you didn't know what to tell an officer it was best to make something up, but when you didn't know what to tell family, the truth was best.

"I have to be an infantryman," Ari said. "I *have* to."

"Why?"

"Because I'm one of the Hanavi brothers." Ari drained his wine and poured another glass, splashing only a little. "You're all fucking heroes, even Shlomo the Asshole. You think I don't notice? You think everybody doesn't measure me against the rest of you? 'Well, Tetsuo may be a staff officer now,' they say, 'but you should have seen him on Endu, back when he was first out.' " He didn't mention what he knew about Tetsuo's other activities, about his suspicions that were just this side of certainty that Tetsuo was one of the nonexistent Metzadan assassins of myth. There were things you didn't ever think about, much less talk about. "Or—"

"Ari—" Benyamin started.

Ari waved him to silence. "—or, 'Benyamin? Benyamin Hanavi? Best damn trooper that ever there was. The bastard's an artist with an autogun, you should see him lay down a covering fire. Solid as Metzada.' Or, 'Ki Hanavi? He was always first in. Always.' " He didn't remember much about Kiyoshi. Ari had only been six years old when Kiyoshi Hanavi died in a muddy rice field on some Randian noble's estate, his legs blown off by a rebel mine.

Tetsuo had drawn his packet of tabsticks and extracted one. Ari took it from his fingers and puffed it to life. Metzada doesn't import luxury items: he'd never tried tobacco before. He coughed hard, and then washed the taste out of his mouth with more wine.

"Then there's Shlomo. For Shlomo, it's always something like, 'I wouldn't share a tent with the pig, and I sure as hell won't leave any prisoners under his care, but did you see what he did on Rand?' Shit, you've heard it, just like I have, that the reason babies on Rand are born screaming—"

"—is because of Shlomo, and that they don't stop until the doctor pulls down the mask and proves that he's not Shlomo." Benyamin nodded grimly. "Who knows, there may even be some truth in it."

"And then there's me." Ari tried another puff of the tabstick. It wasn't so bad this time. " 'Looks good on paper,' they say, 'but paper don't mean shit, now does it? Pissed his pants and froze his first time out,' they say, and they're going to be saying it forever."

"They still call you 'the General,' " Tetsuo said.

"Yeah, sure they do. And they're laughing. Fat chance Ari's going to be a general, they say. Big fucking joke."

Tetsuo shook his head. "If you can't find it in you," he said, his voice low and serious, "fake it."

"*Scusa.*" The maresciallo—warrant officer, second class—at the next table was glaring at them. He was a compact, stocky man, his movements careful and precise, his open collar darkly stained with sweat. "My friend asks, since you cannot manage to keep . . . quiet enough so that we can listen to the music, to please be noisy in Italiano so we that can comprehend it."

The lathe-thin, red-faced man across the table from him was half on his feet. "Cesare, that's not what I said."

The maresciallo made a be-still gesture with his right hand. "Close enough."

"But—"

"Be still, Caporal." He turned to Benyamin and gave an expansive shrug as though to say, *What can you expect?*

A quick look passed between Benyamin and Tetsuo; Tetsuo nodded fractionally, his eyes growing vague and dreamy. They had just picked out their targets, and neither of them had even thought of relying on Ari.

Ari felt like an orphan.

Benyamin nodded, once. "We're leaving, Maresciallo Capo," he said carefully. "My apologies for the disturbance."

The warrant held up both palms. "It's nothing. Sholom, ah?"

Tetsuo cracked a smile. "Indeed," he said, rising slowly.

The warrant shrugged; he gave them something between a deep nod and a slight bow, his hands still open, palms forward. "Buona sera, Sergente."

"Buona sera."

"Che violino," the shorter man hissed.

"Enzo, l'abito non fa il monaco, eh?" said the warrant. "Not only do I want to drink in peace, I just saved your life, and we're not even in combat. Sit down, and I'll tell you about the last war."

As they pushed out into the street, Benyamin frowned. "I didn't catch that last. Either part of it."

Ari forced a smile. "Enzo called you a violin—a toady."

Tetsuo chuckled. "And the warrant quoted an old proverb at him. 'L'abito non fa il monaco'—'the habit doesn't make the monk.' "

The street beckoned to them.

"Tet, what do you bet the warrant's heard a few shots fired in anger in his time?" Benyamin asked.

"And the skinny asshole hasn't? Probably, but not necessarily." Tetsuo shrugged. "I know damn few combat soldiers who like to look for fights in their off-hours, but there are a few."

"Besides Shlomo."

"Yeah, besides Shlomo. And I know a few clerks who don't like the feel of broken teeth—under their knuckles, or in their mouths."

"I like the looks of that bar," Ari said, pointing to a tall building. A red-jacketed doorman kept watch in front of a shiny metal door.

"*Okay.*" Benyamin chortled. "Well, then."

"Well, so much for the enlisted bars," Tetsuo said, leading the other two into an alley and leaning up against the weather-beaten wooden building. He switched the sergeant's insignia for his captain's bars and passed a set of first lieutenant's double bars to Ari. "Put these on."

"Eh?"

Tetsuo beckoned him around the corner and pointed at the sign that said: "UFFICIALE SOLO—OFFICERS ONLY."

"I like the looks of that one, too. Put them on. Take big bites, little brother. Take big bites."

Ari didn't like this. Granted, the regiment played a lot of games with brevets—Ari had heard that Yossi Bernstein was now wearing colonel's leaves—but that was under Shimon's orders, and was surely being done for some purpose. Ari didn't think Shimon Bar-El would approve of them giving themselves French brevets so they could get into a bar.

Still, Benyamin had replaced his sergeant's stripes with a set of major's leaves, and he and Tetsuo were heading through the crowd toward the shining steel door.

Ari hitched at his belt, and tried to glare like an officer as he quickly caught up with them.

The doorman had been briefed on offworld insignia. "Good evening, Maggiore, Capitano, Tenente," he said without a trace of irony, even as he greeted Ari.

Ari Hanavi came awake slowly, regretfully in the dawn light, the back of his mind telling him that he was going to have one hell of a hangover, and maybe it was better to try to sleep it off.

But his bladder was tight as a drum; best to wake up, take a quick piss, and then try to go back to sleep.

There was a bad taste in his mouth, and something soft and cool pressing against his face. His left arm was painfully numb. He reached out and felt a warm softness.

All of a sudden he was very much awake. Gently he spat out the hair, and tried to pull away.

An old story of Shlomo the Asshole's came back to him, about one of the virgins in Shlomo's company. Ari bit his lip.

Whoever you are, please be a girl. Please.

His reaching hand cupped a full, soft breast.

Thank you, God.

She—and who the hell was she? for the life of him

he couldn't remember—snuggled a bit closer, mumbling something.

Although he wasn't quite sure what he was being thankful for. Except for his all-too-quick goodbye from Miriam the night they had left Metzada, Ari was close to being a virgin. It seemed that he'd lost that status in the night, but he couldn't remember it.

God, what was Miriam going to say about this?

That was easy: nothing, because he wasn't going to tell her.

No longer a virgin in either sense, and I probably handled this as badly as the other.

He carefully pulled his arm from beneath her head and slipped out of bed, padding barefoot across the cold tile to the bathroom, closing the door softly behind him with his right hand.

His left arm hung by his side, limp and useless.

As was becoming habit, his education had deserted him in the crunch. His Health instructors had been specific about what to do after you were with a prostitute: remove the condom, urinate, wash yourself. Blood, urine, and semen sample to the chief medician in twenty-four hours, and again in seventy-two.

It was clear that he'd forgotten all the steps last night. The courses hadn't covered what he was supposed to do about the interesting way he ached in unusual places, or the light scratches across his chest, just under the left nipple.

He tried to work some feeling back into his shoulder; the pins-and-needles sensation worsened.

His one-piece was hanging up in the shower, vaguely damp; his commo unit, helmet and pistol hung neatly on the towel rack. His weapons training was still good: he had ejected and checked the magazine, which was full, and pulled back the slide to examine the chamber, which was empty, before he was fully aware of what he was doing.

Rubbing at his arm and shoulder, he looked at

himself in the mirror. He didn't look any different, except that his low-gee acne had finally cleared up.

He washed his hands and face with floral soap. How had this all happened? What you were supposed to do when you were with a prostitute was wrap your valuables in your pants and stash the pants someplace safe—ideally, under the center of the mattress. But it was clear that he hadn't done any of that.

He reached into the back pocket of his one-piece and pulled out his wallet, slapping it once against his thigh before he broke the moisture seal.

Strange, it still contained some of the squarish local currency. Less than he'd started the evening out with, but. . . .

He pulled out the commo unit and slipped the phone over his head, switching it from Standby to On, bringing it up to his lips and puffing for the Admin Freak.

"Kelev One One Two Five," he whispered. "Checking in."

"Mouth Eleven. You're due at Ramorino . . . just less than oh-three hours, Five," a businesslike voice answered immediately, too crisply. "Morning formation —briefing at nine hundred hours. Is there a problem?"

"I . . . don't think so." He thought of asking them to call Tetsuo and Benyamin, but what was he going to say? Hey, brothers, I've locked myself in the bathroom and there's a strange woman out in the other room. Not the kind of situation you wanted to discuss over the air.

The replying voice was too casual as it said, "Say again."

Shit. He just asked me if there's a problem.

Forgetting alert responses wasn't a good way to begin the day.

"Kelev One One Two Five reporting situation nominal," Ari said carefully, and then, with equal care, shut up. The words were important, and so was the delivery.

Translation: I am not being held with a gun to my head, and you don't have to bring the regiment to full alert while you're calling the commanding general, who then gets to decide whether or not to come get me, and with what.

"Mouth Eleven to Kelev One One Two Five. Confirm, please."

The response to that was silence. One word, one grunt, anything—and the voice on the other end would casually accept his word, dismiss him, and then push the panic button.

"Fair enough," the voice of Admin finally said. "You're due in one seven two minutes."

"Understood. Kelev One One Two Five out." He snapped his commo shut.

"Hello?" sounded from the other room.

Great. What was he supposed to do now?

It's amazing what they don't teach you in school, he thought.

He set the equipment down, wrapped a towel around his waist and opened the door.

Her name was Elena D'Ancona, and she was black-haired and lovely, and a few thousand hours short of the twenty standard years he claimed to be, and no, she didn't do this often at all—as she had told him last night, before they broke open the bottle of grappa—she was a sottotenente in the Il Distacamento de la Fedeltà, assigned to Maggiore Zuchelli's detachment, and while last night was fine and all, and she wasn't complaining, they had both had a bit too much grappa and it was all over kind of quick and was the Metzadan Tenente in any particular rush?

Tenente? Oh.

"I'm not exactly a lieutenant," he said. "I'm not even approximately a lieutenant. My brothers had me put the bars on so we could get into the officer's bar."

Her face clouded over for a moment, but then she

laughed. "You look just like . . . a puppy who has made a mess on the floor. You know," she said, "in the Casalingpaesesercito we like to hang sergeants for impersonating an officer."

"In Metzada, we like to promote privates. If they do it right." He couldn't help adding, "And there's been some talk of me getting a promotion." *About the time that the Messiah comes, that is.* "And Zuchelli? Why are you working for that asshole?"

"Oh, the little major isn't so bad." She smiled. "When you do what you're told, we call it obeying orders in the Distacamento Fedeltà, and the Casalingpaesesercito." A sharp fingernail traced down his side. "What do you call it?"

He laughed. "We call it the same thing."

"Why are we wasting time?" she stretched, and smiled.

"I—I've got to be back in three hours," he said, indecently pleased that this time his voice didn't break. "Plenty of time."

She walked him to the shuttle, close, their hips almost touching, but that was all. Metzadan soldiers—be they captains or privates—didn't hold hands in public. Neither did officers in Il Distacamento de la Fedeltà. Bad for the image.

Which helped to explain things, he decided. Fraternization between officers and enlisted was forbidden here—it was part of the local caste system—and while the Distacamento de la Fedeltà was an officer corps, it was not *the* officer corps: regular Casalingpaesesercito officers wouldn't want to associate with the overgrown Inspector General corps that the DF had long been.

At the shuttle, he looked long and hard into her eyes, and then patted his chest pocket, where he'd written down her phone code. "I'll call when I can. If I can, I'll see you tonight."

She nodded briefly, and then smiled. "Luck," she

said. She touched two fingers lightly to her own, full lips.

And then she turned and was gone in the crowd.

He stumbled aboard and found a seat, and then fell into it, trying to reconstruct last night. He could vaguely dredge up a memory of a first round of some fiery clear liquor, and he had a distant image of Benyamin bellowing a Casa captain to attention, but for the life of him he couldn't remember meeting Elena, or what he'd said to her, or how he had ended up in her bed.

There was a tap on his shoulder; he turned to see Benyamin's ugly face split in an almost indecent leer. "Have a good time last night?"

Ari nodded. "Yeah." *I can't remember it, but I guess I did.*

"*Line* up and *shut* up." Peled bellowed, not using commo when ordinary shouting could serve. "HQ there, First Bat over there, then Second and Third. *Move* it, *move* it, *move* it."

Ari shuffled into his place on the tarmac between Benyamin and David Laskov, only two rows back from the front.

Diagonally opposite, a Casa brigade was forming up at right angles to the regiment. They were all clean and shiny, their brass gleaming, their boots mirror-bright, the creases on their utilities knife-sharp. Boots pounding on the concrete, they fell into their places like little toy soldiers.

"If I hear a snicker," Galil muttered from two rows up, at the far corner of the platoon's formation, "I'm going to be real pissed. Keep it to yourselves, people."

"Still, though, don't they look pretty?" somebody murmured.

"That they do." Galil snickered.

Metzadans didn't much practice formal assembly formation. It took a few minutes and more than a few oaths to get the two thousand or so men assembled into lines and files.

The Casas had set up a reviewing stand at a forty-five degree angle to both sets of troops, although what that was all about escaped Ari. Passing in review wasn't one of the things that had been emphasized in school.

Dov Ginsberg stood in front of his seat on the reviewing stand, to one side of Shimon, eyeing the rest of the universe skeptically. Ari could make out Colonel Chiabrera's stout form. The grizzled man next to him appeared to be a general. Probably not Colletta, though—Ari wasn't sure, but he thought he could see only three stars on the general's shoulders.

"Attention to orders," Peled said. He was grim-faced, and his voice was too level, too controlled.

"Stand easy, everyone. This is going to take a few minutes." Shimon Bar-El took Peled's place in front of the microphone. "As you all know, there's been a change of plans," he said, not waiting for Chiabrera's translation for the Casas. "We're moving out in five days to a forward staging area. There's an operation, code-named Triumphant, starting; we're attached to Headquarters, Casalingpaesercito Second Division. Most of you have seen, if not formally met, Tenente Colonello Sergio Chiabrera, formerly the Generale's aide. He's going to be our liaison officer. Standing next to him is Generale Carlo Castiglione, adjutant of Second Division. His boss—our boss—will be Generale d'Armata Giovanni Prezzolini.

"Now, as to what Second Divisione Headquarters is going to have us doing," Bar-El said, smiling, "you don't need to know much. I can tell you that starting tomorrow most of us are going to be doing a solid review of urban assault and street clearing. Sappers are going to be working on occupied demolition. I want the heavy weapons people not only up on local equipment, but local maps and communications protocols, within two days."

"Hey, Benyamin," David Laskov whispered, "you kick in any roofs lately?"

"Shut up." Benyamin sounded more distracted than irritated.

"Now, there's been a lot of shuffling of personnel," Bar-El went on. "I'd like to report that that's all done, but it's not. Effective immediately, Mordecai Peled's relieved of First Battalion and as deputy regimental commander; he stays on as chief of staff. It's my understanding that he's going to put in for retirement when we return home."

Peled's face could have been carved from granite.

Shimon continued: "In case the lesson is lost on anybody, here's the short version. It doesn't matter who you are, or how long you've been my friend, or how well you've served Metzada in the past: when you get a green light on a target, you burn it."

"Bet you Ebi gets the deputy spot," Laskov whispered, probably to Benyamin.

"Five on Sidney," Benyamin whispered back.

"Done."

Shimon Bar-El glanced down at the flimsy in his hands. "Next: Natan Horowitz gets regimental S3. Moshe Kaplan takes over as First Bat commander; he's brevetted to full colonel. Ezer Laskov becomes his deputy, but he's going to have to hold down regimental S2 as well. Sidney Rabinowitz is the new deputy regimental commander, but he's going to have plenty to do with running Third Bat, so let's be sure to keep me alive."

"Pay me," Laskov whispered.

"Shit."

"Aharon Harari is the deputy commander of Second Bat; Benny Elon gets the Third Bat deputy slot." Shimon Bar-El folded the flimsy neatly in thirds, then stuffed it into a hip pocket.

"With all of the reshuffling, all the commo units are going to have to be reprogrammed. Turn them into your platoon leaders at the end of assembly—Sher and his people will have them reprogrammed by evening. Full test tomorrow."

He pursed his lips, then shrugged. "There's one more thing, and it's not a pleasant one. I'd rather not have to do this in public, but if I'm going to embarrass my chief of staff, then I'd best do this publicly, too.

"Brothers and cousins, there's one among us who doesn't measure up. I—no, *we* don't have any use for him. Bring him out."

Ohmigod. Ari's mouth went dry. Shimon was going to march him out in front of the regiment and exile him.

Ari gripped the muzzle of his rifle in his right hand. Better he should pull the charging bolt, stick the gun in his mouth and pull the trigger.

"Stop squirming, asshole. Just stand straight," Benyamin hissed.

Two privates marched Yitzhak Slepak out from First Bat. Slepak moved slowly, jerkily, as though drugged. He wasn't carrying a rifle.

That should be me. Maybe they'll do me next.

No. He hadn't been disarmed, not the way Slepak was. They were going to let Ari get away with it. Ari's stomach twisted itself into a knot. He wanted to vomit, to run, to shout, to do something.

But he just stood there.

Shimon's right hand clenched for a moment before he reached out and tugged at Slepak's uniform, jerking the chain-circled Shield of David patch from Slepak's chest. The threads hadn't been weakened; it took four hard jerks.

Shimon Bar-El shook his head slowly. "I wish there was something I could say to you. Something that would make you understand," he said gently, his voice picked up and magnified into an accusing shout, "but there isn't any point, not anymore. You let us down. We can't afford you." He pursed his lips, then shook his head again. "It's like triage, boy. A medician has to decide who can wait for treatment, who needs to be treated right now, and who is dead, no matter what he does. You're dead weight, and our people can't afford to carry dead weight."

Tears dripped down Slepak's smooth young face, and snot ran from his nose, but he didn't say anything.

"Goodbye, whoever you are," Shimon Bar-El said. "You're no brother or cousin of mine."

Two Casa privates hustled Slepak into a waiting jeep; it raised itself up on its rubber skirt and headed away in a roar of dust and wind.

"What's going to happen to him?" Ari whispered.

Benyamin shrugged microscopically. "I figure the Casas'll put him in the brig tonight, and then offer him some sort of job tomorrow, let him work his way up to some sort of local citizenship. Truth to tell, our training methods are a lot better than what's local; he's worth something to them—as a clerk, if nothing else."

Ari nodded.

I deserve it just as much as he did. I froze like he did.

"Why him and not me?" he whispered.

"Because you're lucky. You've got me and Tetsuo watching out for you." Benyamin sighed. "That poor chickenshit bastard doesn't have anybody."

CHAPTER 9

Training

"Okay, Kelev One One Two Five," Yitzhak Galil, silhouetted in the noonday sun, shouted down from the roof. "Let's see you get up the wall."

Ari couldn't see him but he knew that the captain was frowning. Officially, of course, he wasn't there at all—in theory, they were the first fireteam to try to get on top of the houses.

Hot beneath the glare of sun, the narrow street was done up in pastel and plaster, liberally decorated with signs and bullet holes.

The platoon was halfway down the row of houses that lined the chewed-up street, two fireteams on each side of the street, all except for Ari's watching windows and doors for signs of movement.

It wasn't really much of a street—it was unpaved, with no suggestion of sewer or tube lines below—and only the six buildings at the foot of it were real: the rest of the street was just false fronts. But the real houses were typical of local manufacture: two- and three-story stucco buildings, some windowed on all four sides, some only on front and back. The one Ari stood next to was a compromise: there was only one window breaking the flat expanse of the wall above. Probably a head—a head needed a ventilation window.

Ari hefted his grappling hook in his right hand, the loose coils of rope in his left hand as he stood in the lee of the house.

His first toss went straight up—

"*In*coming," Benyamin shouted.

—and fell straight down, clattering against the wall as it fell to the dirt.

Ari picked it up and hefted it again.

Going in through the top was something that the Sergeant was passionate about—Uncle Tzvi used to embarrass Ari at table by talking about how you take a building like a girl: you start at the top first and work your way down.

It was easy to get to the top of a building if you were already on top of the building next door: most of the time you could jump, or throw a balance beam or a rope slide across. The trouble was the first building. Even that was no problem if you could count on a helo to drop you on it, or if you had a solid ladder.

The trouble with a hovering helo, of course, is that it would draw attention, and fire. The trouble with a solid ladder is that you could never find one when you needed one.

As a last resort in the field, and as a first resort in practice, there was always the grappling hook for the first man, who would secure the rope ladder on top.

The rest of the platoon, spread out along this side of the street, eyed the windows and doorways with practiced attention.

This wasn't a live fire exercise, and Galil hated running blank ammunition through the Baraks—he thought it wore the barrels out—so Ari's efforts to throw the grappling hook were accompanied by constant shouts of "Bang, bang" and "ratatatat," interspersed by the occasional laugh.

Ari's second throw caught on something, but when

he started to put his weight on the rope, he could feel the hook tear free and slide.

"*In*coming."

"Again." Galil's voice was flat and emotionless; Ari could barely tell from the tone that the captain despised him. "This your idea of suppressive fire, people?" Galil shouted. "I can see hundreds of Freiheimers sticking their heads and guns and putzes out the windows, looking at you and shooting at you and pissing all over you. Let's hear some shooting."

"Bang. Bang. Bang."

"Bang, bang, bang, bang, click, chick, chick, slide, reload, bang. Bang. Bang."

"Ratatatatat, ratatatatat, ratatatatat. Five-shot groups okay, Captain, or should I be only ratatat-ing three times?"

Galil laughed. "Very funny, Skolnick."

The third throw worked: the grapple caught tightly on something, and even with Benyamin's and Laskov's weight added to Ari's it didn't come loose. Not a great location, but not bad—the rope was just to the right of the third-floor window.

"Grenade," Benyamin called, and Lavon easily arced a dummy grenade up and in through the window, while Laskov pitched another in through the front door.

Ari worked his shoulders as he slipped his hands into his climbing gloves.

"No." Benyamin said. "David."

"From each according to his ability, eh?" Laskov quickly shrugged out of his packs and tied a coil of light rope to the side of his belt, slinging his assault rifle across his back.

"Take a strain, now."

Ari admired the quickness with which Laskov swarmed up the rope: he made the ten-meter climb to the window in well under a minute.

Just below the window, Laskov freed one hand to

toss a dummy grenade into the room, momentarily flattening himself against the wall before following it in.

One end of the rope dropped out of the window; Ari quickly made it fast to the rope ladder, which Laskov hauled up. In just a few moments, the whole team was inside the room, which did turn out to be a head, the porcelain sink dry and dusty, the bowl half-filled with murky, foul-smelling water.

"My bladder's going to bust." Laskov jiggled the trip handle, considering. "Think there's a chance the plumbing's hooked up?"

Benyamin shrugged. "What do you care? Just piss real quiet. If Galil hears you, he'll make us run through the whole thing again."

"Mm. I'll wait."

The room had been built for training, not maintained for living: the walls were pocked with bullet holes—the Casas were heavily into live fire exercises, and the door to the hall beyond had been kicked off its hinges once too often.

Benyamin put his lips against Ari's ear. "Hallway goes about four meters, past a closet, I think, to a room overlooking the next building."

Ari flattened himself against the wall and pulled a dummy grenade off his belt. He caught the firing pin against the hook on his belt and pulled it out one-handed, then tossed the grenade out into the hall.

"Three, two, one," Benyamin said. "Bang, the grenade explodes, *go.*"

Ari came through the doorway, low, and dashed down the hallway, past the closet, and—

There was a clatter behind him. "Bang, bang, bang, you're dead," sounded from the closet.

"You're all dead," Yitzhak Galil said, stepping out into the hallway, "because I just threw a grenade into the toilet and blew your assholes up around your necks."

His right leg was clamped into a walking brace, and

beneath the carefully groomed beard his face was pale and sweaty, but his voice was strong, his tone biting.

The ceiling of the closet had been smashed through and opened to the attic. Galil had entered through the roof, and then silently made his way through the attic and into the closet.

Benyamin made a fist and banged it against his thigh. "Dammit, Captain, that's a judgment call—"

"Yeah, and his judgment sucks. So does yours. I've done more house-to-house than you have, and if you don't start listening better, more than you'll ever live through. Believe you me: the opposition will be hiding in every nook, under every desk, in every closet, trunk and suitcase you don't blow away, so you *will* throw a grenade through each and every window you pass, through each and every door. You let me worry about supply, understood?"

Benyamin nodded. "Sure. So when we run out of grenades you'll be right there to give us some more?"

"Count on it. Rappel down and do the next house. I'll get Lipschitz started on this one."

"That'll make four times today."

"Right. You count real good. But since we're likely to be clearing out whatever building Shimon chooses for the Tactical Operations Center, I think we may as well do it right. Again, Hanavi, again."

Benyamin didn't want to go into town after supper, so Ari went with Tetsuo and Shalvi. As the bus hissed to a stop, Shalvi, his trumpet case in hand, was out the door.

"Been nice traveling with you, Pinhas," Tetsuo said to the empty air. "Where do you want to go, little brother?"

"Café D'Oro. I may have a date."

Tetsuo was amused. "Hey, it may be the only officers' bar in this part of town, but there's lots more places to drink and, well, whatever," he said. "Or is it just that you like playing officer?"

Elena D'Ancona sat by herself in a dark corner, hunched over a tall frosted glass. Maybe it was just that when she straightened, it brought her back into the glare of an overhead spot, but her face seemed to light up when she saw Ari.

Her glossy hair was tied back in a bun, but stray wisps toyed with her cheekbones, framing her face. The set of her full mouth was a bit hard, perhaps, but that went with the mannish cut of her black uniform, tight in the chest, loose in the waist, as though denying that there was a woman's body underneath.

"Maybe you do have your reasons," Tetsuo said. "Very nice," he muttered, "although packaged like a boy."

Ari glared at his brother as he slid into a chair beside her. Neither imitation Metzadan officers nor officers in the Distacamento de la Fedeltà fondle each other publicly, but her hand was warm on his thigh beneath the table. He let one of his own hands rest against hers. She stroked it gently.

Ari tried to keep his voice from cracking—"Elena D'Ancona, I'd like you to meet my brother, Tetsuo." —and succeeded.

"Delighted," Tetsuo said.

"Ah," she said with a smile, dismissing Tetsuo's offer of a tabstick with a quick toss of her head. "Another . . . officer in the family?" she asked.

Tetsuo smiled absently. "Appears so."

"Perhaps a real one this time?" she murmured.

"Everything about me is real, lady," Tetsuo said.

"Please. Sit with us, for a moment."

As she turned to beckon to the bartender, Tetsuo gave Ari a glare that made it perfectly clear how he felt about unnecessary truthfulness.

The bartender came over with three short, thick

glasses, and set them down, no napkin, on the polished wood.

Idly, Ari stroked at the water beading the side of his glass.

"Your good health, Tetsuo," Elena said.

"Ah. And good evening to you," Tetsuo said, taking it as a dismissal. He dropped a bill on the table, rose, and walked away.

She smiled. "I hoped he'd leave." She raised an eyebrow. "Well?"

"Well, what?"

"Well, what are your plans? Do we have the night, or do you have to be back?"

He shrugged. "Reveille's and morning formation is at oh-six-hundred."

"Plenty of time."

"The long run," she said, reaching across his chest for a tabstick, and puffing it to life. "Tell me about the long run." Her hair, long and glossy and smelling of flowers and sunshine, was smooth against his face as she leaned over him.

The hotel room was lit by a glowplate next to the bathroom door, and intermittently by the hissing and crackling neon sign outside.

He took a puff. "Long run. Well, I go out and prove myself, then I go home, eventually—"

"Soon."

"—and you get to decide if you want to come with me."

She laughed. "Ari! We spend two nights together—"

"One and a half."

"—and do we now have to decide to get married?" She sat up straighter in bed, sweat-dampened sheets piled about her in some absent attempt at modesty. "Do we?"

He shrugged. "Maybe. The regiment isn't going to be here forever. We always have some empty spaces going back, and some of those are, sometimes, filled with immigrants."

Space was on a priority basis, and a shit-listed green private didn't have any priority, but if Ari could prove himself during Triumphant, he wouldn't be a shit-listed green private, not anymore. She brightened, but he put a finger to her lips. "Think about it. There's a lot you don't know about Metzada, a lot you'd have to think through. Just the security problems alone. . . . You'd never be able to leave the rock. Then there's the social problems. . . . You'd have to be a second wife, and that starts to get complicated."

"Second wife. Oh?" She stabbed her tabstick out in an ugly ceramic ashtray, perhaps too violently.

"I'm engaged." How would Miriam take his coming home with a war bride? Of course, he could always call off the engagement; multiple wives were not required, after all. Sure. Then he would get to explain to Miriam's brothers why he preferred an offworlder shiksa to their sister. "Does that bother you?"

As the Sergeant always said, you make your decisions, and then you live with them. He had known Elena for only a little more than a day, and much of that time was blotted out in an alcoholic haze, but there was one simple, basic fact of the universe: he wasn't going to be without her.

He drew her to him.

He made it back just in time for morning assembly. While Peled droned on and on about training schedules, Ari was barely able to keep his eyes open.

"You look tired," Benyamin said, as they walked to breakfast with Laskov and Lavon. "Get enough sleep?"

Ari nodded. "Yeah."

"Good boy. Quick, yes-or-no question—can you spend the rest of the nights this week wherever you were last night?"

"I think—yes."

"Good. Do it." His big brother left unsaid the obvious, that he wanted Ari invisible and out of the way. "Another thing—Galil took me aside; we're switching from urban assault to OP training. You and Tetsuo hear anything about it?"

Ari shook his head. "Not me. Tetsuo didn't say anything. What do you think it means?"

"It means we're going to be running an observation post, and that we'll be told where we're going when we're on the way to it. But you tell your girl even this little and I'll have your balls, understood?"

"She doesn't ask me about that kind of thing."

"Good. One other thing," Benyamin said. "About Slepak."

Ari looked over at his brother. Benyamin's face was flat and impassive; no trace of a smile creasing it. "Yes?"

"He hanged himself in his cell last night."

CHAPTER 10

Yitzhak Galil:
Pieces in Place

A hard rain clawed and hammered at the helo's windscreen, but it couldn't touch Yitzhak Galil, not yet.

The helo shuddered and lurched in flight.

And then the rain stopped, again. Coming off the ocean far to the southwest, a massive storm had met a cold front moving in from the west. The front had shattered the storm into minor stormlets, spinning them off across the Plano Amiata.

Yitzhak Galil pulled the cheap plastic lightscreen around his seat, running his fingertips all along the edge of it before he turned the overhead light back on.

He didn't hear a cry of protest from the helo's pilot, so he pulled out his maps and took off the heavy combination headset/helmet/nightgoggles, wiping his eyes with the back of his hand. Not good to start an observation post mission tired, not good at all. What passes for rest in an OP isn't.

Without the headphones clamped on his ears, the din of the helo was deafening. The roar pressed down on him, making his ears ring.

It was probably worse back in the cabin, although that didn't have anything to do with why Galil was up here. Yitzhak Galil didn't normally insist on the per-quisites of rank.

In garrison, insisting on special treatment was bad practice, an abuse of power. For Metzada, the pur-pose of rank and the chain of command is to get the job done, not to enforce class distinctions between officer and enlisted.

In the field, demanding perks was usually a bad idea, often a dangerous one. A company-grade Metzadan commander usually went in first. It was in many ways a safety mechanism—an officer whose troops thought they could live better without him might not come back out.

Still, this time Yitzhak Galil rode up in the right-hand seat of the helo instead of in back, with the platoon. For one thing, he could prop his bad leg up a bit better, without everybody bumping into it back in the passenger compartment.

More importantly, he still had to figure out where on the ground to put everybody. He wasn't pleased with himself. Looking at it objectively, as though he were his own rating officer, he decided that he should have done that already. Hell, he *had* done it already, but he wasn't satisfied with the locations of some of the OPs.

Reaching into his khakis, he unzipped his exposure suit all the way to his crotch and scratched at the itch over his belly.

Enough dawdling, he decided. Back to work. He zipped himself back up and spread the maps across his lap.

Damn it—being an officer, being in charge, was supposed to get easier. He was supposed to, eventu-ally, be able to look at a map and figure out where to put his people.

His stomach wobbled with every lurch of the helo.

Nap of the earth flying or no, there was a fair chance that a Freiheim skywatch was somewhere along their twisting route, and that any second thousands of silcohalcoid wires would be cutting through the hull while the skywatch's computer took an extra couple of milliseconds to lock its 20mm main gun onto the bird.

His stomach threatened to rebel. Dammit, you were supposed to get used to this after awhile.

Just didn't work that way. He bent back to his maps.

It had sounded so simple at the staff meeting.

"Mopping up," shit.

Not that he objected to house-to-house fighting, particularly when you had an enemy that had been cut off. It was the only assault situation where technique reigned supreme, and where Galil knew that if everybody did their part by the numbers, one step after another, he could keep casualties low. You cleared a town street by street, entering houses from the top, working your way down, driving those who didn't surrender out into the street to be cut apart by your waiting autoguns.

He was good at house-to-house. He knew that his platoon was good at house-to-house.

So, of course, he wasn't fucking getting it. Shimon had given him recon.

And babysitting.

Shit.

"I've got an easy one for you. Foreplay, while the rest of us get fucked." The old bastard hadn't had the grace to blush. "Sit down," he had said. "I know your leg's hurting."

It was; he sat.

Shimon had been given a small, windowless office, probably intended for two staff officers to share. The brick walls were covered by an awful yellow paint that looked almost wet in the light of the overhead glowplates, and there was barely enough room for three chairs in front of the desk.

Mordecai Peled had set up a worktable next to the door and was hunched over a haphazard pile of maps and tech reports.

Peled looked even more tired than Galil felt: his lined face seemed to sag, particularly around the eyes, and his shoulders tended to hunch.

Poor bastard. It would have been kinder to stick a pistol in his ear.

Shimon Bar-El cocked his head to one side, as though he was trying to figure out what Galil was thinking, then shrugged, as though it wasn't worth the effort. "Prezzolini," he said, "the general running Second Division, knows his shit. Good soldier; he's doing the mech assault through Sector Three right. I think."

Peled nodded. "Classic armored cav tactics—smash through, then let somebody else clean up the mess behind you." He straightened. "You don't need to know the details, except where." He tapped a map, fingernails on the paper like ticks on a drumhead.

"Don't worry about it, Mordecai. Yitzhak won't be talking to anybody." Shimon Bar-El turned back to Galil. "The Freiheimers have been patrolling heavily all through here," Shimon said. "The Casas can't keep an OP manned, and I don't want them going in blind, or without good, accurate arty prep. Since we're going to be clearing the town—call it Trainville—after they crash through, I need some idea of the local order of battle so we'll know what kind of clearing job we're facing."

Peled tapped the map again. "Three observation posts scattered across here, each with a Casa forward observer."

Shimon took another puff of his tabstick and shook his head. "Not enough, Mordecai. I've called for six posts. Six FOs."

"Yes, General." Peled's lips whitened. "Each OP has about a ten percent chance of being discovered, even assuming that the Casas are up to sneaking around the woods at night. With six posts, General, it's about a fifty percent chance that at least one is discovered."

"So minimize the chances of discovery, but give me the six." Shimon turned to Galil. "Double some of them up, Yitzhak. We're attaching them to us, so they're under your orders. Put the worst FOs in three of the distant posts, and put your best teams up close. We'll pass fire orders from those through Greenberg, and Deir Yasin—I'll have them liaise with divisional arty."

Galil nodded. It meant that, once the assault started, the wrong people—the Casas—would have priority of mission, but that was to be expected.

Shimon pursed his lips. "Another thing. You're going to figure a lot of this out yourself, so I may as well tell you straight out: they're doing it right. Diversionary assault in the center sector—and there'll be heavier arty prep over there, to keep the Germans sure of their clever guess that the Casas are going to try to punch through in the wrong place.

"At zero minus one hour, your Casa FO takes over and he spots for the arty while they start rolling the tanks. The tanks punch through the right flank; rest of division bypasses the town, while we secure it. They're buying the real estate; we have to take it."

Yitzhak Galil looked at Shimon Bar-El, long and hard. "How sure are you of all this?"

Shimon Bar-El waved away the possibility that he was trying something tricky. "Sure enough to tell you I don't want you captured. And that you'd better locate your own exit-pill. Understood? Soft touch, Yitzhak. That's what I need from you—a nice soft touch. You get your people in there, and you keep them watching and waiting until you get further word. Then you report, spot, and get your heads down. Things have to roll through. Got it?"

"Got it."

"Anything special you want?"

Yeah, he wanted to say. *I want that Ari Hanavi the hell out of my platoon.*

But Shimon Bar-El already knew everything that Galil did; if Shimon wanted the asshole out, the asshole would already *be* out. Should have drummed him out of the family along with Slepak. Would have, if Ari didn't have connections that poor cowardly bastard Slepak didn't.

On the other hand, this was Galil's command.

"Damn it, yes, Shimon. Give me two good sharpshooters from Ebi's battalion, and give *him* the Hanavi brothers. You're talking about me going in with about thirty people, and six of them are Casas. I've got to be able to count on my people, and Ari Hanavi just doesn't measure up."

"I understand he had a head injury. Is that his fault?"

Galil didn't answer.

Shimon Bar-El toyed with a stylo. "Mordecai? You got an opinion?"

"Shit, I don't know." Peled shrugged. "I'm just the chief of staff—"

"Don't," Shimon Bar-El said. "Don't do that again, Mordecai, or I swear I'll relieve you on the spot. You're a full colonel, you were my deputy, and you flinched on a green light. I had to fire you, and you know it. Our friendship, if there's anything of it left, doesn't mean anything. Your hurt feelings don't mean anything. The question in front of us is whether or not the regiment is better off if I do what Yitzhak wants, *and nothing else.*"

Yitzhak Galil felt like he used to when his parents had argued in front of him.

"Very well, sir." Mordecai Peled drew himself up straight. "Then I'd say that we're marginally better off with two sharpshooters in the main force, and not in an OP. The Hanavi kid's scores are good; odds are he'll do fine."

"So be it," Bar-El said. "Request denied."

Shit. Well, if it had to be done, Galil would do it himself. "When do we go in?"

"One squad in three days, to lay the groundwork and site the OPs."

Galil stood. "Then I'd better get some rest."

"No. Not you, not this time—Doc Zucker says you need the full five days to heal. You'll do that here. Skolnick can handle this."

"*I* choose who goes in first, not you." Galil shook his head. "You've already overruled me on personnel; don't try to micromanage my platoon, General. Recon squad goes in three days—the rest of us follow two days later?"

"Right. You've got five days to train your people. You think maybe a quick review of OP selection and setup is in order?"

"Yeah. It'll be a change from urban assault." Galil was already on his feet.

"How are they handling it, by the way?"

"In truth, not bad. I caught some of them with a cheap trick today, but they're pretty good." Galil shrugged. "If they do as well in OP, I'll be happy. I'm going to keep it simple and light. They're in good shape, and OP is a matter of endurance more than anything else. Two, three days of reasonable work, then let them rest." He tottered off toward the door.

"Good. Yitzhak?" Bar-El's voice stopped him.

"Yes?"

"Who are you sending in?"

"Skolnick." Yitzhak Galil smiled. "But it's *my* call, not yours."

Of the six Casa forward artillery observers assigned to him, two were absolutely useless—stumbling oafs who hadn't been able to go through the forested areas of Camp Ramorino without tripping over their own putzes.

The only thing Galil could think to do with them was stick them in an out-of-the-way OP, with their radios under the control of the two Metzadans, and with the firm hope that they wouldn't get caught.

Not that they'd stay caught: Sapirstein had specific orders on that score, and the only phut gun. If necessary, their bodies would be captured. Let the Freiheimers make corpses talk.

Orders might be orders, but Galil was taking only a minimum of shit.

That left four Casas that might be able to tell their left foot from their right, and could be reliably expected to call in the arty into roughly the right hex, if everything went right. If they didn't panic, if the radios were still working, if, if, if. . . .

He shut off the reading light and pulled up the screen.

The rain hammered down at the windshield, coursing off in manic rivulets.

It was dark in the cockpit, the faint glow from the instruments and the almost invisible flicker of the windshield display barely relieving the inky blackness.

He pulled the copilot's helmet down on his head and turned the screen back on. The cabin sprang into relief, the dim light of the helo's instruments flaring like a red beacon, the windshield display becoming a twisting net of paths and flashing crimson sources.

The pilot sitting next to him looked like some enormous insect, wires coming out of the top of his helmet like antennae, the oversized lenses of his night goggles riding high on his forehead, the screen in front of his face flat and blank from this side.

Beyond the rain-streaked window, the enhanced night was harsh whites on black, skeletal trees poking bonily from rolling, corpse-white hills.

"Thirty seconds to Site One," the pilot announced, his voice clear in Galil's ears. "No lights. Do you still wish me to dip and bypass? Or can I just bypass?"

"Dip and bypass," Galil said. "Maybe they're at Site Two."

The idea was simple: the helos would simulate dropping them off at one or more sites before and after actually dropping them off. If there were Freiheimer observers out there, they'd have only a twenty percent chance of guessing where Galil's people had been left.

Of course, it did make the chances of the helo getting blown out of the sky a lot worse, which was why the Casa pilot hated it.

The pitch of the blades deepened as the helo slowed. Galil shut the screen off and patted the panel the helmet was plugged into, wishing he could take it with him. The Freiheimer watchers in Menadito would have night goggles. Granted, not the super-light models that you could use on other worlds, but that was an advantage for the defenders: they could afford the thirty kilos of circuitry it took to process a starlit image into something usable. Galil couldn't afford to haul it—there was already too much mass in his Bergen.

The helo settled toward the ground, dropping rapidly until Galil could feel the surge as it went from true flight into transitional lift, riding almost like a skimmer on the cushion of air between the rotor and the ground.

Too soon, the helo started to move.

"No. Give it thirty seconds." It would take at least thirty seconds to disembark, if this was for real.

"Capitano—"

There was another helo two minutes behind this one, also half-empty.

"Count it out. Twenty more seconds."

With a muttered curse, the Casa pilot pushed the cyclic forward, jerking up on the collective. The nose dropped and the helo moved forward, quickly picking up speed as it climbed.

There was a phut gun in his thigh holster, but Galil didn't reach for it. Galil knew which part was which, but he couldn't fly a helo, dammit, and the Casa knew it.

"We spent long enough there," the Casa said. "Site Two in five minutes."

The helo roared through the night.

Shit. This asshole wasn't going to fake stops at the other sites—he was just going to drop them off and fly his ass back to safe airspace.

Maybe that could be fixed. Galil punched for the cabin intercom. "Anybody here checked out on a helo enough like this?" he asked, hoping that the Casa pilot couldn't understand Hebrew. It was a good bet.

There was a moment of silence, then: "Laskov. I can fly it, although I don't know how well. Hang on a sec." There was a long moment of silence. "I've got the most flight time in a helo, but Edel has more simulator time."

"You take it. Orders: you're going back with the pilot. Make sure the bird fakes stops at Sites Three and Four. Hoist a drink for the rest of us."

"Yes, adoni. Will do."

Galil could tell that Laskov didn't like it—trading off more time in the air for the safety of being relieved of the OP mission—but he was reliable. It cut Galil's strength by one man they might not be able to spare, but this pilot was too tentative to be trustworthy. It was a bad bet that the Casa was willing to play target, to fake landing at other sites in the hope of keeping the Freiheimers ignorant about if or where Galil's commando had been dropped off.

Ahead and below, five lights blinked on in a T-shape. The night outside was wet, but Galil's mouth was dry.

"Set it down there," he said.

The Casa pilot flared two meters off the ground, hovering in ground effect.

Galil exchanged the wired-in copilot's helmet for his own, zipped up his ex-suit, then velcroed his khakis over it. "Set it down."

"Never mind that," the pilot shrilled. "We're here. You get out, out, get out."

"I said, set it *down*." Galil reached forward and snapped the power off, slamming the edge of his hand down on the pilot's wrist—hard enough to bruise, not quite hard enough to break—when the Casa reached for the starter. Choking, the engine died. The helo splashed down, hard, on the dark, wet ground, half-knocking the wind out of Galil.

He snatched up for the intercom microphone. "Kelev One Twenty. Go."

The Casa pilot was grabbing for the starter; Galil slammed his elbow into the side of the pilot's head. The Casa subsided long enough for Galil to unbuckle the pilot's holster and relieve him of his automatic.

Galil kicked the door open, tossed his Bergen out, and launched himself into the dark and the rain.

The ground squished under his feet, and he slipped on a slimeleaf plant. He hit rolling, his mouth full of bile. If Skolnick and his scouts had been found and tortured into giving out the drop zone, here was where the bushes would open up with autogun fire, cutting Galil and his commando into little bloody chunks.

"Am Yisroel chai," a voice called out of the night. *The people of Israel live.* It was a password, and likely to choke in a Freiheimer throat.

As the two squads moved off into the dark to secure the perimeter, Skolnick, his face black with paint and slick with rain, his arms held high over his head, came out of the trees, stepping over a clump of deathly white cadapommidor.

Ari Hanavi brought his rifle halfway up, but Benyamin caught the muzzle, forcing it down.

Galil clasped hands briefly with Skolnick.

"Perimeter secure. We're clear—a patrol passed down the road half an hour ago," Skolnick said. "Got the OPs picked out and assigned."

"That's my job," Galil said.

"You think you can do better in this shit?"

"Sorry." Never apologize, never explain—except always apologize when you're wrong, or the troops will think you don't know what you're doing; always explain when they don't understand, or they won't know what they're doing.

Behind Galil, the helo's right-hand door slammed shut after Laskov. The engine stuttered back to life, the rotors, which had never quite stopped rotating, speeding up.

"Faceplates down," Galil said, obeying his own order.

The engine screaming in protest, the helo pulled straight out of the mud, spun quickly around, dropped its nose and lifted off into the rain and the dark.

Galil pushed his faceplate back up, shouldered his Bergen—damn, the thing seemed to gain mass by the second—and followed Skolnick off into the trees.

It always happened, even after years in the field. You feel like everyone and everything is looking at you, aiming at you. The night has a million eyes and each one is looking at your back through a set of crosshairs.

But the night was silent, and dark. He waited.

There was a low whistle to his left, somewhere off in the rain; it was immediately answered by another from the darkness, and then another, as the fireteams counted off.

So far, so good. Galil pulled off his helmet and ran his fingers through his hair.

The other helo roared down out of the rain, quickly disgorging its three fireteams as it hovered above the flattened grasses.

Thirty seconds later it was back in the air.

Galil gave the short whistle that meant prepare to move out, with the two-minute suffix.

He wiped the rain from his face. His exsuit and boots did a fine job of keeping most of his body dry, but his hands and face were bare, and cold. Galil's bladder was tight. He unzipped his khakis, and then his exsuit, and pissed against the nearest tree. As he fastened himself up, he caught one of the Casa lieutenants, a gangling man named Andreotti, grinning at him.

Asshole. "If you've got to go, go now," Galil ordered. "From here on in, you barf, piss and crap into a plastic bag." The whole idea behind an OP was to dig a hole and pull it in after you. Nothing was expelled from the OP unless necessary.

The rain eased, just a little. It was time to get moving.

Galil would have whispered; "Move out," but they all knew their jobs. They moved out, across the slimy floor of the forest.

His exsuit had kept him dry through the night, the fabric breathing enough so that he wasn't swimming in his own sweat. But that didn't do anything for his feet; by the time the sky to the west was graying toward dawn, each step was agony.

Galil should have argued with Shimon about who went in first: Skolnick had spread out the other four posts too far along the hillsides, and had sited the last two OPs too near each other. That last was understandable, though: Galil would have been tempted to situate himself so another post could give him covering fire. It was the right move for almost everything except an observation post.

Still, Skolnick had picked out a good spot. Flat on his belly on the slick melfoglia leaves, Galil could make out most of the town square and the chewed-up ground to its north, where the Freiheimer tanks huddled in the dark, waiting.

He had seen worse places for an OP.

"Go," he whispered. He gestured at Benyamin Hanavi and Lavon to cover them. Not that a couple of phut guns could make any difference if a Freiheimer jumped out of the bushes, but there wasn't much you could do.

Skolnick and the rest of his team crept off to the east, quickly vanishing among the trees.

Galil gave a single quiet hiss. All of them shrugged out of their Bergens and propped them up against the base of a bifurcated tree stump, quickly covering them with the spare blackscreen-backed camo net.

Not a bad match, Galil decided, although it might be visible in the daylight unless it was properly covered.

Carefully, gingerly, Yitzhak Galil worked his shoulders and arms, trying to loosen them at least a little. Their tendons were stretched as painfully tight as his nerves.

"Let's get to it," he whispered.

Galil wanted badly to take the first watch himself, but it was better practice to give it to somebody else. Get himself real tired, so that he could sleep during his offshift.

Working with Marko Giacobazzi, the lanky Casa FO, Galil put up the vision screen, a strip of black cloth one meter high and four wide. In dim light, the human brain sees movement much better than colors or shapes; as long as they kept quiet, they could move behind it without being spotted from the town, at least for a while.

Galil consulted his thumbnail watch. They should be able to work behind it for an hour, at most. Not nearly enough time to dig themselves in; they'd have to camouflage themselves as best they could, and then dig in the next night.

In a few minutes, they had the cover tarp pitched, then covered with quickly chopped leaves. That would do for the day, he hoped.

He gestured at the others to get themselves and their gear under the tarp, then moved away to get some perspective. Not bad—he could just barely make it out in the dim light, and probably couldn't have spotted it from more than ten meters away.

That would do, for the time being. They were close

enough to the edge of the woods, where the trees gave way to the deeply furrowed ground of a field ready for planting, that the Freiheimers would likely patrol near them—but, with luck, they'd get through the day.

In any case, there was nothing to be done about it.

He slipped back to the tent and slipped underneath, into the mass of bodies and Bergens. There was barely room for the six of them to curl up in the rear of the tarp; they had to leave an observation bay in the front.

Galil cut it too close; it was already getting gray outside, enough light that he didn't have any trouble locating his own Bergen. He pulled out two black boxes, one containing the squash radio, the other the demo charges. The green flash that answered his quick push of the radio's test button told him that the circuitry thought it still could work.

He unrolled the wires to the pincer-like dead-man switch, then stuck the prongs carefully into the front of his pants before arming it. Galil couldn't guarantee that his OP would not be found. But he could guarantee that they wouldn't be taken.

Ari Hanavi swallowed; Benyamin Hanavi smiled. "Captain, do me a favor and don't forget to disarm it before you unzip yourself for a quick piss, eh?"

"Shut up," Galil said. "OP rules—silence. Lavon, first watch. Chamber empty. Wake Benyamin, then Ari, then me."

"And me?" Giacobazzi snorted.

"Nothing. You just do what the rest of us are going to do in our offshift: lie still for the next sixteen hours and don't make a sound."

Clumsily, painfully, awkwardly, he stretched out on his belly atop his sleeping bag, the dead-man switch pressing against the pit of his stomach in a cold reminder.

CHAPTER 11

Banked Coals

1315.

Shit. Only two minutes since the last time he looked.

The day was dragging on, Ari was sweating, and time itself was slowing down.

It was still 1315.

Ari had thought it was bullshit when the Sergeant used to talk about how he preferred any other kind of work—even urban assault—to covert OP duty. Ari was beginning to understand it. Not agree with it, mind, but understand it.

Unmoving, they lay under the camo cover like rounds in a clip, waiting. Or maybe more like rolls in an oven.

Ari always hated being crammed in. His universe had shrunk to the few centimeters from the kipmat under his sleeping bag to the underside of the tarp, maybe twenty centimeters over his face.

The day was heating up outside, and so was the space under the tarp. He lay in his sleeping bag, which was always unzipped, just in case he had to get out of it quickly. Metzada didn't expect you to be able to survive anything and everything, but the rule was that you were to die trying, their throats in your teeth, and not bagged and ready for delivery to a prisoner camp or a grave.

Once every fifteen minutes he was permitted to shift position slightly, to let the rocks under his bag and mat press up against a different part of his aching body. There was one sharp rock that kept poking him in the right kidney when he lay on his back, and when he tried to pretzel his body to avoid that, the blunt rock to the right of it pressed hard against his spine, even through the kipmat and bag.

Once every four hours, at the change of watch, he could take his turn to work his way across the prone bodies to the rear of the OP, slide out of his khakis and exsuit, and stretch out to use the bedpan-shaped toilet, then carefully dump the mess into a plastic bag, tie the bag shut, and spray a neutralizing chemical over the slickened toilet to keep the smell at a minimum. Chemicals or no, the smell never quite went away.

Living in the OP was living in a fart.

On his left, Benyamin was asleep, snoring lightly. He'd come off watch a few hours before, and had immediately fallen asleep and stayed that way with a resolution that Ari could only envy.

Ari had barely been able to sleep at all. A pill from his belt kit would have put him out; on his last turn to sleep, he had asked Galil for permission to take the morphine, and had been told no.

Ridiculous. A shot of naloxone could bring him out of a morphine nap as quickly as a shaking would waken him from normal sleep.

He didn't really understand why Galil had said no. It wasn't as if they were expected to defend themselves. If they were surprised, Galil would just blow them all up.

Ari shuddered. He hadn't really thought about that before. He tried to think about something else, anything else. But he couldn't. No wonder the Sergeant said that OP duty combined "all the thrills you get from spending hours locked in a skipshuttle with all the warm feeling of safety you get in combat."

It was hot under the tarp, and getting hotter. Ari glanced down at his thumb.

1317.

He loosened the waist vents of his exsuit. He couldn't get comfortable no matter what he did: when he kept himself sealed up tight, he got too hot, and began to sweat. When he opened his vents, the ground stole the heat from his body too quickly and he started to freeze. Damned kipmat wasn't any good.

When he tried to find some way to get comfortable by opening and closing the vents every few minutes, Galil, on watch, reached out and slapped him on the ankle, shaking his head in a definite order.

It would be Ari's watch next. Then he could at least have something to do while he was miserable.

1325. Thirty-five minutes to the start of his watch. They staggered it so that there were always two men on duty at a time. In another . . . thirty-four minutes now, Marko Giacobazzi would come off shift and crawl back, Galil would take over the squash radio and Ari would get the observer's slot. At 1500, Benyamin would come on and Ari would get to play with the squash radio, compressing their observations for later retrieval.

Best to think of something else. He tried to concentrate on Elena D'Ancona, recalling the firm but silken feel of the skin over her hip, the awkward but strangely erotic way her belly creased when she bent forward, very soft and real, not at all like a frozen holo in a pornographic picture book, her long hair streaming down over his face, or brushing against his chest and belly.

Great. A hard-on in an OP. He rolled over onto his stomach.

What would the Sergeant do in a situation like this? He tried to remember. That was the big advantage that Metzada had, of course: with a constantly employed military, you were being taught by people who had done it—not just studied it—and had probably done it recently, and at least well enough to live through it.

"Lesson time," Uncle Tzvi had said—and Ari could almost hear his voice grate, like oiled gravel. "There I was, and I couldn't do anything. Shit, I didn't have anything to do. So I did a mental review of some skill I wasn't going to need on this one. When you don't know what to do next, or now, think about something you can do some other time."

Tzvi Hanavi had been on Endu, putting down the Kabayle revolts. They were chasing some now-itinerant tribesmen all over the central highlands, and had gotten stretched past their supply line, then pinned down when the natives attacked. The central highlands were rocky, and there were no real roads at all. Overland travel was by foot or sure-footed mule.

So Uncle Tzvi had spent the week doing a mental review of vehicle checkpoints, something totally irrelevant there—the locals' idea of a luxury vehicle was a cart with some other asshole pulling it.

Uncle Tzvi had chuckled as he told the story. "Even did me some good," he had said, "although not on Endu. Next time out, I swear: the captain asked for a squad to run a nice, safe VCP instead of squatting in the mud with the rest of us, and since I'd worked out how damn boring they are, I gave it a pass, and ended up not getting blown up with your cousin Avram and the rest of his fireteam. So, the trick is to think about something that doesn't apply. Got it?"

Okay, Ari decided. He would try a review of the aims of vehicle checkpoints in a counterinsurgency situation.

Well, the book said that VCPs could prevent insurgent movement in general, and reinforcement in particular; it could interfere with insurgent logistics, preventing them from moving supplies and arms around; it could provide subjects for interrogation; it could—if done right—impress the local inhabitants that the controlling forces were in control. . .

Blah, blah, blah. Didn't help.

Okay. Try visualizing a hasty search—no, a thorough search, just this side of a workshop search.

The Renault 220 was a common alcohol burner—burned petrochemicals, too, if available.

Forget setting up. Privates didn't have to decide on the setup, although Ari knew you were supposed to set up a VCP just around a bend, with a light machine gun group in concealment on the other side, just in case the insurgents tried to escape when they saw the checkpoint.

But never mind that—visualize a Renault 220, a blocky automobile, obeying the traffic sentry's instructions to slow down and stop.

Ari would approach from one side while his partner approached from the other. Combat conditions—rifles charged, safeties off and fingers the hell off triggers. Keep the rifles pointed to one side, but just barely so.

Check the registration first. If you're computerized, there may be a flag.

Then check the driver, make sure he's not wearing anything that passes for body armor, while checking him for weapons. Yes, he's entitled to have a pocketknife —but it'll be given back to him after the search, if he's allowed to go.

Then start the search, keeping the driver—no. Then Ari would safe his rifle and hand it to the third member of the fireteam before beginning the search. No weapons within reach of the driver, and always keep the driver covered by a good shot, sighting firmly on the driver's center of gravity.

Ari would start with the outside of the car, and keep the owner with him.

Then underneath. If they'd had time to prepare the

site properly, the driver would have been forced to stop over an improvised lubrication pit.

Ari would look up, looking for paint; for too much grease—it could cover the scratches of some recent work, and the work might have been hiding a bomb or parts of a gun—for extra pipes in the exhaust system. . . .

He came awake suddenly, trying to suck in a breath. He couldn't; something was clamped over his mouth. He brought up his hands.

"*Easy*," Benyamin whispered, sharply but quietly. "Your stag now. You fell asleep," he said, just a trace of pride in his voice.

Oh. He glanced down at his thumbnail. 1403. Right.

He worked his way over to Benyamin and Lavon, stretching out next to Galil as Marko Giacobazzi spidered his way to the rear of the tarp.

His mouth tasted of salt and dust.

Galil wore the squash radio's facemask, his jaw muscles working as he dictated, his stylo checking off items on the sketch pad in front of him.

He scribbled on the pad and showed it to Ari.

NO BINOCS, NO SIGHT. SUN BAD ANGLE.

Galil tabbed the note into oblivion when Ari nodded his understanding. They didn't need light flashing off the binoculars or the sight of the sniper rifle in its case to his left. As long as no Freiheimer patrol stepped on it, the OP was effectively invisible—unless they earned some attention.

He folded his hands and started to crack his knuckles, but stopped himself before Galil could. No. Granted, there wasn't any patrol within range, but on OP duty you don't make any noise that you don't have to.

He stretched out in front of the viewing port, feeling his muscles unkink.

Viewing port, hah. That was far too dignified a

name for something that was only a camo net covered by grasses.

It was dark and dank in the OP; Ari drank in the fresh air and golden sunlight that trickled in through the netting.

Almost a klick beyond, across the rolling, weed-choked fields, the town stood at the junction of two roads—one running east-west, the other north-south—and a rail line that ran from the northwest to the southeast. The town's operational name was Trainville, but the Casas called it Menadito. The locals grew corn and wheat—*had* grown corn and wheat, until the Freiheimers had punched through almost to the Pecatrice River, leaving Menadito behind enemy lines, its residents sent scurrying as refugees.

There had been a stand of tall pine trees to the south of the town, but all that remained were even rows of stumps, and logs lying on the ground. Ari wondered if the Casas had done it themselves, to spite the invading Freiheimers, or if the Freiheimers, not finding any use for a pine forest, had cut them down, spoiling what they couldn't use. A real terran robin—Ari stared at it until he was sure; he'd only seen them in textbooks—flitted in and out of the leaves, probably trying to rebuild a shattered nest.

Ari tried to feel sorry for the Casas—both of his mothers said you were supposed to—but he couldn't muster any real sympathy. When the Casas were driven out of their homes, at least it was into an atmosphere they could breathe. Fuck 'em.

Ari had enough problems of his own. It looked like he had gotten away with screwing up during the ambush, unlike Slepak, may the poor bastard rest in peace.

But forget about all that. This should be easier. If only he could do things with the sureness and self-confidence that Galil had, that Benyamin and Lavon had. Hell, even Lieutenant Giacobazzi seemed to fit in here better than Ari did.

Ari didn't have the style down. Everybody else did. Hell, somebody had made up a range card, just as if they were in an autogun emplacement, and oriented a standard hex overlay over the card's distance and angle coordinates. It was all probably Galil's work—the town was sketched in with almost feminine accuracy and care, down to the trio of dug-in skywatches that guarded the skies overhead.

The buildings were mainly two-story, of weather-darkened stucco, although a four-story red brick building dominated the middle of what probably was the town square. At the west edge of town stood a tall, white spire topped by an elongated pyramid. Ari thought he saw a flash of light from an opening in the pyramid, but he wasn't sure.

Ari made a note. FLASH OF LIGHT IN PYRAMID AT R 030 DEG. DX 1200 METERS? BINOCS?

Galil nodded, and crossed out PYRAMID, substituting CHURCH STEEPLE.

ALREADY NOTED. Galil added. OVERT OP. WHAT FIRE PRIORITY YOU GIVE IT?

Ari shrugged. MEDIUM. CAN'T MOVE. BEFORE ASSAULT THO.

HIGHER, Galil wrote. DON'T ASSUME NOT DUMMY, THO. LOOK FOR OTHERS.

Ari watched for a long time, but he didn't see anything of importance. They weren't here to see nothing of importance, though. Better look closer.

Okay. Arbitrarily but reasonably, split the field of view into foreground, middle distance and background. First get rid of the periphery on both sides, then concentrate on the core of the matter.

Foreground was nothing. From where the forest left off and the fields began, there wasn't anything except plowed ground for two hundred meters at least, broken only by a running wire fence. Mines could be hidden in the ground, of course—mines could be hidden anywhere—but the main purpose of mining was psychological, which was why most minefields were marked. If an assaulting force didn't know it was going over mined ground, it just might charge across it and make it.

Besides, the Freiheimers wouldn't be expecting an assault from the south, and with good reason—infantry needs armor to defend it, just as armor needs infantry, and armor needs open country or roads to move along and fight on.

Hmm . . . the fence could be barbed wire, and it might be booby-trapped, but it wouldn't matter if it was; there wasn't going to be an overland assault through—

There was something at one of the low buildings at the edge of town, off toward the south, something in the window. He stared at the window until spots danced in his eyes, but it was gone. POSS. MOVEMENT IN WINDOW AT –45 DX 850.

He kept looking, though. Nothing.

Ari glanced down at his thumb. 1414. This was getting to be as boring as being off stag.

Back to first principles. The duty of a forward observer is to observe and report. Ari checked the range card. The wire fence was marked, and noted as being barbed. Enough to stop a cow, but nothing that would make troops hesitate.

In the far distance, Ari couldn't see anything but the brown hills. Hmmm . . . not true. There was a twin contrail near the horizon, stretching out to the east. He noted the time and direction, wondering whose it was.

The middle ground was where the action should be. The Freiheimers were dug in for defense. Ari could spot two, no, three anti-tank emplacements, and he was suspicious about the hole in the back wall of the garage at the edge of town. This area hadn't been fought over recently, but there was both a man-high hole in the brick and a pile of rubble near it. It could be just an honest bit of construction, or it could be a hole cut in the wall so that the backblast of a recoilless rifle or an anti-tank rocket wouldn't fry the users.

There were maybe three dozen people moving in the street, most of them in the too-dark green field uniforms of the Freiheimarmee, bulky with their draped body armor.

For a moment, Ari could make out one of their oversized six-man fireteams crossing the street, the autogunner trying to hold his weapon chest-high, like a rifle, making himself look like just another rifleman. Freiheimer discipline was good, but that could also mean that the defenders feared they were under observation.

Feared, rather than knew, or even suspected. If the Freiheimers suspected that the hills around them held observation posts, they'd probably send out patrols to examine closely.

Or, possibly, send out an artillery barrage. Impact fuses triggered as shells dropped into the forest would send down cones of killing splinters and fragments. Tomorrow, they might be able to live through that— they were going to attempt to fill the sandbags and dig themselves in tonight, to get at least forty centimeters of overhead protection for the sleeping area of the OP.

The Freiheimer patrol vanished behind a building and didn't reappear.

More likely it was just good discipline, and the Freiheimers had good discipline.

Ari made a note of where they had disappeared. Odds were fairly good that they were based on the street that Galil had named Avenue C, somewhere here between Fourth and Fifth Street.

Six Freiheimer tanks, their main guns pointing rearward, rattled out from a warehouse at the edge of town and moved slowly away, turning left behind a block of apartment buildings and disappearing. All hatches were open, helmets and shoulders peeking out. One of the tank commanders was standing up, his body armor gleaming.

Ari didn't understand why he was wearing it while in the tank. Anything that could crash through the ceramic armor plating of the tank wouldn't be stopped by another couple of millimeters of baslyn, and the ninety percent or more time that tankers spend outside their tanks only account for about a quarter of their casualties.

SIX[-]—POSS. TANK COMPANY, Ari wrote, then traced their path on the map. FL4; GUNS REARWARD; UNBUTTONED; PLT LDR(?) STANDING IN HATCH.

Identifying them as the Funcken-Leopard IV had been easy. The Mark IV had the stubby Rheinmetall 100mm smooth bore main gun, instead of the longer 120mm rifled gun of the Mark III. Military utility tends to run in cycles; in another ten years the locals would be producing the double- or triple-charge HESH loads that would make spin-stablized ammunition again preferable for tanks, counting on multiple shaped charges to do the job of crashing through armor, instead of the kinetic energy of the Hivel rounds the smoothbore gun had been designed for.

Still talking into the squash radio's facemask, Galil shook his head.

REINF PLATOON, he wrote.

Ari didn't know much about it, but he didn't remember hearing that Freiheim was using the overstuffed five-tank platoon. They didn't try to cram in all that sort of data in school; there were too many armies on too many worlds for you to remember the TO&E of all of them, or even most. Ari's teachers had concentrated on the principles of organization, not on memorization of details. He hadn't cross-trained in armor, but from what he could remember about tank organization, pretty much everybody had long been convinced that the basic fighting unit was three tanks: one to attack, one to cover it, and the third as a spare—a necessary spare, given that you tended to lose about ten percent of even well-maintained tanks for every hour of travel. Finicky beasts; they needed a lot of service.

LOOSE DEUCE PLATOON? Ari wrote.

Galil pulled the mask from his mouth. His lips pursed in exasperation, he picked up the pad, pulled the tab to blank it, then put it and the stylo down. He opened his mouth and then with a visible effort closed it, before beckoning Ari closer to him. Galil pulled the speaking mask from the radio and fit the rubber collar tight over Ari's ear.

"Screw it," he whispered, "I'm getting writers' cramp.

"First, asshole, you'll note that the Freiheimers are protecting the town with an infantry battalion. If you were listening to any of the briefings, you'd know that Frei doctrine calls for a maximum of a tank company integral to a defensively positioned infantry battalion. If you'd been paying attention to the previous reports, you'd know what we already spotted another six tanks on the other side of town, operating together. If the Frei are moving them around for our benefit, we're in deep shit.

"Simple conclusion: what you're looking at are reinforced platoons. Platoons. Figure six tanks times three platoons plus a company command tank and one for the exec and you've got maybe twenty tanks defending the town. It's likely the other platoons are out preparing defensive positions, accompanied by bulldozers we know ought to be in Trainville, but which we haven't seen, either.

"Second. Tanks break down. Nobody good switches to loose deuce *before* combat—it's better to make do with fewer three-tank platoons. Frei armor commanders are good; they know all that.

"Conclusion: you don't see two-tank platoons here.

"Lastly. The job of observer, particularly when the observer is a green private, is to observe. Not argue." Galil pulled the speaking mask gently from Ari's ear and fitted it back to the squash radio before picking up the stylo and writing:

CONCLUSION: YOUR CONCLUSIONS NOT WORTH SHIT.

ORDER: STOP ARGUING, ASSHOLE. KEEP EYES OPEN, NOTE WHAT YOU SEE.

Ari finished his shift with his eyes open, noting only what he saw. No conclusions. He mentioned that the tanks used the tarmac roads, and that the roads were not apparently damaged, but not his conclusion that that meant the tanks wore the heavily rubberized treads that wouldn't chew roads.

But he didn't pull the tab to erase the notepad. He wasn't sure whether it was an act of bravado or cowardice not to hide Galil's stinging message so Benyamin wouldn't see it, but he couldn't do it.

A day of boredom and embarrassment was followed by a night of work and agony, and then another.

The book said that it was supposed to take anywhere from a half hour to two hours for two men, working overtly, to move the bit more than a cubic meter of soil that clearing a fighting position required. The amount of time depended on the soil.

Ari had spent some of his off-time performing the mental calculation as to how much soil they'd have to move, and had come up with about two cubic meters. The resting bay of their OP would be a shallow, box-like hole, a bit less than two meters wide, half a meter deep, the side-by-side observation posts an inclined plane leading down to it.

The ground was practically ideal—the melfoglia that covered the floor of the forest rooted only shallowly, and choked off everything else; there were no root systems to hack through in the soft soil. It should have been easy, neat, like the book, and like one of half a dozen positions Ari had helped dig during training exercises.

A lot of work, granted, but with five to help, it should have gone quickly. Figure four to six hours, max.

He hadn't thought it through. For one thing, there weren't five to help. An OP is maintained around the clock. Even combining the observer and recorder into one job only left four men.

Then subtract two others, out in the night with phut guns, watching for Freiheimer patrols.

And, unlike when Ari had practiced digging a regular fighting position, there still wasn't enough room. Whoever was digging had to work under the tarp, and without making noise.

And then there was the damn dirt to get rid of. They had to keep some, of course, and had hauled hundreds of thin urlar bags along in their Bergens. While bagged soil wasn't as good overhead protection as could be manufactured, it was already there.

But most of it had to go, and go somewhere inconspicuous. Ari was going to suggest that they sneak out to the edge of the woods and dump it on the plowed ground, but Galil had other ideas. Fresh soil from the floor of the forest would be of a different shade than the dirt in the fields. It would look different, to an alert Freiheimer.

So two of the Bergens were filled with dirt—easily 60 kilos each—then strapped to the backs of two men and hauled off into the night half a klick away, spread or dumped somewhere away from the edge of the forest.

Ari had figured on it taking four to six hours, but it took all of that night, and all of the next.

* * *

He came awake painfully, Benyamin's hand on his mouth yet again. *Your stag again,* Benyamin mouthed. *Five minutes.*

Benyamin looked like shit in the light streaming through the vines covering the observation port at the front of the OP. His eyes were red slits in dark hollows, and his face was greasy with sweat and dirt. The hand that helped Ari up to a sitting position trembled. He probably smelled bad, too, Ari couldn't smell anything, which was just as well.

Ari looked down at his thumb. 0755 was the time, but what day was it? It had to be the fifth, or maybe the sixth. No, maybe the fourth. Two days ago there'd been the flight of Casa attack airplanes overhead, only two of them peeling off to lightly strafe the town.

Or was that just yesterday?

He couldn't be sure; time had become an unending chain of sleep and wake, work and watch, always surrounded by a haze of pain, and of weariness. Sleep didn't refresh. Neither did food. Nothing could, nothing ever would.

Ari tried to stretch, then thought better of it. A permanent pain had taken up residence in his upper back, just under his left shoulder blade. Probably tore something, he decided. It felt different than the bruised spot over his left kidney. Worse. More of a deep ache than a stabbing. He was becoming quite a connoisseur of pain.

His lips were dry and cracked, his mouth tasted of salt and dust, and the daylight hurt his eyes as he sprawled out in the observer's spot. His eyes immediately started sagging shut.

No. Keep awake. Don't give the bastard the satisfaction of waking you up on stag.

He looked down at the notepad, amazed at the date. It was only the fourth day, after three nights of digging.

NO DIGGING TONITE, the notepad read, under the words STANDING ORDERS.

EVERYBODY TOO TIRED TO KEEP SILENT.

INCLUDING YOUR FEARLESS LEADER.

If anything, Galil looked worse than Ari felt, although not much.

His eyes seemed to have trouble focusing. His hair and now ragged beard were matted with dirt and oil, and his hands were seized with occasional tremors. He had cut his right hand digging two nights ago, and even though it had been washed and bandaged, it had still somehow become infected. Farabuttocillin had the infection under control, but the hand was still swollen, leaving Galil barely able to write, his stylo clamped awkwardly in a fist.

Like the rest of them, Galil had long before stripped off his exsuit for the heat of the day. His khaki oversuit was damp at armpits and waist, where it had already long been stained white with salt and spattered with dirt.

But he still held the squash radio's mask against his mouth, and referred to the notepad as he dictated his report. Even though he was only a few centimeters away, Ari couldn't hear his voice, but he would have bet that Galil's tone was flat and steady.

Ari eyed the sun and decided that he had at least a half hour of binoculars until the angle became dangerous. He brought the set up to his eyes, and felt them start to sag shut again.

He could probably close his eyes for just another minute or two, but he wouldn't.

It was no big deal; nothing much would be happening below. The tanks would make their daily run out of the OP's line of sight, presumably into prepared forward defenses, and then practice a classic mobile ambush retreat.

Ari was sure he had pinpointed the command tank—and yes, it appeared to be a reinforced platoon, not a stripped company; Galil was right. Twice he had seen the platoon commander turning toward the 297 tank before issuing a hand order, as though he were verifying instructions received.

TANK #297 PROB. COMMAND TANK, he had written, and put his initials after it. Not that that would matter much. Galil wasn't listening to him, anyway.

He woke with a start. Galil was shaking him, frowning.

DON'T FALL ASLEEP, he wrote.

A distant whistle grew louder, becoming a scream that ended in a flash in the town below, and followed, seconds later, by a distant *crump!* It was followed by another explosion, and yet another, then by the crackling thunder of several detonations coming all at once.

"I think," Galil said, his voice cracking around the edges, "that we've got a war on our hands." Galil tapped at the binoculars; Ari put them back to his eyes. The skywatches had tucked themselves down into their holes, which could easily go down as deep as ten meters, maybe more. Unlikely targets for artillery, it would take armor and infantry to dig them out—or aircraft, but the trick of using drones to lure the skywatches out of their holes had long been countered by pop-and-fire.

The transmit plate on the squash radio went green—a flat green, not a glow—and stayed that way for more than five seconds before the bottom of the display went back to being a clock, the top half now announcing RETRIEVAL 08:22:01. Remotely triggered data pickup —and from the length of time it had taken, RHQ had polled them for everything.

Galil put on the earphone and listened, then passed it over to Ari. "Begins," it whispered in Peled's crisp syllables. "Triumphant is go. OP mission concludes as of 0830; FO mission begins as of 0900. OP Four is off the air; all others have reported in. Continue mission. Good luck, all. Ends."

"Shit." The tank platoon was rolling down the road, buttoned down except for three of the tank commanders, who stood upright in their hatches. The tanks were rolling forward to defensive positions. The best tank killer has long been another tank, and hull down behind prepared defensive positions, a retreating ambush was about the most effective way to use that tank killer.

Galil rolled over for the sniper rifle's case and opened it. The snap of the catches sounded like shots in Ari's ears. He cradled the weapon in his arms, then handed it to Ari.

Three shells blew on the edge of town. *Blam. Blam. Blam.*

And then there was silence.

"You'll have two shots, at most," Galil whispered. "I want the armor company CO. Do it."

This was crazy, Ari thought, as his hands went through the motions with the rifle, snapping a magazine of match-grade 7mm ammunition into the receiver.

This didn't make sense.

Ari started to bring the rifle up.

"No," Galil whispered. "Move back a bit."

The captain was right; Ari would have poked the barrel through the grasses covering the observation port. Do it by the numbers.

He rolled over on his left side, working the charging bolt, ignoring the way the muscles in his back protested, using his right hand to force the butt of the rifle into his right shoulder, gripping the stock with his right hand as he rolled back on his elbows, his shoulders now level.

"Get on with it, get on with it."

"Shut up, Captain." Ari was a fair long shot with a rifle, but a head shot wasn't trivial, not even at this distance. He flicked the sights to 200 meters.

There were voices and grumbles around him, but Ari concentrated on what he was doing. The world, the universe, was his rifle. It rested on the v of his left hand—on the palm, not the fingers—the butt jammed almost painfully into the pocket where his hunched shoulder met his neck. His right hand held the stock firmly, almost welding it to his cheek, the only part of his body free and loose his trigger finger.

With the tank moving and bouncing, there was no decent chance at a head shot—but if the Freiheimers did what they'd done two days in a row, the tanks would stop at the crossroads, changing from column to a ragged wedge as they left the road for the fields.

He'd have one opportunity.

"Wind at 12:30," Galil announced. "Light—maybe four klicks per hour."

No windage adjustment, but this still didn't make any sense.

They were a lot more valuable as forward observers than they'd be as snipers. Besides, you didn't snipe from a fixed OP—it was take a shot or two, then move, then shoot again. A sniper was supposed to be invisible and mobile.

Maybe ten seconds to the crossroads. He was looking directly into the scope; there was no shadow effect along the edge. Crosshairs were level; no canting of the rifle.

He took in a breath; the crosshairs moved down, through a narrow arc.

Five seconds. He released the breath, took another, let half of it out, and held it. Finger on the trigger, held at the first joint.

The tanks slowed, and Tank 297 rattled into motionlessness in his sights.

"Fire mission, target moving tanks." Galil said. He rapped out a series of coordinates and then listened. "Confirmed. ASAP, fire."

At two hundred meters, even with sight as acute as

Ari's, the face of the tank commander should have been only a blur, a fleshy blob in the sights.

But all of a sudden it was the face of a person, a man of perhaps twenty or twenty-five standard years, his remarkably ordinary face streaked with sweat and dirt, and while it wasn't at all possible that the Freiheimer could see him, he was just at that moment looking directly at Ari.

Ari couldn't shoot him in the face. He couldn't. His fingers trembled, and the Freiheimer's face jerked out of his sights.

But he pulled the trigger anyway.

CHAPTER 12

Yitzhak Galil: Green Light

Three shells blew on the edge of town. *Blam. Blam. Blam.*

And then there was silence.

"You'll have two shots, at most," Yitzhak Galil whispered. "I want the armor company CO. Do it." There was no time; Galil had to use the asshole as the sniper. Galil couldn't shoot, not with his hand swollen and useless, like a pregnant woman's belly; and he couldn't get either Benyamin Hanavi or Lavon up and ready for a shot, not in a minute or two.

Ari Hanavi looked at Galil as if Galil were crazy, but it didn't matter what Ari Hanavi thought. Things were about to get too hot in Trainville for the defenders to be worrying about a stray sniper. It would make the division's job of crashing through easier if the tank company were leaderless. Advancing toward an attacking enemy—even in a tank, even if you were only moving into prepared defensive positions—was difficult to get soldiers to do, and they might fall apart if the leader were gone.

And for sure it would inhibit at least one tank if its commander were dead in the hatch, bleeding out and emptying his sphincters on everything and everybody underneath him.

And, besides, in a half an hour, this would stop being Galil's command and become Marko Giacobazzi's forward observer post. Galil, Lavon and the two Hanavis would just be along for the ride, just to keep Giacobazzi from being bothered or killed while the Casa spotted for the artillery. Yitzhak Galil hated the idea of turning over his command without having drawn blood.

"Do it."

The idiot started to poke the rifle through the grasses covering the observation port.

"No," Galil whispered. "Move back a bit."

Ari Hanavi complied, then started fiddling with the rifle.

"Get on with it, get on with it."

"Shut up, Captain," Ari Hanavi said.

Benyamin Hanavi grumbled something behind him.

"Everybody, wake up," Galil said, unnecessarily. "It's on. Marko, it's yours as of 0900." He took a stim from his belt pouch, slipping it and some grit under his tongue. Galil had held off on the drugs until now; he'd had to. Taken over too long a time, they could screw up your judgment.

It didn't matter which. They all lied to you: morphine told you the world was all cozy and warm and safe. Amphetamines and cocaine only told you that you could do anything. Right now that was a harmless lie. His head cleared and the pain in his swollen hand became a distant ache.

There was no need to be stalling. It was a tough shot, but it wasn't going to get easier. The wind was blowing almost right in their faces and it kept the leaves and grasses in near constant motion. "Wind at 12:30," Galil said. "Light—maybe four klicks per hour."

Fire, asshole. Fire the fucking rifle.

No—it made sense. Maybe the asshole wasn't such an asshole after all; he was aiming a bit to the left, to the crossroads where the chewed-up ground showed that the tanks tended to leave the tarmac for the fields. They'd have to pause for a moment, and unless they buttoned up before they did, it might give Hanavi a decent headshot.

The tanks slowed.

If this worked, it would be a good idea to give the Freiheimers something else to think of. In addition to bossing the regimental mortars, Asher Greenberg was theoretically liasing for division artillery. Only liasing, not commanding—but if Galil knew the squat little man as well as he thought he did, Greenberg would have already built some shortcuts into the relationship.

Galil punched for the RHQ freak and thumbed the squash radio to LIVE. "Kelev One Twenty for Deir Yasin Twenty," he said.

Greenberg must have been guarding the freak himself. "Deir Yasin Twenty," he said.

"Fire mission, target moving tanks." Galil said, looking down at the map, confirming the numbers he already knew.

"I have you on map Zayin Twelve Eleven."

"Confirmed. Crossroads at eight-six, seven-five."

"Crossroads at eight-six, seven-five."

"Confirmed. ASAP, fire."

"Battery one, fire. *On* the way." Even radio protocol couldn't hide the sense of self-satisfaction in Asher Greenberg's voice that he not only could get the Casa arty commander to fire off six rounds of anti-tank without passing it along as a request, but that he could do so immediately. "Spot for me, Kelev."

Galil already had the binocs up against his face as Ari Hanavi pulled the trigger, the crisp snap of the rifle loud in his ears, the expelled shell clicking against Galil's helmet as it bounced away. Galil waited for the company commander to slump down in the hatch, but nothing happened. He didn't even duck down at the sound of a bullet hissing by, or the high ringing of it ricocheting off the tank's armor.

Hanavi fired again, and again nothing happened.

"Hit the bastard, asshole."

"You said two shots—"

"One more, and this time make it count."

Galil turned to look at Ari Hanavi. His rifle was fitted to his shoulder with perfect form, his grip and cheek weld were classic.

But Ari Hanavi was shooting with his eyes closed.

"Relieved, asshole." Yitzhak Galil reached out his good hand for the rifle, but it was no use. Damn, damn, damn Yitzhak, son of Moshe, for not having forced the issue with Shimon.

It was too late, anyway; the tanks were hightailing across the fields, buttoning up at the scream of the incoming rounds.

Something had come over the radio, but Galil hadn't heard it.

"Anybody catch that?" Galil said.

Benyamin Hanavi was grinning, but it didn't mean anything. The ugly man always grinned. "Message begins: 'Shimon to Yitzhak. End of foreplay. Time to fuck them. Careful linking up.' Message ends." He was reassembling his own oily Barak as he spoke, his hands moving swiftly but surely.

Shells screamed downward toward the town, terminating in a flash of smoke and flame. The Casas had overshot the tanks, but that didn't matter. There were men to kill in the town, too. And everyone that the artillery killed now was one more that Bar-El's regiment wouldn't have to kill in clearing the town.

Beyond a low rise, a triple fork of fire lanced into the blue sky, leaving a cloud of smoke behind.

"In case you missed it, Hanavi," Galil said. "That was three Freiheimer tanks firing off rounds toward the line of departure, toward where our brothers and cousins are. You—"

He stopped himself. There was work to do and no time for recriminations, not now. Galil punched for the local freak on the squash radio. "FO's, over to you. Sharpshooters, exit the OP; continue mission as snipers. One man to remain in OP as guard. Acknowledge, no voice," he said, then squeezed the transmit button.

One by one, three green lights flickered on.

Marko Giacobazzi had poked the antenna of his own radio up through the tarp and was stretched out next to Galil, muttering something into his microphone. He raised his head.

"Spot fired," Giacobazzi said. His dirty face was smiling.

"Good," Galil kicked Hanavi. "Get out of Lieutenant Giacobazzi's way—he's got work to do." He turned to the Casa. "Over to—"

Ari Hanavi's face was white. "I tried, I—"

"Shut *up*." Galil helped Giacobazzi forward. The Casa had his own clipboard ready, and was checking off targets with a grease pencil.

"The church first, you think?" he asked.

"Your call, sir," Galil said. It wasn't Galil's observation post, not anymore. All the data he had gathered had been sucked out of the squash radio and was being digested at RHQ for presentation to the Casas. Now it was Giacobazzi's turn to spot targets for the artillery, and the Metzadans were just along for the ride.

Moving around would be dangerous, but there was zero, zip, no chance that the Freiheimers would be out patrolling in the shrapnel rain.

"Well," Galil said, finally letting himself speak with a full voice, "it looks like we made it, so far. Noise discipline is lifted. With your permission, sir," he said to the Casa.

"Permission granted, sir." Giacobazzi produced a canteen and took a swig, then passed it to Galil before turning back to his binoculars, charts and radio.

Galil took a swallow. It was a strong red wine, tannic enough to clear the slime from his teeth. He passed the canteen back to Benyamin Hanavi. Yitzhak Galil was tempted to explain to Ari Hanavi how much trouble he was in, but if Ari Hanavi had known how much trouble he was in, he would have stuck the barrel of the sniper rifle in his mouth and saved everybody the trouble.

Benyamin Hanavi drank, but he had stopped smiling.

Galil was in no hurry to try linking up; it was close to dusk before his reassembled platoon staggered into the town.

Trainville made him feel the way a freshly liberated town always did: why bother?

Thick smoke hung in the air. The burning wood wasn't bad, but occasionally he would get a reek of charred flesh. The streets were scattered with rubble and bodies, mainly Freiheimers, leavened with some Casas. No Metzadans, but that didn't mean anything. The regiment wouldn't leave its dead on the same ground as the Frei.

What walls hadn't been smashed were decorated with bullet holes. The smoldering hulks of two tanks stood squared off in the main street, the Casa tank turretless, the charred mass in the open hatch of the Freiheimer tank only recognizable because Galil had seen bodies burned that badly before.

The Casa armor had already stomped through the center of Trainville and continued onward, leaving the major defenses smashed, but the town was by no means secured: off in the distance, Baraks stuttered, punctuated by the occasional higher-pitched *crack* of Freiheimer rifles on single-shot.

"I get the impression," Skolnick said, "that the Freiheimers aren't going to make this easy on us."

Lavon chuckled. "Gee, that's unusual."

Shimon Bar-El had set up his tactical operations center in an abandoned slaughterhouse and had established his command group two blocks away, in the train station on the edge of town. Outside, a battered tank stood guard, mounted on a pair of field jacks while a Casa team changed a broken set of treads. The tank was wounded, yes, but it was not dead—the engine still chugged and spat, and the turret swung quickly in their general direction as they approached, stopping well before it lined up on them as they were recognized.

The train station was a good place for a command group, Galil decided. The stone building was whole enough and the walls thick enough to offer some concealment and cover.

Then again, nobody was asking his goddamn opinion.

"Take ten, people," he said. "I'll see where we're billeted."

The rest of the men slumped to the ground, but Benyamin Hanavi didn't. "I'll help you, Captain."

Skolnick started to say something, but Galil waved him to silence.

As they walked up the steps, past the guards and into the building, Galil scratched uncomfortably at an itch under his armpit. He didn't like being with the command group. His usual place was in the tactical operations center, keeping things running. The TOC was the usual babble of talk and rattling typers; here, only a half dozen clerks sorted through flimsies coming off the printers, prioritizing them for the general's attention; only three communicators spoke into their masks while their fingers flew across typers.

Somebody had nailed a map of Trainville up on the far wall. While Dov Ginsberg watched the room unceasingly, Shimon was going over the map with Natan Horowitz, Tetsuo Hanavi and Chiabrera.

That was about right, Galil decided. The commander ought to have the liaison officer and the ops officer near him, and maybe the S3's assistant, but it made sense to keep the deputy commander and the chief of staff in the TOC.

Galil would have added the intelligence officer to the command group, but again, nobody was asking him. Nobody was asking him much of anything on this one.

"My guess," Shimon was saying, "is that the Frei are going to counterstrike, somewhere around here. Figure, oh, forty-eight to seventy-two hours."

"Which makes securing this town even more important, eh?" Horowitz was clean and rested and bright-eyed. Hell, he was even freshly shaved, his smooth chin marked by two red nicks.

"Exactly," Bar-El said. He took a good look at Galil, then turned back to Horowitz.

Horowitz nodded. "I should be able to handle things for a minute."

Shimon Bar-El jerked his head toward a doorway, gesturing at Tetsuo to come along. "Then handle things, Natan," Bar-El said, leading Galil and the rest through the doorway into what had been the kitchen of the station.

It wouldn't be good as a kitchen, not soon; strikers had blown two mouseholes in the walls, and followed it with grenades that had shattered every plate and glass in the place, as well as puncturing bags and jars of staples, scattering flour and rice and beans on the floor. The bodies had been carried out, but their smell remained.

Dov Ginsberg followed without asking, standing next to rather than leaning on a wall, his shotgun clutched in his good hand.

"How's your hand, Yitzhak?" Shimon asked.

Galil held it up. Where it wasn't dirty, it was red; the hand had swollen to half again its normal size, and was missing the three outer fingernails.

"You'd better see the medician."

"Never mind that—I want Ari Hanavi out, Shimon," Galil said. "Don't give a shit how good he looks on paper—he froze on me twice. Two out of two. He's gone, General, and I don't care who he's related to."

"You don't think he'll snap out of it?"

Galil scowled. "I—"

"Shh." Shimon touched an index finger to his earphone with one hand while he pulled his microphone down in front of his lips. "No, Hebron Twenty," he said, his eyes vague and unfocused. "You are not, repeat not, to engage in clearing operations, not until 08:00 at the earliest.

"Slow it down, Ebi, slow it down. Get at least two companies bedded down—dammit, I've already got Sidney covering just that possibility. I want your battalion rested in the morning; smashing down and in through the roofs isn't something for sleepy soldiers. Sidney is going to give them harassing and intermittent fire through the night. You get to take them in the morning, when they're tired out.

"You can do a company-sized reconnaissance in force to the granary, but don't pull a stone soup on me. If you meet any serious resistance, fall back. Yes, you can have five minutes to make your case—but in five minutes. I've got to finish something here." He lifted his gaze. "I'm sorry, Yitzhak, but it turns out I don't have a lot of time for this. I've got a town to secure, and then I've got to duck out for a meeting in the morning. You were saying?"

"I'm not risking anything on Ari Hanavi again. Ever. Non-negotiable, Shimon."

"Everything's negotiable, Captain," Tetsuo Hanavi said, his voice studiously level as he squared off in front of Galil.

"Shut up, Tetsuo," Benyamin Hanavi said, setting a hand against his brother's chest, pushing him back. "But please, Uncle, don't write Ari off."

"There's another option." Shimon Bar-El's thin lips quirked into a smile. "I've got a friend, a brigade commander, who's been having a spot of trouble on the northern flank. Way I read the situation, he needs either one," Shimon held up a finger, "a hell of a good company commander, or, two," another finger, "a sacrificial lamb wearing captain's bars."

Galil kept the disgust off his face. You don't solve a problem by sending the messenger out to get shot up. That's been out of fashion since King David.

"I don't know if you've noticed, Shimon, but I'm worn to all hell," Galil said. "What I don't need is a foreign command; what I do need is a hot shower and about three days in a bed that isn't made of stones, shit and dirt. And I swear we'd better settle the Ari matter before you reassign me."

Bar-El allowed himself a brief chuckle. "You're missing the point. Effective five minutes from now, I want you back in charge of RHQ company and straightening out the mess at the TOC. Yeah, you're a good company commander, but I don't have any spare good company commanders—so we give him a sacrificial lamb: Ari."

"You're getting tricky again—" Galil started to say.

"I want the family to have a hero," Tetsuo said. "Live or dead."

"Who's going to make sure he doesn't fuck up?"

"I will," Tetsuo Hanavi said quietly. "Family matter, Yitzhak."

Galil believed him, but he couldn't help adding, "No deal. I don't trust you not to cover for him. I want somebody else in on it, somebody I trust."

Natan Horowitz walked in. "He's right, Shimon. You need somebody trustworthy."

"How long have you been listening?" Shimon Bar-El asked.

Horowitz shrugged. "Long enough to know that Yitzhak's right. You need to send somebody with Ari, to make sure he doesn't fuck up—not successfully fuck up, if you catch my meaning."

Galil decided that he was too damn tired; he hadn't even heard Horowitz walk in.

"You?" Bar-El raised an eyebrow.

Horowitz shook his head. "I've got to figure out how we clear this town for you, and in case you didn't notice, cleaning out a town is tricky. Speaking of which, you're needed—Sidney's on the line again."

"Three minutes?"

"Don't make it four." Horowitz turned and walked away.

"Me, I'll make sure Ari doesn't fuck up," Benyamin Hanavi said quietly. "I talked you into giving him a second chance."

Shimon Bar-El snorted. "It doesn't matter what you talked me into. It's my regiment, Benyamin, and my responsibility."

"Not you, Sergeant." Galil shook his head. "You're too soft on him."

Bar-El nodded. "I'm not about to send out two Hanavi brothers to watch over a third. And if not you, Benyamin, then who?" He glanced down at his thumbnail watch. "You've got thirty seconds, and then I have to get back to work."

"Let it be Dov," Benyamin said, his face grim as though he'd just passed a death sentence.

Dov's broad face was impassive. He might almost have not been there.

Shimon Bar-El raised an eyebrow. "Done. Now, the two of you, get the hell out of here; I've got work to do. Tetsuo, you explain the swindle to Ari."

"You want to reconsider that, Uncle?" Tetsuo asked. "You're going to be part of it anyway—this is Giacometti, remember? He's not going to do any favors for me or anybody else."

"Right." Bar-El frowned. "There's no shooting going on around Jocko's CP—so that asshole Zuchelli will be sticking his nose in it. Okay, give me an hour to get this regiment set up for the night, then bring the poor bastard in and I'll give him the bad news. We'll deliver him to Jocko in the morning. That is *all*, gentlemen."

Shimon Bar-El walked out of the kitchen, Dov falling into place behind him.

PART THREE

ASSAULT

CHAPTER 13

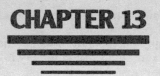

Promotion

It was the only time that Ari had ever been alone with his Uncle Shimon.

"It's very simple," Shimon Bar-El said. "I need to swap favors with an old friend of mine, and you're it." He idly sketched a map in the dust on what probably had been a baker's table. "Main assault is along here, but the Casas are expecting a . . . Freiheimer counterstroke anywhere along here. Doesn't much matter where. If they can have the lines fluid and choppy when the truce starts, they can dicker with the TW busies and win by negotiation what they can't by force.

"Minor sore spot is *here*. The town, call it Anchorville, sits just on our side of the military crest of this ridgeline, which means that it'll be a nice place to put some arty—if we can own it. What with other commitments, though, there just aren't enough free forces in that sector to stomp in and take it, which is why an old friend of mine has been reduced to sending the same company up against it, again and again."

Shimon Bar-El shrugged. "Way I figure it, it's a morale problem. If we give them a magic Metzadan miracle-worker to lead them, they just might be able to take the town. Or, at the very least, give the

Freiheimer defenders reason to panic and divert, say, a battalion of reinforcements.

"Then again, maybe not. Maybe they'll just blow him and that ratty-ass Casa company into bloody little chunks."

He handed Ari a sheaf of flimsies. "So . . . instead of kicking your ass out of the Metzadan Mercenary Corps, we're brevetting it up to captain. Do a good job, and I'll see what I can do for you. Now, all we have to do is sell the idea to the Casas—including that asshole Zuchelli."

He patted Ari on the shoulder. "As of tomorrow, you're an officer. For tonight, you'd better get some sleep, boy. You're going to need it."

The reassembled Kelev One didn't have any formal assignment, not yet, but they had been billeted in the basement of the house next to the operations center. By some standards it was crowded, but it didn't feel that way: Ari had a gloriously roomy three- by one-meter sleeping area on the concrete floor all to himself, a soft, firm, sleeping pad underneath him—and no rocks to torture him.

But he couldn't sleep. Every time he closed his eyes, all he could see was that Freiheimer's face in front of him, and he couldn't shoot, he couldn't pull the trigger.

Buck fever, they called it. Just another form of cowardice.

He heard Benyamin turn over.

"Can't sleep?" Benyamin whispered.

"No."

Lavon turned over and glared at the two of them, but then went back to sleep.

"Here." Smiling, Benyamin held out a white tablet. "Take this."

"What is it?" Ari asked. It looked like—

"Morphine. Just a sleepy dose—I'll stick a naloxone

needle in you in the morning if you're still groggy."
Benyamin shrugged. "Worked for me in the OP."

"I—never mind." Ari had asked Galil, and had
been ordered not to take drugs. To hell with it. He
swallowed the tablet dry.

Benyamin's whispered chuckle was warm in the dark.
"I know: you asked Galil if you could. I didn't. Like
the Sergeant says, it's always easier to get forgiven
than to get permission. 'Night, little brother. Do us
proud."

Sleep was a long, black, warm thing, punctuated
and terminated by the prick of a needle.

CHAPTER 14

Assignment

Hanging by the neck from the improvised gallows, the captain's corpse turned slowly in the early morning breeze. It wasn't a pretty sight, and it wasn't a pleasant smell. His fatigues hadn't been spotless to begin with; his sphincters, in his last moments, had relaxed in the mindless reflex that tries to make all animals less tasty to the predators that bring them down.

Ari doubted that the particular predators who had brought the captain down cared much about how tasty he was. The Casalinguese army's Loyalty Detachment was cannibalistic, but only metaphorically.

As they passed the gallows, General Shimon Bar-El paused at the steps of the former schoolhouse that High Colonel Giacometti was using as his brigade command post. He gestured at Major Zuchelli, Tetsuo, Dov and Ari to precede him, pointedly ignoring both Elena D'Ancona and Zuchelli's two Distacamento Fedeltà sergeants.

Ari had hoped to get a few moments alone with Elena, but that hadn't happened, and wasn't likely to. She had nodded pointedly at his bars, and when Shimon had mentioned that Ari's captaincy was a brevet, she had smiled broadly enough to earn a glare from Zuchelli.

Halfway up the steps, Shimon stopped and turned to stare at the body for a moment before he turned to Ari, a momentary frown quirking across his leathery lips.

His eyes always bothered Ari. Not because he had the epicanthic folds that should go with a Nipponese name like Tetsuo's. The problem was that Shimon's eyes saw too much. Right now, they were looking at a seventeen-year-old boy pretending to be something he wasn't, a phony in more ways than the obvious one of wearing the triple bars of a captain on his shoulders.

But that wasn't special. Anybody could have seen that Ari was just playing officer, that he was a coward, a failure.

"Ari, do you know what bothers me about death?" Shimon Bar-El asked, his eyes searching Ari's, maybe for a sign that this time Ari wouldn't fuck up, that somehow he would find the inner resources to do the right thing, or at least get himself killed trying to do the right thing.

Ari didn't say anything at first; he couldn't answer the unasked question, and the spoken one didn't matter. Then he decided that it couldn't hurt to answer: Shimon Bar-El was always tolerant of subordinates misunderstanding him; he said that it was his fault, not theirs.

"No, sir," Ari said.

Shimon clicked his tongue against his teeth. "It's undignified, death is," he said. "Horribly, dreadfully, uncontrollably undignified." He shook his head sadly. "What do you think, Ari? Do you think that Captain Tommasino has learned his lesson?"

"Tommasino?" Ari's voice almost broke.

Shimon jerked a thumb at the gallows. "Tommasino. He commanded F Company. Until yesterday, Captain

Hanavi." His uncle smiled genially at the brand new triple bars on Ari's shoulders. "Correct, Zuchelli?"

"Major Zuchelli." The Casalinguese scowled, touching at his bristly mustache; the DF officer had a face like a ferret. "And you seem to disapprove, General Bar-El."

"I do, at that."

"Captain Tommasino declined to order his company to attack the enemy, General," Zuchelli said, raising his voice. "Is pusillanimous conduct in the face of the enemy encouraged in the Metzada Mercenary Corps?"

Shimon didn't answer the Distacamento de la Fedeltà officer as he dipped two fingers into a pocket of his khakis, coming out with a brown, half-crumpled tabstick. He flicked it to life with his thumb and stuck it between his lips.

"No," he finally said, watching the body dangle. "No, it isn't encouraged, at that." He turned to Tetsuo. "What do you think, Tetsuo?"

"About the hanging? I think it's a good idea to hang a man for refusing to make a worn-out company engage in a futile attack." Tetsuo nodded soberly. "A wonderful idea, sir. I am sure that Tommasino will never do it again."

"Dov?"

"I agree, Uncle Shimon." Master Private Dov Ginsberg didn't bother to keep a twisted grin off his ugly face. "That will teach him."

"Pour encourager les autres," Elena D'Ancona put in, very seriously, even though her voice seemed to tremble at the edges. "Orders must be obeyed."

"Or is the concept unfamiliar to you?" Zuchelli asked. The Distacamento de la Fedeltà major hitched one thumb under his glossy leather belt and stroked at his three-day beard with his free hand. The scraggly beard was clearly an affectation: Zuchelli's mustache was neatly trimmed, and his nails were recently manicured.

Tetsuo shrugged. "I don't understand. Why did he decline to attack? Just to give the DF pigs practice in hanging someone? Not that they did a decent job." He spat, more in contemplation than in disgust. "See how straight the head is? If you hang them right, the drop is supposed to snap the neck; this one was strangled. Very sloppy."

Zuchelli and his baby-faced junior bodyguard glared at him, but neither of them said anything. Zuchelli's senior bodyguard, a fortyish sergeant with a well-scarred face, suppressed a smile; not all Distacamento de la Fedeltà personnel are Distacamento de la Fedeltà types.

Elena caught Tetsuo's grin and, perhaps deciding that he was just kidding, returned his smile.

"Maybe," Shimon said, "he just got tired of seeing men die for nothing, watching them carved into bloody pulp by autogun fire and artillery barrages."

The MPs at the table just inside the archway at the top of the steps had been eyeing them and each other.

Ari figured the private was debating with himself whether or not offworld officers' uniforms necessitated a salute. The MP's immediate superior, a corporal with a DF brassard on his left arm to balance the MP one on his right, smiled in self-satisfaction and took out his notebook as though he was going to make a note to report the private for insubordination if he didn't salute or for suspected disloyalty if he did.

When he saw Zuchelli's DF brassard, the private almost voided himself in relief. He snapped a salute at Zuchelli; the DF corporal followed suit, visibly irritated at being unable to come up with grounds for complaint. *"Sir."*

"Major Zuchelli and a party of five to see the Colonel. Send a runner, and tell him to get his ass out of bed and into his office."

"Major, I've had about enough of you," Shimon said. "Repeat after me: 'Private, you will please convey the following message to High Colonel Giacometti:

Major Zuchelli's respects to the high colonel. Major Zuchelli, General Shimon Bar-El, Captain Tetsuo Hanavi and Captain Ari Hanavi urgently but respectfully request an audience with the colonel, at his earliest convenience. Thank you, Private.' "

Tetsuo didn't make a move toward unslinging his rifle; he just took three slow steps away from Shimon's side until he was within reach of both of the MPs, his hands open and relaxed, his weight on the balls of his feet.

"Stand very easy, if you please," Tetsuo said.

Ari's brother may have spent his career as a staff officer, but there wasn't any trace of a staff officer's tentativeness in his manner now.

Zuchelli looked from Shimon to Dov to Tetsuo to Ari, which was sort of flattering; at least Zuchelli included Ari as a real Metzadan.

The senior of Zuchelli's bodyguards shook his head minutely.

If you ignored his size, Dov didn't seem particularly threatening; he just stood there, flatfooted, a vaguely bored expression on his face. He wasn't even looking directly at Zuchelli's bodyguards, although he could have reached either with a back-kick. He just faced the junior MP, looking at him as if the boy had crosshairs painted on his forehead.

Not that they were wrong to leave Ari out of it. Not that somebody who froze, the first time he heard a shot fired in anger, who couldn't even come close to a 200-meter head shot—not that somebody like that would be a big help in an intimate firefight.

Ari was useless. But, in front of a pretty girl, Ari could fake being something that he wasn't. He tried to mimic Tetsuo, and gave Zuchelli his best I'm-baring-these-teeth-to-bite-out-your-jugular smile.

"Well, Major?" Shimon asked.

Numbly, Zuchelli echoed Shimon's words while Tetsuo nodded approvingly at Ari. Dov just looked bored.

Ari didn't understand it, not at all. He didn't know why Shimon had forced a showdown with the Distacamento de la Fedeltà major—

—until he saw the left breast of Giacometti's uniform blouse.

The lettering on the open door of the inner read DIRETTORE. When this had been a school, it had been the principal's private office. Books, papers and other detritus were strewn to one side of the desk, beneath the black-curtained window.

In contrast to the brightness and airiness of the operations center beyond the busy outer office, the inner office was stuffy and dark, the only illumination provided by a hissing lantern on the desk and two others mounted high on the walls. A slick cable snaked in through the open door from the outer offices, running to the printer and commo box on the gray desk where Giacometti sat.

High Colonel Vittorio Giacometti was a funereally thin man. From the pinched face and the loose uniform, Ari decided that he had once been rotund.

"Shimon," Giacometti said. "I didn't expect you in person." He rose slowly, carefully to his feet, looking not at all like a man grabbing at a life preserver as he clasped Shimon's hand.

That was when Ari spotted it: among a scattering of local ribbons that he didn't recognize there was the blue-and-white decoration that represented the Two Swords, with three of the unauthorized red stitches that Shimon Bar-El always put on the ribbons he awarded. The Two Swords was the only medal that Metzada gave out—campaign ribbons, qualification badges, specialty warrants and such aren't medals— and was given only to foreign soldiers serving under Metzadan officers.

While it could be awarded at the discretion of senior field-grade officers and generals, Shimon had never been known for passing out the Two Swords for ordinary efficiency, or even for tactical or logistics genius.

It was a blood award.

Which began to explain why Shimon had volunteered to lend an officer to the Casas. He was taking care of his own: Giacometti.

For that matter, in a different sort of way, it explained Ari. After all, there are all sorts of ways of taking care of your own. One of the things they teach you in school is not to tell battle-hot troops to "take care of" captured prisoners, or you'll likely end up with a war crime on your hands.

"Vittorio," Shimon said, smiling like a Buddha. "It's good to see you again. What's left of you."

"Colonel," Zuchelli said, nodding briskly.

"You didn't salute, Major," Shimon said out of the side of his mouth.

Zuchelli didn't answer. "Get it over with," he said.

Shimon smiled tolerantly. "Very well," he said softly. "As you like."

Ari hadn't heard that note in Shimon's voice before, not even when Shimon had taken him aside to pin the captain's bars on his shoulder. Tetsuo returned his look blankly.

"Enough ceremony, Vittorio." Shimon waved Giacometti back to his seat, taking another one for himself. "I need to trade favors with you."

"Ah, good." Giacometti's smile was weak. "You have a deal." He raised an eyebrow. "May one inquire as to what the deal is?"

"Divisione is stripping me of my tank company as of 1300. I had Chiabrera on the line all yesterday, but I can't get anybody to even consider leaving me a platoon. I don't need the whole company, but I could use a few rolling pillboxes for clearing the town. Can you get to somebody?"

Giacometti nodded. "I have a cousin in Divisione

G1. I'll see what I can do." He spread his hands widely. "I make no promises, except for my effort."

"Fine. Now, as to your problem, can you give me a quick tac briefing, please?" he asked, as though it were more of an order than a request—although, technically, there was no chain-of-command authority between a Metzadan general of a regiment under contract to the Casalinguese General Staff and a Casalinguese Regular Army high colonel.

On the other hand, Shimon was wearing stars on his shoulders, while Giacometti had only four gold bars. More importantly, he was Shimon Bar-El. Ari figured that was enough.

"It's bad, Shimon," Giacometti said, ignoring the way Zuchelli scowled and began writing something in the black leather notebook he always carried.

Tetsuo leaned over to Dov and said in a stage whisper, "I guess in the Casalinguese army, you're not supposed to notice when the situation sucks."

"We're stretched just about as far as we can take it," Giacometti went on.

"So I hear," Shimon said. "And this Second Battalion of yours sound like a bunch of losers. Where did you get this battalion commander, anyway?"

"It is not Verone's fault. The Second was engaged for three solid weeks, with no rest—"

"And no success." There was no trace of accusation in that tone; Shimon was just pointing out a fact.

"—and when they were moved back to Divisione reserve, all the supposed rest they got was trying to sleep through artillery fire. The TO shows them at about eighty percent strength, but a lot of them are green replacements whose only experience under fire is being hit by artillery."

That sounded bad. Infantrymen hate and fear artillery most. You can outshoot or outplan infantry; you can avoid or trap armor; but the only thing you can do with artillery is outluck it. Too much artillery fire can turn good troops sour. It said so in all the textbooks.

It didn't say in the textbooks what it was supposed to do to soldiers like Ari.

"We have to take Anchorville," Giacometti said. "I don't know if the whole battalion could do it, and how the hell can I do it if Divisione won't give me permission to use the battalion? All I'm allowed is a company."

"You're not looking at it from Generale Prezzolini's perspective." Shimon shook his head. "The real final push is going to be over on the other flank, just to the south of Trainville—but he can't have the herrenvolk figuring that out, not if you're going to end up with a decent border when the Commerce Department closes you down in a couple weeks. So he's got to keep them busy on this flank, but he's still got to keep something in reserve for their final push.

"I'm no Montgomery, but tidying up the lines is the order of the day—and it's better to tidy forward. Besides, the Freiheimers in Anchorville are probably just as tired as your men are. Tetsuo?"

"If that's so," Ari's brother said, "a company might be able to take the town."

"Casualties?"

"I don't know," Tetsuo said. "Looking at the map, if that company is going to do it at all, they're going to do it as some sort of frontal attack. A banzai charge, and you know what that means."

Ari knew from his schooling that the casualties could be anywhere from negligible to total. If a charge quickly turned into a rout for the defenders, it wouldn't cost the assault force much blood. But if the defenders held firm, if their discipline was decent, their autoguns would carve the attackers into bloody pulp.

"You're not worried about Freiheimer reinforcements?" Shimon asked, a teacher looking for the missing steps in a logic problem. "Do you think that the herrenvolk won't care if we stomp on some of their own?"

"General, Freiheimer commo is as bad as Casalinguese. It'd be all over—either way—before any in-person relief arrives, although they can call in artillery with a signal rocket." Tetsuo shrugged. "You might be able to outrun the artillery, if you surprise them."

"Wait." Giacometti lowered his voice. "What do you think they'll do when we throw in our own artillery prep? Do you perhaps think they won't notice?"

"There is that," Shimon said. "There is that. So perhaps we'll do without prep fire." He turned and looked Ari in the eye. "Well, Ari, are you ready to take command of F Company?"

He wasn't, of course. A seventeen-year-old, offplanet for the first time, shouldn't have been offered any kind of command at all. Unless he were an exceptional soldier, and under exceptional circumstances.

This was exceptional, but not in the good sense. Offworlders tend to overplay the influence of Metzada's Nipponese heritage. There had only been a few Bushidists transported to Metzada, along with the Children of Israel, and their influence is more apparent than real: his uncle's epicanthic folds, his brother's name. But sometimes the influence is there.

There was a time when his Nipponese ancestors belted some of their young men into stubby-winged gliders called bakus, each with a half ton of explosives in its nose. When they did, their faces may have looked like Shimon's did as he asked again:

"Well, Ari? Are you ready?"

Ari drew himself up straight. "Yes, sir," he said slowly, "I'm ready."

"We'll see how you do," Zuchelli sneered. "We'll see about that when you're under Distacamento de la Fedeltà discipline—"

"Wrong." Shimon shook his head. "We're not attaching him to F Company. Just the other way around. I'm not going to see my nephew swinging from your gallows if the attack fails and he's lucky enough to survive."

"Eh?"

"It's simple, Major. You don't have authority over my men; you do over CPE forces. So instead of loaning Jocko a company commander, I'm having him loan me a company." Shimon Bar-El smiled. "Which puts paid to your meddling, doesn't it?" He pulled a sheaf of flimsies out from his breast pocket and slammed them down on Giacometti's desk. "Sign this, Vittorio. It attaches F Company to my Thirtieth—"

"Mm." Giacometti smiled. "Putting Casalinguese forces under Metzadan control?" he asked, toying with the idea.

Shimon shrugged. "Those are the terms. Those are *my* terms. How's your comm to Divisione?"

"At the moment? Land lines are up; soon as you get out of here, I am going to use one to call up my cousin in G1. It's all I have: radio truck got hit by a cruise two days ago, and plexlase went down last week. Any spare 'tronics techs handy?"

"Sorry. All the fancy electronics looked so nice in the showroom, didn't it?"

"Very pretty, indeed." Giacometti almost smiled. "Ah, well. That still doesn't solve the problem."

Bar-El snorted. "So get off the pot and get your general on the line. If you don't think you have the authority to detach a company," Shimon said, smiling to take the sting out of the reproach.

Zuchelli had been holding his peace impatiently. "I object," he said. "I refuse to permit any operation that involves separating our forces from the watch of Distacamento de la Fedeltà troops."

"Shit, Major," Tetsuo said, "in another couple of weeks the whole damn war is going to be over—the TW is shoving a cease-fire up your ass, remember? Why not just grease the way a bit and make it easier on yourself, eh?"

"Gracious as always, Tetsuo," Shimon said. "Still, Major, his point stands."

Zuchelli tented his fingers in front of his face. "If we had known about the cease-fire, I hardly think that your regiment would have been hired."

"So? You offering us two weeks off, with combat pay?"

"Don't be silly. I don't have that kind of authority."

"So shut up." Shimon Bar-El turned to Giacometti. "Decide, now."

Giacometti looked from Shimon to Zuchelli, and then back to Shimon. Giacometti would have to live with the Distacamento de la Fedeltà for the rest of the war, and well into the scapegoat-hunting period of the truce. Right here and now, Zuchelli couldn't overrule him directly. But he might be able to see that Giacometti was hanged later.

"You want to go with them, Major?" Giacometti asked.

"Of course."

Giacometti pursed his lips. "I'll give you the company, Shimon. But you'll have to take Major Zuchelli and a Distacamento de la Fedeltà squad, too."

"That seems a reasonable compromise." Zuchelli turned to Ari and nodded. "We'll help you chivvy them along in the attack."

"No." Shimon pulled out a tabstick. "You can bring up the rear, Major. But not Ari." He looked at Ari. "This will be my nephew's command, Major Zuchelli. Tell him, Ari."

"None of the men," Ari started, "will—"

"No," Shimon said. "Again."

"None of *my* men," Ari said, parroting the words he had learned in school, "will set foot on hostile ground before me. I lead the attack, Major Zuchelli."

And I'll not disgrace my family again, he thought—terrified that he was lying to himself.

He was able to get a moment alone with Elena in Giacometti's outer office, while Shimon and the others were going over details of the assignment and orders. Zuchelli's two guards had been loitering in the outer office, but left at a twin glare from Ari and Elena.

When the door closed, she came into his arms. She smelled of soap and lemon.

"Stefano—I mean, Major Zuchelli—I know he won't let me come with you. I can come out after, probably." She ran her fingers through his hair, her nails gentle against his scalp. "I can see you after you've taken a town for me."

He forced a smile, "Of course. You can wear it on your finger."

Her lips were warm against his for a long moment, but they jerked apart guiltily at the sound of a creaking chair. They were still alone. "You asked me about the long term," she said.

He nodded. "Yes, I did."

Her eyes brightened. "I took out my Bible the other day. Remember the part from Ruth? 'Wither thou goest. . . .' "

"She was talking to her mother-in-law."

"I'm talking to you."

He was reaching for her when the door creaked opened, and he tried to turn the motion into something more natural, sure that he ended up looking like a puppet on a tangled string.

Zuchelli nodded at him. "Are you ready, Captain?"

"Always, Major."

CHAPTER 15

Tetsuo Hanavi:
Keeping the Faith

HEADQUARTERS

Thirtieth Regiment Metzadan Mercenary Corps,
Operational

Menadito, Casalingpaesa, Nueva Terra
Special Field Orders 10/28/32
To: Captain (brevet) Ari Hanavi, MMC

Assignment

1. Effective immediately, by order of the commander of the 2nd Division of the Casalingpaesesercito (hereinafter CPE), Company F of the 21st Battalion, 10th Brigade CPE is detached from the CPE and attached to the MMC Expeditionary force for a period of five (5) days.

2. You are herewith detached from present duty, designated as commanding officer of this company, and so assigned.

3. You are reminded that during the period in which you will be serving as commander of Company F, the company is attached to the MMC and is to be considered as though it is a part of the MMC. It

is your responsibility to conduct yourself and
your company accordingly.

Mission

4. On 10/30/32 at 0230 local time, your company
will capture Anchorville (Correggio).
5. Artillery preparation will be at your discretion.

Forces

6. Enemy forces:
   a. Direct opposition:
      1) The enemy force in Anchorville itself con-
      sists of a reduced-strength company of Frei-
      heim troops. Ten crew-served automatic
      weapons of standard type are emplaced in a
      rough arc approximately 250 meters to the
      south of the town. (See map)
      2) All indications are that the herrenvolk
      are in just as tired and sorry shape as are
      the Casalinguese.
   b. Supporting opposition:
      1) Supporting enemy forces appear to con-
      sist of two artillery batteries, capable of
      laying down a barrage approximately 200
      yards in front of the auto emplacements.
      2) Freiheimer communication is known to
      be inadequate. It appears that the signal for
      the barrage is the firing of a green rocket,
      which results in a Battery Ten along the
      indicated area (see map) on the south side
      of Anchorville.
7. Friendly forces, Supporting:
   a. Three batteries of the CPE Twenty-Fifth Artillery Battalion. Note: Company G (Heavy Mortar) of the 21st Battalion CPE has been detached
   and will NOT be available for supporting fire.
   b. Daleth Party (see below) will consist of a two-
   person detachment from Eighteenth Regiment

HQ, consisting of Captain Tetsuo Hanavi and
Master Private Dov Ginsberg. These will be
supplemented by Casalinguese DF troops.
8. Friendly forces, Adjacent:
   a. Company E of the 21st Battalion CPE (see map).
   b. Company H of the 21st Battalion CPE (see map).

Allotment of units

9. Platoons 1 and 2 are designated Aleph Party;
   Aleph Party will be under your direct leadership.
10. Platoon 3 and the First section of Platoon 4 are
    designated Bet Party; Bet Party will be under the
    command of Lieutenant Paulo Stuarti.
11. The second section of Platoon 4 is designated
    Gimel Party. You will designate a senior NCO to
    lead it. You will also, on a one-for-one basis,
    exchange all armed medic personnel from other
    sections for non-medic personnel in Gimel Party.
    In effect, Gimel Party will be the medic section.
    However, your attention is drawn to the Casa-
    linguese practice of unarmed medics and the
    wearing of brassards; as all personnel will be
    armed, the brassards MUST repeat MUST be dis-
    carded to avoid violation of the Conventions of
    War.
12. The two-person detachment from Eighteenth Reg-
    iment HQ plus an unknown number of CPE DF
    troops are designated Daleth Party.

Execution

13. Company F will, under cover of darkness, insert
    itself onto north face of Hill 201. Should you
    choose to employ artillery preparation, upon the
    firing of a red flare from Hill 201, the support-
    ing artillery will engage in preparatory fire on
    the autogun emplacements. Either after or in
    the absence of preparatory fire, Company F will
    advance, assault, and take Anchorville.

14. Mission of Aleph Party:

    a. Aleph Party will approach Anchorville, in staggered line deployment, as the first wave.

    b. While the advance will be silent, it is anticipated that you may be able to get no closer than fifty meters from the defensive perimeter without drawing enemy attention and fire; accordingly, when the lead elements are fifty meters from the line, Aleph Party will take cover.

    c. If the defenders observe Aleph Party prior to that, you may exercise your option to call in preparatory fire, and will in any case take cover. The actual line at which Aleph Party takes cover will be considered the line of departure.

    d. Upon your voice signal, Aleph Party will rise and, maintaining moving fire, overrun the autogun emplacements and assault Anchorville. You will overrun any opposition, and strike into the heart of the town.

    e. After securing the town, you will prepare defensive positions against a possible Freiheimer counterattack.

    f. Pursuit and exploitation are forbidden; the limit of your advance will be the northern outskirts of Anchorville.

15. Mission of Bet Party:

    a. Bet Party will be positioned at the military crest of Hill 201.

    b. During the assault by Aleph Party, Bet Party will advance to engage the enemy autoguns in suppressive fire. After the autoguns are overrun, Bet Party will complete the tactical elimination of any opposition on the outskirts of Anchorville, and then proceed to coordinate with Aleph the final reduction of the defenders.

16. Mission of Gimel Party: Gimel Party will function as armed medic and support, giving first aid

to casualties from the first two assaults, and will also function as the reserves at your option.

17. Mission of Daleth Party and CAF DF troops: Daleth Party and the CAF DF troops will engage in any measures necessary to encourage soldiers and officers in the performance of their duty.

Logistics and Support

18. All supplies will be furnished by the CPE QM Corps. Medical evacuation via skimmer will take place once the town has been brought under your control.

Command and Signal

19. Signal instructions and information: It should be noted that local commo is unreliable, and is not to be depended on.

   a. A red flare will instruct your supporting artillery to engage in or repeat its preparatory fire mission. For the sake of simplicity, the fire mission will be a Battery Three.

   b. A blue flare followed by two yellow flares will signal the completion of the mission.

   c. A double white flare will call for final protective fire beyond the town.

   d. (Special) You are reminded that, in current local Freiheim usage, a green flare is the order for a Freiheim defensive barrage (see map for rough area of barrage.)

20. Location of commander: During the assault, you will be located at or near the point position.

Special Order: If all else fails, improvise.

(signed)

Shimon Bar-El

Shimon Bar-El
General, MMC

Across from Tetsuo in the cramped passenger compartment, Ari was going through sheafs of flimsies—mainly personnel reports—as though they mattered.

Tetsuo sighed and shook his head, then picked up his copy and read the orders again as the skimmer rattled along.

They were a standard set of formal orders, old-style, just like he studied in school. Nicely done, very nicely done—Shimon had even been careful enough to keep the brevetting orders separate. Ari might have to show these to some Casas; best they keep thinking Ari was a first lieutenant who had been brevetted to captain, and not a green private.

The last line was one of Shimon's trademarks. There's an old saying to the effect that a battle plan never survives the battle; the last line was Shimon's guarantee that his would.

Tetsuo didn't want to admit it, but Ari was bringing off the commanding officer bit quite well: there was a confident air to the way he flipped through the flimsies, pausing occasionally as though he could separate what was revealing from what was just pro forma paperwork.

No, that wasn't true, Tetsuo *did* want to admit it: he was happy that Ari was faking it well.

Ari probably wasn't thinking it through, though. Tetsuo was willing to bet that baby brother hadn't noted that both skimmers were overloaded, which didn't bode well. When you're near the front, overloaded transport usually means that supplies are coming through on an irregular basis. The Casas were throwing everything into Triumphant, down south: The northern front was suffering, and not just in supply. He could hear the fluttering whine of the forward fan, clear evidence that routine maintenance was going by the boards. The Casas were overusing equipment, expending it instead of maintaining it.

Not the only thing that was being expended.

Tetsuo admired the old man, but this was raw, even for Shimon. Might work, though, if Ari could get his head out of his ass long enough to lead a charge.

Just one time, little brother, just once. That was all Tetsuo wanted.

After that, he thought, drumming his fingers against his thigh, a disabling wound—in the legs, say, or the gut—heroically received, and Ari could go back to being the clerk that he clearly was destined to be.

Tetsuo shrugged. It might be worse. They'd called Ari the General when they all were boys, but they weren't boys anymore. They were men, with men's responsibilities to the family. Here, Benyamin was head of the family, and Benyamin had told Tetsuo to make sure that if Ari fucked up this time he didn't have the chance to do it again.

We take care of our own. He wouldn't stop Dov from killing Ari if Ari froze again, but that was where he drew the line. Tetsuo would take care of his own.

Besides, all Ari had to do was stand up and shout *Follow me.*

Once.

He could do that.

Through the window to the skimmer's cargo compartment, he could see Dov sitting on the large aluminum case containing his personal supplies. It took a lot of ammunition to keep Dov in business; Tetsuo thought of the ugly man as a human weapons carrier.

Dov was also one of the few men who could take Tetsuo in a fair hand-to-hand, although if Tetsuo ever had to go up against Shimon's pet psychopath, it wouldn't be a hand-to-hand affair. Tetsuo would prefer a sniper rifle at four hundred meters, but he would settle for a flamethrower at a hundred.

There was a certain something about the times when you're moving out, Tetsuo decided. There was something special about traveling in the direction of an armed enemy. His stomach was always tight, of course, and he knew that if he didn't control each and every word he spoke there would be a tremor in his voice that could be heard a klick away, but there was something special about it, too. The air tasted sweet, and rare, and precious. The only time it tasted sweeter was *after*.

Zuchelli held out a pack of tabsticks to Ari—who declined with a shake of his head—and then to Tetsuo. "Would you care for one, Captain?"

"Yes, Major. Thank you." Tetsuo thumbed a stick to life and inhaled the rich smoke. Tobacco was one of his offworld vices, and the Casas had good tobacco—mainly burley, with just a spicy hint of perique.

"Might I examine your sidearm?" Zuchelli asked Ari. "Looks like an expert's weapon to me."

Tetsuo kept his face blank.

"Certainly," Ari said, loosening the tie-down thong, then slowly drawing the Desert Eagle. He thumbed the clip free and worked the slide, making sure the chamber was empty before he handed the weapon to Zuchelli.

Zuchelli examined it with a smile. "Classic, Captain, a classic. Desert Eagle, I believe?"

Ari nodded sagely, "Very early. It's a Belge copy of the one that originally had a reversible safety," he said, as if he knew what he was talking about. It was something that Benyamin had once mentioned.

"Eh?"

"Originally, if you stripped the piece and put the safety in backward, you could find that what you thought was putting the gun off safe had just the opposite effect. It's important to know when a weapon's live."

"It is, at that. Is this your regular sidearm?"

"Yeah."

Zuchelli nodded, his face impassive.

Tetsuo wondered if he was impressed. "Major," Tetsuo said, soberly, "when you're the kind of pistol shot that my brother is, carrying a rifle is redundant."

There was a tradition in the clan for officers to carry old weapons instead of modern ones, which went against the standard Metzadan notion that an officer's personal weapon is a device intended to be used in assault and defense, and not the equivalent of a swagger stick. There was Grandfather Yitzhak's 1911 Colt, and Shlomo's bowie knife that supposedly had been used by Jim Bridger himself, and which somebody in the family had looted from a museum during the suppression of the NAF Rebellion. There was also Tetsuo's penchant for his ancient daisho, but that was different, he decided. He was quite good with the paired swords. They weren't for show.

But, mostly, the clan's officers' weapons were for style rather than effect: for serious work, most of them had no problem picking up an assault rifle—and using it to good effect.

In Ari's case it didn't matter, not if he couldn't even make a decent shot with a sniper rifle. So he carried an expert's weapon. A bit of a bluff.

And a bit of style, Tetsuo had to admit.

Again, Zuchelli smiled his approval. "I was on our Olympic team, myself, back before the war started." He sighed. "I was getting ready for the trip to Old Greece when the war broke out. Perhaps, if we have a bit of free time, we could shoot for fun."

"Perhaps," Ari said noncommittally.

Tetsuo didn't like the DF officer, and he didn't think much of Zuchelli's coarse attempts to ingratiate himself with him and Ari. He guessed that Zuchelli figured that he couldn't manipulate them with fear. With Dov and Tetsuo unofficially guarding Ari's body, and with Shimon's protection against the official wrath of the DF, they were immune to his displeasure.

And since fear wasn't available, perhaps a bit of camaraderie might work.

Or maybe nothing would work.

Ari held out his hand for the pistol, slid the clip in,

then holstered the weapon with the chamber empty. Tetsuo approved. Some people carry pistols with a round chambered, but anybody as clumsy as Ari was more likely to shoot himself in the leg than be able to take advantage of the slight reduction in alert-to-first-shot.

Dammit, little brother, you do everything right except fight when you're supposed to.

Finally, the pitch of the skimmer's engine slowed and the vehicle ground to a sluggish halt. The other skimmer—the one carrying the DF squad—stopped behind them.

Tetsuo clapped a hand to Ari's shoulder. "You're on, little one."

Ari shoved his hand away.

"Fuck you, too, brother," he said. He swung the door open, vaulted to the ground and walked around to the cargo compartment.

"Captain Tetsuo Hanavi. Private Ginsberg. Get out here."

Dov visibly considered it for a moment, then nodded. "Yes, sir," he said, exiting the compartment, not quite slouching.

"I know what your job for Shimon is," Ari said in a low voice that couldn't have carried further than a few meters. "I'm not quite as stupid as you think I am. It's was obvious: Captain Ari Hanavi is either going to fight bravely and effectively, or he is going to die bravely in combat. No problem. But until those orders of his apply, you obey mine. Understood?"

"Captain. . ." Dov started slowly.

"I'll handle this." Tetsuo hitched at his rifle's sling. "If you'll remember, Ari, Dov is under my command, not yours. Understand me?"

Ari smiled as he turned to Tetsuo. It was Shimon's arrogant smile. "And if you'll remember, Captain, I am a line officer. You are staff. And this is my area of operations, not yours. You will release Dov to my service, now. Do you understand me?"

Zuchelli and his bodyguards had been watching the discussion with interest, and a few dozen grimy, weary soldiers had gathered, clearly preferring to watch an argument between officers to unloading the supplies that still stood stacked in the skimmer's cargo compartment.

Tetsuo looked at Ari, and then at the crowd, and then back at Ari. Officially, Ari had no right to make any sort of demand like this; Tetsuo wasn't under his command, wasn't subject to his orders. Maybe Tetsuo could make him back down—he'd always been able to do that when they were younger—but he couldn't make him back down publicly and then expect him to lead the company.

Tetsuo let a thin smile spread across his face. He nodded. "As you will. You're working for Ari, Dov."

"Yes, sir." It didn't really matter to Dov. He would do what Shimon had ordered him to do, and when he ordered him to do it, and it didn't matter who pretended to command him until then.

"Try again, Tetsuo," Ari said. "I'm the commanding officer hereabouts. You're not, Captain," he said. "That makes me senior, regardless of time-in-rank, no?"

Tetsuo was getting irritated, but this wasn't the time to show it. "Yes, sir. As you will, sir."

It's just form, Ari, and it doesn't make any difference. Just remember to shout, "Follow me," Tetsuo thought.

Please.

CHAPTER 16

Flares

"Try again, Tetsuo," Ari said. "I'm the commanding officer hereabouts. You're not, Captain," he said. "That makes me senior, regardless of time-in-rank, no?"

Ari Hanavi considered the soldiers crowding around the skimmers. They were all dirty, and he couldn't see among them a set of shoulders that wasn't stooped. Some of them, staring blankly, were just too far gone to do anything without orders. For the others, it was probably more tired fun to see if they could spot the new company commander as a fraud than it would be to unload some cargo.

"Yes, sir," Tetsuo said. "As you will, sir."

The skimmers had stopped on what probably had been a helo landing zone—a fifty-meter clearing in the slimy forest, hidden from observation on either side by rises in the gently rolling ground. Ari looked around for watch posts on the rises, but couldn't see any. Which meant that either they were well-concealed or that they weren't there.

That a new commanding officer has to establish himself as being in command was something Ari had learned in school. Needling his big brother came naturally.

"Better." Ari turned to the nearest of the Casalinguese soldiers, a ragged private whose long face was stubbled with beard and caked with dirt. "Your name and unit, soldier."

At that moment, Zuchelli and two DF storm troopers stepped into sight, their uniforms clean, their brass sparkling.

The soldier was silent for a long, long moment. "De Sanctis," he said, slowly. "Private Rafael . . . De Sanctis. First . . . Platoon." He passed a tired hand across the deep black pits of his eyes.

"Easy, Ari," Tetsuo muttered. "Burn-out case."

"Hey, Captain, you got a problem with Rafe?" A scraggle-bearded corporal interposed himself between Ari and De Sanctis.

"You are?"

The corporal tapped at the nametag over his heart. "Rienzi, Dominic. Fireteam B, Second Section, First Platoon. What's it to you, Captain?"

"Corporal—" Zuchelli started.

"I'll handle this, Major," Ari said. He wasn't a real officer, but a real officer wouldn't let somebody else discipline his men. He turned back to Rienzi. "Fair question, Corporal. My name is Hanavi; I'm the new CO. Three things, Corporal Rienzi. Number one, except in a combat situation, every dog gets one bite. You've just had yours. *Dov*."

He had heard that tone in Shimon's voice a couple of times; he wanted to try it on for size.

Rienzi started as he heard the *chick-chick* of Dov's shotgun being pumped.

"As you were, Private Ginsberg. Number two, Corporal: you keep your eyes on me when I'm talking to you."

Actually, number two had been intended to be something about sirring and saluting an officer, but Ari was improvising. It was more important right now that he seem to know what he was doing than anything else.

"Number three, and last: while I'm in command of this company, you don't have to worry about Major Zuchelli and the Distacamento de la Fedeltà having you hanged. You don't have to worry about protecting your friend De Sanctis from them. That's an order. Understood?"

He didn't know whether Rienzi's smile came from relief or exhaustion. "Yes, sir."

"The reason for that, Corporal, is that dead men don't get hanged. If anyone gives me any trouble," he said, drawing the Desert Eagle and working the slide, pumping a round into the chamber, "I'll burn him down where he stands."

The 10mm Desert Eagle had more of a maw than a bore. Although Ari kept it carefully pointed to the side, it got Rienzi's attention. So did the flat tone with which he delivered the threat.

If I can't really be an officer, I can at least fake it, he decided. It didn't matter that his heart pounded in his chest, and that his palms were slick with sweat, not as long as he kept his voice level, not as long as he didn't wipe his hands. "I can't hear you, Rienzi. You understand me?"

"Yessir."

Ari raised his voice. "Pass the word. The Metzadan bastard is here, he knows what he's doing, and he's in charge."

One, maybe two out of three wasn't bad. He turned to one of the open-mouthed NCOs. "You, sergeant . . . Adatzi, is it? Good. Senior NCO call in ninety minutes—section leaders and up. I want to see the officers half an hour before. Tell the first sergeant and the exec that they're to find me on the double; I'll be looking over the camp. And tell the cooks three things: first, that they'll be in the assault. Second, if the food—anyone's food—is as badly prepared as everything else around here seems to be, they'll be part of the force *leading* the assault, right behind me. Third, tell them if I don't see a bunch of well-fed soldiers by nightfall, they'll be wearing day-glo orange rompers while leading the assault,"

This sergeant broke into a broad smile. "Yes, sir. Do you want those calls in the mess tent, sir? Or—"

"Mess tent. Move out. Rienzi, don't you have anything better to do than stand there with your thumb up your ass? Enlist some volunteers and get those skimmers unloaded."

He turned and started to walk away, Zuchelli and his men walking with him. "Dov, stay close by. Tetsuo, you go find Major Zuchelli and his men a place to pitch their tents. I'll see them and you after the staff meeting."

Zuchelli opened his mouth to protest. But Ari turned his back and walked away, opening the chamber of the Desert Eagle, ejecting the round. He stooped to pick the cartridge up, then removed the clip and thumbed the round back in. 10mm ammunition wasn't easy to get hold of, but that wasn't why he was going to the trouble.

It gave him something to do with his hands. Besides trembling.

He slammed the clip home and holstered the pistol. This hadn't meant anything. He knew he could handle himself in bivouac. That had never been an issue. There was only one real question: was he going to freeze in the face of the enemy?

No, that wasn't the real question: when he froze, how long was it going to be before Dov burned him down?

Nobody was looking, but he didn't wipe his sweaty palms on his khakis.

Aaron Leumi's *Commanding Foreign Troops* has a long chapter on how a Metzadan officer often has to lower his expectations and standards when commanding foreign troops. Metzadan officers are all too used to Metzadan soldiers, who are not only better-trained than all but elite offworld troops, but who are usually contractually protected from being on active status for more than five hundred consecutive hours.

Downtime is just as important for men as it is for machines. More important: men are more valuable than machines. On Metzada, it takes about nine months plus an additional seventeen years to make a soldier. Machines can be made much more quickly.

But the Casalinguese army was not giving time off, at least not on the north part of the front. Casalingpaesa had been in a war with Freiheim for better than two years, Giacometti's brigade had been engaged for almost a year, and Company F hadn't been out of contact with the enemy for better than a hundred of the overlong local days, and they looked it. There is a kind of impenetrable dirtiness that a worn-out soldier gets, where the grit seems permanently bonded to the flesh and the soul. Maybe that was it. It wasn't just the stubbled faces, the lukewarm food, the clothes in rags. It was the lack of hope in the faces, the conviction that all they had to do was go on for a while, for just a little bit longer, just stumble for a few more hours, until they met the only real rest they would find, in the grave.

He didn't really have a company. What he had was a collection of the walking dead.

There were some exceptions. The first sergeant was one.

While the Casalingpaesesercito was a people's army, with all its flaws, First Sergeant Luigi Matteotti was the kind of professional NCO that the Sergeant used to talk about.

"You'll see them in a lot of places," he'd said. "Mainly around the sort of gentleman officer setup like they have in New Britain, over on Thellonee. Make no mistake—their NCOs are one of the main reasons the New Brits consistently kick the shit out of the 'Zbaallah: if you're going to handicap your army by effectively restricting your officer selection to unblooded members of your upper class, you'd damned well better have superb company-level NCOs."

Like Matteotti. Not that he looked like much, unless you looked close. He was a pudgy little man, round-faced under a hairline that was racing for the back of his neck. His camouflage-mottled ODs wouldn't have looked particularly neat when new; he was the sort that could wrinkle a brand-new formal mess uniform just by looking at it.

But there was something in his eyes as he drew himself up straight and threw a measured salute, holding it until Ari returned it.

No, it wasn't that bullshit "look of eagles" Ari had read about. He didn't know what that look was. What he saw in Matteotti was an absence of panic, worry, desperation.

It was the way his brother Benyamin used to look at him.

"First Sergeant Luigi Matteotti reporting to the commanding officer, sir," he said, handing him a clipboard with a flimsy on it. It was a standard assumption-of-command-and-acceptance-of-responsibility form. Ari scribbled the usual subject-to-subsequent-sight-inventory codicil, signed his name and handed it back, trying to look as though he had done it a thousand times before.

"Very good, sir," Matteotti said. "Orders?" he asked, perhaps a touch too crisply.

"Standing orders remain in force, until I have a chance to review them," Ari answered, as custom required. "I've set up an officer's call for—" he glanced down at his thumbnail "—seventy-three minutes from now. I want you to be ready for a few changes. And for an attack order." He pulled out the flimsies and handed them to the sergeant. "You can take a look."

"Now, sir? Or—"

"If I wanted you to look later, Sergeant, I would have *told* you later."

Matteotti nodded, his face studiously blank as he looked over the orders.

Ari let himself smile. So far, so good. It wasn't important to Matteotti whether or not he liked Ari personally, but in any case Matteotti didn't hold it against him. An officer taking over a new outfit always has to step on a few toes to assure everyone—including himself—that he's really in command.

"Tomorrow night, sir?"

"That's right, First," Ari said, hoping he sounded more than confident, less than cocky. It sounded crazy to him, too. But Meteorology reported that storm clouds were rolling in from the west, and it would be best to get the assault over with before the storm.

Or maybe it was just best to get it over with. Period.

"As far as the watch goes tonight, I don't want any laxity," Ari said. "I want a half hour of full darkness prep—none of this red-goggle nonsense." Actually, there's nothing wrong with twenty minutes of red goggles followed by ten minutes of darkness prep. But a new commander must take command.

Ari was sure that Matteotti knew what his new CO was doing, but all the sergeant said was, "Yes, sir."

"You can take it easy on the 'sirs,' First Sergeant. Now, I want you to set up a new watch list for tonight. Other than yourself, there are to be no exemptions. Everybody else in the company stands a watch tonight. The company clerk, the cooks, the exec—everybody. Specifically including me."

Matteotti muffled a complaint.

"Well, what is it?"

"Two things, sir. First, we don't have near enough slots where we need to put everyone on watch tonight. Second, if I put sergeants on guard tours, we don't have enough officers for corporals-of-the-guard—"

"Well, then you'd better go designate some more

watch posts, hadn't you? Second, this is guard duty, not combat—rank isn't an issue. You can put Private Ginsberg and me on—" he glanced down at his map "—Post Three. The midnight to 02:00 watch."

Matteotti hesitated, then seemed to decide not to ask who to put on as corporal of the guard over him. "Yes, sir. If everybody else is taking a watch, sir, maybe it would be better if I did, too?"

"No; case closed," Ari left it at that. He didn't plan on spending the rest of his life explaining orders, and he particularly didn't want to have to explain even that. "Now, I sent for the exec at the same time I sent for you. Where is he?"

"Sir, Lieutenant Stuarti may be sleeping in his tent. He was in charge—"

"Captain," Dov put in, "I got the word. He's a drunk."

Ari sneered. "And Shimon put him in charge of Bet Party? So much for the famed Shimon Bar-El intelligence. First Sergeant, you've got things to do. Dov and I will go wake the lieutenant."

Matteotti straightened. "Yes, sir."

"Okay, First, you look like you've got something on your mind. Spit it out."

Matteotti shrugged. "Nothing much, Captain. It's just that, shit, Captain, I know you're doing the best you can, but I don't know that these guys have any more in them."

"They'd better, First. Dismissed." Ari turned away, trying to look theatrically lost in deep thought. A commander was supposed to think deep thoughts.

Ari hoped that, at the least, both Dov and Matteotti were thinking the same thing that he was: that he didn't do a bad job of imitating a company commander. At least, as long as there weren't shots being fired in his ear.

Of course, that was the only time that mattered. The rest of it didn't count, unless he fucked up.

Now let's see if I can tear my exec a new asshole, and then bullshit my way through a staff meeting.

Paulo Stuarti lay snoring in his tent, a carefully corked bottle cradled in one arm, the other flung over his eyes to ward out the mottled daylight. He was a tall man, his thin, mustache several shades darker than his sun-bleached hair.

Dov, as per Ari's orders, had procured a bucket of water.

"Do it."

Dov dumped the pail over the Casa's torso and tossed the bucket aside.

Stuarti straightened with a jerk. "Basta—" he was reaching for his pistol belt when Dov caught his hand with a meaty thunk.

Stuarti sputtered and coughed as Dov jerked him to his feet.

"Get control of yourself, asshole," Ari said. "My name is Ari Hanavi, I'm your new commanding officer, and you've got one hour to report to the mess tent, looking like a good imitation of this company's exec." He spun on the balls of his feet and stalked away.

The NCO meeting broke up slowly, sullenly, until Matteotti cleared his throat, cueing the rest of the sergeants to get out.

Ari jerked his head at Lieutenant Stuarti. "You may as well go sleep it off," he said, letting disgust drip from his voice. "I'm not going to replace you as exec; I wouldn't know what to do with you if I did—"

Stuarti started to smile, relieved at getting off so easily.

"—except turn you over to the Distacamento de la Fedeltà."

That wiped the smile off Stuarti's face.

"Which," Ari finished, "I'm not going to do. One

thing, though. You're not leading Bet Party; I'm giving that to Romano. You're going to be right up front,
by my side."

Paulo Stuarti started to open his mouth, then closed
it. Officially, the Casalinguese army had strong penal-
ties for drinking on duty, and even an exec who is only
acting as CO is always on duty. Facing Ari's disap-
proval wasn't quite the same thing as facing a DF
hangman.

"Now get the hell out of my sight." Ari turned his
back on him, watching Dov watch him go. He beckoned to Tetsuo, who had been taking it all in.

"So." Tetsuo quirked a smile at Ari. "You want to
know how you did, eh?"

"Yes. Both at the officers' call and with the NCOs."

"You did well, I think."

"I hear a 'but'?"

"You're right to play it hard because you don't have
any other choice, not with an assault tomorrow." Tetsuo
looked from him to Dov. "But I think you'd best not
let this go to your head, Captain."

"True. Particularly since I've got a favor to ask. I'd
like a nice quiet recon of Anchorville, with special
attention to its southern perimeter. Tonight."

Tetsuo started to look from side to side, then caught
himself.

"Relax, Tetsuo, nobody else is going to know. I've
got me and Dov on Post Three from midnight to two.
You can slip out just after dark; that'll give you plenty
of time to make like a ghost and give you a nice wide
re-entry window, without anyone being the wiser."

"If you think it's so easy, would you like to come
along?"

It was starting to look like Tetsuo was going to do
it; Ari forced himself not to let out a sigh of relief.
"No, I don't think it's so easy. As Galil was kind
enough to point out to me, I'm a clumsy asshole. Even

forgetting that I'm the CO, I couldn't go." He shook his head. "I wouldn't be any good."

"That's true," Tetsuo pulled a tabstick out of his pocket, puffed it to life and exhaled a deep cloud of blue smoke before answering. "Why not?"

Ari leaned on the side of the trench, looking out at how the field spread out under the stars. He was still vaguely disappointed by the sky; he had been hoping that he would see a world with a real moon before he died. The Sergeant used to talk about standing out in the light of a real moon at night, how special it was.

But there were only stars. Nueva Terra had three moons, but they were tiny, with a low albedo. Occasionally you could see lights moving in the sky at night, but those were as likely to be TW observation sats as they were the natural satellites. There was nothing romantic about either.

It was too dark, Ari decided. A guard post was different than an observation post: it was like being a hunted animal, not a hunter.

Sometimes Ari really liked the Thousand Worlds Commerce Department's restrictions on the importation of military tech, particularly on worlds of lower tech levels than Nueva. The restrictions were always on weaponry and support—but medical supplies weren't ever considered support, and communication gear usually wasn't.

Idiots. Everything has a military application, or implication.

If a Metzadan took a jecty arrow in the belly, he wasn't in the same position that a gut-wounded medieval peasant would have been. Not only would he be unlikely to die, but the battlefield medicians would have his bowel resected and patched and have him up on his feet and back in combat in less than a hundred hours.

Sometimes the rules favored the soldier. A set of

night goggles would have been awfully handy, and never mind that the pack to carry them around weighed better than thirty kilos. But they were expensive pieces of equipment, and were not available to a line company in bad odor at Divisione HQ.

So he swept his eyes across the night. It didn't merely require wearing a blindfold before guard duty. He had to adapt to a whole different way of seeing. The area of the retina used for central vision was heavily laden with cone—color—cells, which needed plenty of light to function. At night, a watchman had to depend on the rod cells of his peripheral vision—he had to look without quite looking.

Ari kept his eyes moving constantly, in short, quick, jerky movements, hoping to pick up any strange shape or movement with his peripheral vision, and hoping that there wasn't anything there.

"Captain," Dov hissed, his voice pitched to carry a couple of meters, no further. "I see him."

"Close an eye." Ari checked to see that there was a round in the flaregun he carried—at close range, they were a not-bad substitute for a rocket pistol, and would temporarily blind any open eye—and thumbed the safety off.

"Ari," a voice whispered from off to his left, "if you shoot me dead, I'll tell our mothers on you."

Dov made a patting motion. "It's him. Only him, Captain."

Wearing mottled fatigues, soft shoes and carrying nothing that resembled a weapon, Tetsuo stepped out of the darkness as if he were stepping out from behind a curtain. Ari didn't really know how he did that, but the black bundle he was arranging under his arm probably had something to do with it. There was a lot about his brother Ari didn't understand, and didn't want to know.

Without being asked, Dov pulled the canteen from

his belt and tossed it to Tetsuo, who unscrewed the top and took a long pull.

"That cuts the dust," Tetsuo said. "I have a little good news and a lot of bad news. The bad news is that they've strung commo wire all over the place—even from the autogun emplacements." He shook his head. "Typical Frei discipline: even though they've got beaten fire zones as nice as I've ever seen, they've set up range cards for the guns. With their comm setup, unless you overrun them damn fast, they'll be able to walk artillery fire all over the place, using the autogun nests as forward observers. Spot for effect, eh?"

"What?"

"Old, bad artilleryman's joke. They're using white phosphorus rounds for spotting."

"So? Everybody does."

"Yeah. So the joke goes, if you've got a target that's mainly infantry, and you don't want to *just* kill them, you don't call in a load of frag—you call for the whole battery to fire the white phosphorus rounds, at three rounds a minute. Spot for effect."

Ari had seen the burn victims hauled out of the buses after the ambush. Horrible sight, and a worse smell. There was a sickly sweet odor that almost made him gag, even just remembering. He tried to change the subject. "What do you figure it'd take to neutralize the town?"

"Artillery?" Tetsuo shrugged. "Five hundred tons, minimum. Possibly a thousand. You're authorized around—"

"Ten tons. Eight battery threes. Just enough for harassment, and maybe a spot of interdiction—and then the battery's going to pull out. Meanwhile, they'll be able to call in whatever they want, and put it wherever they want."

"Perhaps," Tetsuo said. He broke into a crooked smile as he pulled a black plastic box out of his bundle. "Unless, of course, right before you assault, you were to flip up this guard and press this button. There are strong Commerce Department sanctions against the import of certain kinds of devices to some worlds. Of course, those sanctions apply if and only if you're caught."

Ari took the box and tucked it into a pocket. "And if I were to do that?"

"Well, the first thing I'd suggest is that you get rid of the box; it'll self-destruct about ten minutes after. Don't forget, now, you might get distracted—because as soon as you press the button, a small explosion will have taken out the Freiheimer central commo office. They've got it in the basement of the old church."

"That was the good news, I take it."

He shook his head. "Not really. I don't think it'll make much difference. They can still call in a barrage with a green flare, no? The last of the good news is that the Freiheimers are as tired-looking a bunch of soldiers as I've ever seen." Tetsuo sighed. "Almost as bad as your own, but only almost." He raised an eyebrow. "You want to argue for a change of plans? We've got about twenty-four hours until H-hour."

"No," Ari said, still wondering if he could do it. "We go."

Tetsuo raised the canteen. " 'Everybody comes back,' " he said, pronouncing the words the way they're supposed to be pronounced: matter-of-factly.

It was called the Mercenary's Toast. It was just a wish, an ambition, not a prediction, and certainly no promise.

Ari took the canteen.

"Fat fucking chance." He drank, but only a little.

"Beggin' your pardon, Captain, but it isn't going to work that way," First Sergeant Matteotti said. "I'm not in the habit of bringing up the rear." If anything, Matteotti looked more harmless than usual in full combat get-up—his bulky plastic body-armor parka and

leggings made him look inflated. On the chance that
he wouldn't want to keep his helmet on, he'd streaked
camouflage paint on his forehead, all the way up and
into his receding hairline.

"What are you saying, Sergeant?"

"You've assigned me to Bet Party, sir. And that
isn't going to happen. Sir." He beckoned to a bulky,
tired-looking private, almost Dov's height and weight,
who was shouldering an autogun.

"Salute the Captain, Sbezzeguti," Matteotti said,
shaking his head at the half-hearted response from the
soldier. "Back before I got all the stripes, sir, I was a
damn good assistant gunner. And you're going to need
a damn good assistant gunner on your right flank.
Sir."

Ari started to open his mouth to say no, but stopped
himself. Why was he tempted to overrule Matteotti?
Because he didn't need a good man on his flank,
laying down an autogun barrage to close down the
western exit from the town and divert attention from
the main charge? No. He wanted to overrule him
because he didn't want Matteotti see him turn coward
when the shooting started. Ari hitched at the box of
flares hanging from the left side of his belt. To hell
with it.

"You've got it, First." He glanced at his thumbnail—
0137—and up at the night sky. "Pass the word down:
Aleph Party's moving out."

It's dangerous to leave an outline against a sky,
even a night sky, so they crossed the crest of Hill 201
on their bellies and then rose into a crouch as they
moved through the tall grasses.

The wind rose from the north, caressing his face,
whispering vague threats and imprecations. Spread out
on his right, Matteotti, Sbezzeguti, Stuarti and a pair
of fireteams from the First Platoon plodded slowly,
like men walking toward the gallows. They moved

silently, except for the quiet swish of boots in the grass, and the occasional half-grunt as someone came close to stumbling into a shell crater.

The field had been well-chewed by artillery. Whether it was Freiheimer defensive barrages or Casalinguese prep fire didn't matter; it still looked like a wasteland. Five hundred meters out, he signaled for everyone to drop down. The grasses were starting to thin out and the detachment had to make the rest of the way low.

The repeated artillery barrages had left the ground heavily cratered, but the craters made decent cover. They slipped from one shell crater to another, working their way up until they were a little more than a hundred meters from the nearest autogun emplacement.

Almost losing his footing, Ari staggered into a crater, Dov and three Casalinguese following him.

He turned to look at them: Rienzi, and the rest of his fireteam. Ari took off his helmet and ruffled his hair—helmets have sharp outlines—and raised his head over the edge of the crater. Ten meters away, in a giant of a crater, Matteotti and his autogunner had a whole crowd with them, including Lieutenant Stuarti. Ari was wondering if that was a coincidence, if Matteotti didn't have a dual purpose, one he should have picked up. He wanted to be sure that, if things went to hell, Stuarti didn't end up in charge.

Paulo, looks like you and I have something in common.

He closed his eyes and listened. While he couldn't make out the words, off in the distance he could hear voices. Close enough. He pulled the black box out of his pocket and flipped the cover off the button. He rested his thumb on it. The demolition of the Freiheimer comm shack would do fine as a start signal. . . .

But he just couldn't press the button. His thumb wouldn't move.

Again. I'm doing it again.

He beckoned to the First Platoon communicator—a

skinny kid, even younger than him, and gestured for the headset. The kid carefully paid out more comm line, and handed Ari the set.

He slipped it on. "F-six," he whispered, trying to force some calmness into his voice. "Give me Big Brother."

Tetsuo was on in a couple of seconds. "I'm here, Ari. You calling about the support barrage?"

His heart was pounding so loudly that he was sure the soldiers in the crater with him would hear it, if not the Freiheimers.

But he couldn't tell him. He couldn't do it.

"Yes," he whispered, trying to get some moisture in his cotton-dry mouth. "Yes. I'm calling about the barrage."

"Do you want me to launch the flare for it?"

Ari just didn't know; he couldn't think. He knew that he was in the wrong place, the wrong person to be doing this. He couldn't press the button; he couldn't answer. He couldn't stay there, he couldn't make the others just stay and wait, but he couldn't go on. He was supposed to set up the line of departure from twenty meters away from the line of Freiheimer autogun emplacements, but here they were fifty meters out and he didn't know if he could do it and with four sets of round eyes looking at him he was freezing. Again.

"Brother," Tetsuo said. "I'm sorry. Here it comes."

From the crest of Hill 201, a signal rocket screamed into the night and exploded overhead in a green shower.

What? It wasn't the red flare, calling for support fire—it was a green flare, the Freiheimer signal for a defensive barrage.

Around him, three soldiers, their faces white under the camouflage paint, stared wide-eyed at him, their eyes seeking Ari's for some sort of reassurance, some sort of explanation.

He didn't have anything to give them.

"What are you doing?" he shrilled, his thumb coming down on the button, rewarded by a *crump*! from the town.

"Run for the town, Ari, take the town. It's your only chance. There's a Freiheimer barrage on its way. If you can't find it in you, brother, fake it."

Ari tossed the plastic box aside and tore the headset off as he leaped to his feet.

He wasn't a soldier, he wasn't a commander, he was a fraud. That wasn't just his problem—it was his secret, his solution.

In the green light of the flares, he rose to his feet, the way a real commander would, and shouted, the way a real commander would have.

"Run for the town," he shouted as the bright lines of tracers drew their way through the night, clawing toward him. *"It's our only chance."*

He wasn't a soldier, not anymore—they weren't soldiers, they were screaming madmen. And as shells roared down from the sky, a reinforced platoon of screaming madmen sprinted for the town, overrunning the Freiheimer autogun emplacements and sending the survivors running for their lives.

Few could stand against such madmen.

Those who stood, died.

CHAPTER 17

Company C: Assault

Caporel Dominic Rienzi:

No shit, there I was, running like a rabbit, with incoming screaming at me. The Boche autogunners must have been too busy jerking each other off or something —by the time the bugger finally opened up, my squad is mebbe thirty, forty meters away, each of us running like we have rockets stuck up our asses, screaming like we was crazy.

We probably was. I know I was.

I'm not sure what I was aiming at—and I don't remember reloading my piece, not until later. Aw, to hell with it—truth to tell, I don't think I *did*, at least not until I reached the pit. Asshole that I am, I'd probably fired off the first clip, and was running and shouting, not stopping to reload.

Well, come to think of it, it was probably just as well I didn't stop to reload, 'cause then I hear the fart of one mortar, and then another, and then the whole sky lights up with illum rounds coming from shit knows where, and it's practically daytime. I mean, I could have whipped out a book and fucking *read,* you get the idea?

You know that funny hissing sound wire makes when

it gets close to you, the way the wires scream higher, like a trumpeter on a sweet riff, then drops off? Well, I musta lucked out, 'cause the loudest, wildest, jazziest scream cuts off just as something chews through de Sanctis, armor and all, and then rips my right ear off. I couldn't tell where it was coming from, and I wasn't exactly going to ask him—he was too busy drowning in his own blood, you know?

My ear still hurts like a sonofabitch, by the way—yeah, yeah, I mean the ear itself. I know plastic isn't supposed to—well, never mind.

Well, Gambetta's ahead of me, at least in the initial deploy, but I'm the first one in, with what was left of my squad right behind me—six of us.

And it's one-on-one, because there are six of them, and one of the Boche draws the longest mother fucker of a knife I've ever seen—wish my cock were half the size of the damn thing—and jumps me.

I swear to the Virgin I don't remember what happened next, except next thing I remember, I'm sitting on his chest, pounding his face with my rifle butt. I think he was dead by then, but I wouldn't swear to it. I *know* he was dead a few seconds later, but I couldn't stop. I mean, the fucker's face is, like, a bloody *paste*, and I'm still pounding on his brains with my rifle butt.

I had just about figgered out that killing a dead man is stupid when somebody jumps me from behind, and I think I'm cooked, sure as shit, and I scream even louder, but then he, like, shudders, and *he* screams, and lets me go. Then I hear another shot, and I realize that it's *loud*. A lot louder than a rifle. I can't see much because the somebody in front of me shoots something to the side of me, and the muzzle flash burns out my eyes for second.

So I turn, and the captain's—no, not the capitano, the *captain*: Hanavi—he's standing there, that big motherfucker of a pistol in both hands, and his face is all lit up by the illum rounds, and the fucker's *smiling*.

He's got the first sergeant with him, and the exec, and both of them are just crouching there, looking at him.

He says something like, "I guess a body *will* stop a hollow-point, eh?" and then he mutters something in that Jewtalk of his, and then he tells us all to reload—which we do, and quick.

Now, by this time, not only do we have enough illum floating in the air to light up a medium-sized country, but there's wire and lead flying around us in all directions. I guess that the Boche are as bad fuckups as our own quartermasters, 'cause one of them's firing off a lead autogun—not wire—that looks like it's all tracers. I think somebody nails him, 'cause it stops traversing, but it doesn't stop firing. Just sends out a solid stream—you know, in one direction? Really kind of pretty.

I coulda stayed and watched it for hours.

Like I say, I wasn't eager to leave—I mean, like, nobody was telling me to leave, you know? He doesn't do that. Giving an order would be too fucking easy for him—yeah, him: Captain Hanavi.

He says, "We're not doing any good here, friends and cousins," and then he stands up and then I see him—I see him pull a grenade and toss it into the autogun's ammo box as he jumps over the sandbag wall.

I can tell you that Enzo and Anna Rienzi's baby boy was *out* of there.

Just as well, because right after his grenade goes off and the ammo box blows, something *big* hits the gunpit, blowing it to all hell. I got some sand driven hard into the back of my neck and my ears are still ringing. Yeah, both of them.

"Just as well we left, eh, Rienzi?" he calls out as he runs for the town. The bastard was smiling.

And the first sergeant, too—Matteotti was one step behind him, and he was laughing as he ran, I swear. I mean, first sergeant is a tough bastard, but I never knew he was crazy, too.

The big surprise was Stuarti, the exec. I always thought of him as a lightweight, but he starts laughing, too, says something like, "Hey, a guy could get killed out here," and the three of them are laughing while they're running into town.

Shit.

No, I don't know anything about what happened later. But you can't get every sniper, you know. I heard they were still picking a few out three days later, when the company was on R&R, and I was up spending half my time and money in the bar and the rest in the whores.

Nah. I don't know nothing. No, maybe I do know two things. First is that we took that town with only eleven KIA, when I thought we all were walking dead.

The other thing I know is that the captain, he may be a crazy mother fucker, but if the crazy bastard ever wants a ride on *my* mother I'll hold her ankles, you hear me?

Soldato Scelto Aldo Cartage:

I very much hate crossing streets. You've got at least ten, fifteen meters with no cover, and everybody and his mate shooting at you. Or maybe there's nobody shooting at you until just before you reach the other side. I wish I was a better shot; I could have qualified to be a sniper instead of a sniper's target. Being a line infantryman is just pasting a big set of crosshairs on you.

It was toward dawn. We had a sniper in a big building, you know, the alley near J Street? It must have been an office building or something, back before the war. When we finally got inside, the fourth floor was filled with desks, maybe two hundred of them. I'm a country boy—my family are farmers along the southern branch of the Baby Dora—and I've never seen anything like it.

But I'm getting ahead of myself.

There was this big building across the street, and we couldn't spot the sniper in it, see—although we pretty much knew he was on the fourth floor. There'd been two squads that had tried to rush it, one by one, and some of them had made it.

We were pinned down behind a dumpster, over near the loading dock. We very much had to get across the street . . . do something.

Now, we were hiding in the loading dock of a building that had been pretty badly chewed up. It was the alley, am I right? My sergente hadn't even gotten into the street when he got himself shot—and nailed good. Bullet went in his mouth and out his kidney. He'd forgotten that snipers use holes in the wall as aiming points; he'd been too busy moving us along to pay attention. You can get killed easy enough when you are paying attention; it's kind of silly to forget shit like that.

We'd dragged the body back in, but you know how it is. You can't do anything for the dead, and I was more worried about the living. Every time somebody made a run for it, this sniper in the building opened up, or when he missed, then what's got to be at least three, fireteams in the building we're next to shoot at us.

Then *he* showed up. The captain, I mean, and he's got the first sergente and the exec with him, along with that bodyguard of his, the one with the name like a bird in Basic. Yeah, Dove. Him. He doesn't look like a bird to me.

So I explained the situation to the captain.

"It's my turn, Ari," the exec said quietly. "I'll take it."

"No, Paulo, this one's on me," the captain said. "Matt, you go back and hurry the First Platoon along. Tell Romano I want him to clear out this building," he said, slapping at the wall. "Just like you're undressing a girl—work from the top on down, then stick it in hard. We'll fuck 'em when they try to get out."

The first sergente tried to argue with him, but the captain just smiled and said that he'd be fine, and sent the first on his way. Then he turned to me.

"You tried to cross the street one at a time?"

"Yeah," I said. "So that the rest of us could cover the guy who was running. You hear of covering fire on Metzada, Captain?"

"Yeah, heard all about it," he said, and his eyes went a bit vague and distant and he looked, I don't know, about twenty years older. "Lesson time, chaverim: when you're crossing a street under fire, split your force in two. Bounding overwatch." His voice sounded kind of funny, a bit deeper and, I don't know, sort of gravelly. "Stationary group divides targets, then the moving half goes right across—fast, and all together—then covers the other group. And make sure the second group crosses from a different part of the street. Don't give them time to react, and don't give them any easy aiming points. You taking notes, soldier?"

I didn't know what to say to that, so I didn't. Figured it was safer.

"Now," he said, "we've got a problem. Romano and Matteotti are going to be driving the ones in this building down and out. I figure that either they'll come out through the east archway or," he said, rapping on the steel door of the delivery dock, "out here, right on top of us. So we'd better get across the street and set up a position where we can do to them what that sniper's doing to you, eh?"

Then he turned to Piscatore, and said to fire some RPGs into the fourth floor, near wherever he thought the sniper was.

"You're not listening, Captain," Pisser said. "We haven't been able to pinpoint him—he keeps moving around. The bastard's a sniper. What do you want me to do, pop up and draw his fire so that you can pinpoint him?"

"Fuck, no," he said. "The sergente will do it."

I looked at him like he was crazy. The sergente was dead.

He sent Pisser and his launcher around to the other side of the dock—telling him to keep low, not that Pisser needed the invitation—and then the captain muttered something to that Dove of his.

"You ready, Piscatore?" the captain calls out.

"Well, yeah."

"Good man. *Dov.*"

Well, the big fucker picked up the sergente's body by the back of his shirt—and the sergente was a big man, too, easily a hundred kilos—and held it out like it was a hand puppet.

The sniper put two holes through the sergente's body before the RPG launcher roared. The charge must not have gone off until it hit the back wall, because it took a long time.

And then, *whoom.* I would have been watching, but I like to keep flying glass out of my eyes, you know?

"Look at that. Mother of Christ, would you *look* at that," Pisser said. The sniper was lying in the street, a bit bloody, but with all the parts there, far as I could tell. The grenade had kicked him right out of the window, neat as you please.

"Easy, Piscatore," the captain said. "Don't assume that's the only one. Fire another while we move out."

Well, we crossed the street—in two groups, each group all together in a clump, the way the captain told us to—and set ourselves up.

When Romano and most of First Platoon had driven the Boche in our building—I mean the one we'd been under for a good ten, fifteen minutes; shit, that's enough to feel right at home—we were set up in the office across the street.

Cut the bastards to ribbons, we did. Then Lieutenant Stuarti and I went out and finished the job. He had a rifle in the crook of his arm, strolled around like a trapshooter, except instead of shooting skeet, he would just casually blow the backs of some dead men's heads off.

Shooting the injured? Nah. I didn't see him shoot anybody who was just injured. They were dead. I've never seen anybody shoot anybody who was just injured. That's against the law, isn't it?

I stripped them of grenades. We weren't short of grenades, not then, but the captain said to, and we did it. The Boche didn't need them anymore. You got a problem with that?

No, I don't know anything about the snipers. I wasn't there, and I don't listen to gossip. Talk to the captain about it. Or Lieutenant Stuarti.

Sototenente Luigi Romano:

We didn't have any experience in city fighting, because we'd never made it into a town—we'd been pushing the Frei across the farmland and back for the past forty days. No, it wasn't covered in training, not in the eight weeks of Fundamentale, or the next eight weeks of officer training I signed up for, hoping that the war would be over by the time I got out.

I thought it was crazy when he sent us in through the top. But he ran it down by the numbers, just like this was a classroom.

"One," he said "the stats say that they will—ninety-five plus percent of the time—go out to the street if you drive them down. The stats say—ninety-nine percent of the time—that they'll fight like cornered rats if you don't give them a place to run. So we give them a place to run.

"Two. You've been out in the country, so you're thinking rifle fire instead of grenades. Rifle fire is better in the open, but in any enclosed space, grenades do it—let the pressure wave do the work for you. Send one into a doorway or window before you go through, then follow the explosion in. When you get inside, throw a grenade into every room, every hall, every closet. Rifle's to clean up after grenades, just like the Sergeant says."

I was going to ask him which sergeant he was talking about, but he just said, "Let's do it."

So we did.

Some of the houses were real pretty, with vines and trellises. I thought we were going to lose a couple of men to broken legs when trellises weren't as strong as they should be, but you know how *they* are—they always overbuild.

One thing that happened was funny as all hell. We were working our way down a street, one squad on each side of the street. We were still having some trouble with supply—you wouldn't believe how many grenades and RPGs you can use up clearing a town.

Now, the way you're *supposed* to do it is to throw a grenade in through each window as you go past. It doesn't quite secure the street—you've still got to go through each room later—but it does keep them busy.

Now, if there are soldiers inside, they'll usually manage to beat the grenade out. Nobody likes sharing close quarters with a fragmentation grenade.

So . . . we were working our way down the street, and I was busy doing a quick sum of windows and doorways versus grenades, and I calculated that we were about twenty percent short. I told him that.

Ari started laughing. "So, you play a practical joke on them," he said. He pulled a Frei grenade out of his pocket and pulled the pin, then tossed it in through the nearest doorway.

There were shouts, and two Frei soldiers crashed right through the window. I think they were going to surrender, but they didn't have their hands up—shut your hole, Martoni, or I'll shut it for you: I said they didn't have their fucking hands up—when Sbezzeguti, *hot* gunner, stitched right through the both of them, pinning one of them square up against the wall before he slipped to the ground, lying in his own blood and shit.

I'd flattened myself against the wall, and I must have been flattened there for about ten seconds when I realized that the grenade hadn't gone off.

There was a strange grin on Ari's face. "It's a dummy," he said. "I took a few tools and pulled the charge on a couple of grenades," he said, handing me another one. "Left the fuse."

I showed him, though—I found an even better trick, which we needed when we ran out of dummies, but still were short of grenades. Remember, soldiers don't like seeing grenades come in the window, so one out of five times, I'd, well . . . it's easier to show you.

Here, *catch*—hey, it's okay, it's okay. I didn't pull the pin now, either. Scared the hell out of them, just before we killed them.

You don't think it's funny? Well, I guess you had to be there. You should have seen the expression on the face of this one Frei . . . well, like I say, I guess you had to be there.

And yeah, I got there just after Ari and the rest had brought down the snipers. What the fuck do you expect? You want it to be safe in a *combat zone*?

Capitano Paulo Stuarti:

No, I don't know anything about anything. Now, if you'll excuse me, I've got a company to run, and I don't care if you're from Brigade, Divisione, or a messenger of God. First Sergente, get these assholes out of here.

CHAPTER 18

Warrior's Reflex

General Shimon Bar-El came out to see them early in the morning, as they were clearing the last of the Freiheimers from the town. It was a family affair: he had brought Tetsuo back, as well as Elena and two more DF troopers.

Ari had set up a command post in an old house at the edge of town, but he hadn't spent much time there. Mainly it was a place to assemble the Freiheimer prisoners; two dozen of them were held on the other side of the building, cuffed to each other on the dirt, casually covered by twin autoguns in a captured gunpit twenty meters away.

He had taken time out for a very quick sponge bath in the Freiheimer commander's former quarters and a change into a fresh set of khakis. He wasn't sure whether that was for Shimon or Elena or himself.

The hard part was over, thank God, although it was going to take at least the rest of the day, and probably most of the next two, to finish clearing out the town. Even when you're only up against a few snipers, street fighting is slow work if you want to do it with reasonable safety.

Off in the distance, assault rifles hammered out three-shot groups, punctuated by the thump of grenades.

"I heard you did it well, Ari," Shimon said. Tetsuo stood at his side, grinning like a fool. Elena stood next to Tetsuo, stifling a smile. It wouldn't do for an officer of il Distacamento de la Fedeltà to giggle like a school-girl in front of the troopers.

"It worked well, Shimon," Ari said. "Eleven dead, total. The Freiheimers panicked. As you knew somebody would, eh?"

"Naughty, naughty, Ari," Tetsuo said. "A nasty trick to play on your men, though, calling in an enemy barrage on your own position, forcing your people to attack."

"Oh," Ari said, "is that the way it's going down? *Freeze it*, Stuarti," he shouted. "I want to see another grenade in that house before you go in."

The procedure for clearing a street is just a variant on the basic pill box technique: you move carefully down the street—one party on either side—trying to draw hasty fire, carefully checking out apparently un-occupied houses after tossing in a frag grenade or two. When you run into enemy fire, you pour your own fire at the window to suppress it, then bring up a grena-dier, rocketeer or flame-thrower.

Paulo Stuarti grinned back. "Hey, whatever you say, Ari," he shouted.

He took out a grenade, held it so a private could snatch off the ring, and then carefully tossed it into the window of the nearest low stone house before taking cover. One of Stuarti's arms was in a dirty, bloodied sling, anesthetized by a medician's nerve-block and, Ari suspected, aided by his hip flask. It also gave him a place to stash a few extra grenades. Stuarti liked grenades.

Flame roared out of the window, followed by silence.

"See, Captain, I *told* you it was unoccupied." Ari remembered reading something to the effect that the old United States President Abraham Lincoln, when told by some snitch that U.S. Grant drank whiskey, ordered some of the same for the rest of his generals. Ari wasn't about to encourage drinking on duty, but if Stuarti could function as well as he did with a bit of liquid encouragement, the least Ari could do was pretend not to see it.

Ari turned back to Shimon.

The general was smiling at him. "Yes, Captain," Shimon Bar-El said, "that's the way it's going down. You seem to have thought your men were too . . . uninspired to attack, so you tried to inspire them. That's official." He shrugged. "High Colonel Giacometti is due out here any time to put his imprimateur on it, and a medal about, oh, there," he said, tapping Ari's chest. "Ari, a hero is just a coward who got cornered. The question is: what will you do the next time you're cornered?" He smiled genially. "I hope you do as well as you did this time."

Dov eyed Ari carefully, so he kept his hand well away from the open flap of his holster. Wouldn't want the big man to think he was threatening Shimon.

Elena beamed.

Matteotti, sweaty and grim, threw him a quick salute as he jogged up, an assault rifle slung over one shoulder. "B Street cleared, sir." He looked at Shimon and then back to Ari. It was hard to read his expression: his face was still mottled with brown and green camouflage paint. "Permission to speak frankly, sir?"

"Granted. And don't wait to ask permission next time."

"That was a fucking mean trick, Captain," he said, his face somber.

And what am I supposed to say to that? It was a mean trick but—

"Fuck it—it worked, didn't it? You didn't think you had any more in you. I proved you wrong, First," he said, as Shimon smiled.

He didn't have any choice. They were, if only for another two days, his men and his responsibility. If there were going to be any repercussions from the men, he was the proper target.

My responsibility. Not anyone else's.

Matteotti's paint-darkened face broke into a broad smile. "That you did, sir. That you did."

As the smoke from the latest grenade cleared, Zuchelli and his five DF troopers walked out of the nearest safe house. Zuchelli gave Elena a quick glare for God-knew-what. The major had a sheaf of blue personnel flimsies in one hand and a grim smile on his face, as he turned to the nearest of his bullyboys. "Sergeant, bring me that drunk Stuarti—"

"Major," Shimon said quietly. "He's under Metzadan command."

"General—"

"Peace, Major," Shimon said, holding up a hand. "Ari, would you be kind enough to send for Lieutenant Stuarti? Please."

Matteotti's face was ashen under the paint and dirt. Last night, Lieutenant Stuarti had calmly shot through the head a Freiheimer who had at the time been busy sweeping an autogun toward Matteotti.

"Please," Shimon said.

Stuarti and his team had worked their way down the dusty street.

Ari called for Stuarti's group to hold in position, then called out, *"Paulo.* Now." Ari made a fist and pumped his arm.

Paulo Stuarti gestured at the squad to keep moving on, then trotted over, his face grim.

"I understand," Zuchelli said to Ari, "that one of your officers has been drinking on duty. A lieutenant named Stuarti, I believe?"

Ari looked at Shimon, who spread his hands, almost helplessly. "Rumors spread, Captain."

Matteotti started to open his mouth; Ari gestured at him to shut up.

"Major Zuchelli says you've been drinking, Paulo," he said. "I'm about to tell him that that's none of his damn concern, that what an officer in a Metzadan company does isn't any of the Distacamento de la Fedeltà's fucking business."

Stuarti pulled the flask out of his sling and smiled crookedly. "Figured you might, Captain."

"Although," Ari said, holding out his hand for the flask, "I don't approve of drinking on duty. And that's to stop. Understood?" Stuarti handed over the bottle. He tucked the flask into his hip pocket as he turned to the DF major. "Can we just forget about all this?"

"Not near good enough." Zuchelli shrugged. "Although I won't push it now. They'll all be back in the Casalingpaesesercito in three days, Hanavi. Then I'll see him hang."

"You're being silly, Major," Tetsuo said, but they were just words thrown into the air. "The war's almost over. The truce will—"

"What of it? We haven't finished things with the Frei. There will be another war and then, perhaps, the officers and men will know that they must do their duty, by the rules. Being unfit for duty in a combat zone? Unacceptable, Captain Hanavi." Zuchelli smiled. "You must trust me on these things, Captain."

Ari didn't like the way Zuchelli smiled, or how his DF troopers looked as though they were some sort of superior breed, able to execute brave men at their own discretion.

He didn't even like the way Elena looked at him now, like he was some sort of alien creature. Didn't she understand?

The phrase from the orders echoed in his mind: ". . . the company is attached to the MMC and is therefore to be considered as though it is a part of the MMC.

"It is your responsibility to conduct yourself and your company accordingly."

He couldn't tolerate it. You don't let foreigners discipline your people; you don't let them hang your men. It's bad for morale; it's against the rules.

There was a technical way out. He could just freeze—he could just ignore it for now, he could just close his eyes for the moment and maybe try to reason with Zuchelli later. But there wouldn't be any way to stop Zuchelli in a few days; then, Company F would be Casalingpaesesercito troops once again, and both technically and practically under DF control.

Yeah. He could freeze again.

Protecting your people isn't just a technicality. There's nothing more real. But his pistol was in his holster, and it might as well have been a light-year away.

He was cornered, again. As he always would be, one way or the other.

He looked over at his brother. Tetsuo's blue eyes had gone vague; he deliberately didn't meet Ari's gaze. Tetsuo wasn't going to fire off a green flare, not this time.

Elena's brow was wrinkled. She should have been white-faced, terrified. She didn't get it, either.

Look, he wanted to say, *I can't let him get away with it. It doesn't matter how I feel about Stuarti. It's irrelevant. But I can't let the idiot you work for threaten my family, and for the time being he's family. We take care of our own. We have to.*

It should be so simple. All he would have to do was stop Zuchelli. But he knew that while he could start things, stopping them was something else entirely.

"Look!" Ari shouted, pointing with his left hand while he reached for his pistol with the other. "A green flare!"

It barely fooled anyone as the Distacamento de la Fedeltà soldiers went for their weapons. All but one was looking at him, not at where he was pointing.

But Shimon stepped back while Tetsuo and Dov stepped forward, and Stuarti and Matteotti brought their weapons up.

Tetsuo reached for one of the DFs while he booted another into Matteotti's line of fire. He only seemed to touch the DF he'd grabbed, but there was a bone-crack in sharp counterpoint to the *rrrip* of Matteotti's rifle.

"*Dov*," Ari shouted, clawing for the pistol that seemed glued in its holster, "leave Elena alone. Don't hurt her."

Stuarti shot Zuchelli in the chest and then turned to help Dov, but it was too late: the big man's three opponents were already down, broken like discarded dolls.

Ari had managed to thumb his safety off, work the slide and get a shot off, but he missed, as usual.

And then there were six bloody DF corpses dirtying the road, and a crowd of dirty, tired soldiers crowding around, panic written across their faces, looking at him . . . wanting something.

Elena lay crumpled on the ground with the rest of them.

Ari dropped to the dirt and knelt by her, feeling for a pulse. But her slim neck was bent at an impossible angle; Dov had gotten to her.

"*Dov*," Shimon said, "he told you to leave her alone."

"Maybe he should have told her not to go for her pistol," Dov said, kicking at her hand, toeing the automatic away from her dead fingers.

"Good point. Good boy."

Maybe Elena had been reaching for her pistol to help them, or maybe she had been reaching for her pistol to help Zuchelli, or maybe she had just been reaching for her pistol because everybody else was. Why didn't matter now. It would never matter.

What was the point, Elena? Why?

Ari wanted to shout at her, to lift her up and slap her awake, to *make* her tell him why, to make her take it back, but he couldn't. Not even the best commander nor the most convincing phony can breathe life back into the dead.

It hurt, but there was a cure for the hurt. It would have been so simple, so easy to bring up his pistol, point it at Dov and pull the trigger. Either he would kill the ugly bastard or Dov would kill him, and it would be all over.

No, that was silly. He had no chance of moving fast enough to kill Dov.

"No, you couldn't beat Dov." Shimon Bar-El's eyes could see everything. "I'm not going to make it that easy." Bar-El's eyes never left Ari's as he said, "You are not to harm Ari, Dov. No matter what he does. It's an order."

"Yes, Uncle Shimon."

Just at the edge of Ari's vision, Matteotti and Stuarti had squared off opposite Tetsuo.

"Ari, dammit," Paulo Stuarti said, "you'd better tell me what to do."

Shimon Bar-El smiled, "So, Ari, what will it be?" he whispered.

Kill Dov, kill Shimon, kill his brother, kill everybody in the whole damn universe, and it wouldn't breathe life back into Elena's chest. Throw everybody he knew on the pyre of his anger, and her breath would never be warm in his ear again, her mouth would never be wet and alive against his.

But, damn, killing that simian psychopath of Shimon's would feel good.

"Ari."

A real commander would tell his people to stand easy, would cut all their losses now.

Ari Hanavi let his gun hand drop down to the side. "Stand easy, the two of you. Matt—go make sure we're not interrupted. I need a minute to think."

"Captain—"

"*Go.*"

Reluctantly, his eyes never leaving Dov, Matteotti backed away, then turned, broke into a trot.

"This isn't a problem for junior officers," Shimon Bar-El said. "I'll handle it."

"Zuchelli's alive, Uncle Shimon," Dov said. "Want me to fix it?"

"Well, maybe—"

"It's Ari's command," Tetsuo said softly, and there was a grim note in his voice that brooked no argument. "This is my brother's command. You will wait for him—I swear, you *will* wait for him."

Stuarti grunted. "Count on it."

Zuchelli was still breathing as Ari knelt beside him. The Casa's chest pumped blood in a slow, idle fountain. His eyes were wide and filled with pain. His mouth worked in a silent plea.

This wasn't the same thing as charging through a town, shooting at vague shapes in the dark. You didn't have to look at their faces.

Bar-El towered over Ari and Zuchelli. "Friendly fire, Maggiore Zuchelli. Remember what you told me once? 'These things happen, as well you know,' " he said, his face a grim mask. "Well, Ari?"

"You leave my people alone," Ari said dully. He tried to bring up the pistol, but all the eyes stared down at him and he couldn't move. The Desert Eagle was a heavy pistol, but it wasn't supposed to be this heavy. He swallowed. "You leave my people alone."

"It was snipers," Shimon Bar-El said. "I'll fix it, Ari. We'll find some bodies. Giacometti will be here in a while, and he and I will set it all up. You just tell your men to keep their mouths shut; everything will be fine. You don't have to do this."

"Nobody will say anything, General," Paulo Stuarti said. "Nobody saw anything."

Ari couldn't move.

"Ari," Tetsuo said, gently, "it's a hard thing. You can let me do it. Or Dov."

"Captain Hanavi," Dov said, "I don't mind. Cold blood doesn't bother me."

No. He wouldn't leave it to Dov. A real commander wouldn't leave it to Dov, not when he could do it so easily himself.

"I take care of my own," Ari said, lifting the heavy pistol, putting the barrel against Zuchelli's head.

He wasn't sure whether he was talking to Bar-El, Tetsuo, Dov—or to Zuchelli. Or to Stuarti. Or himself.

He hoped he was talking to Shimon, Tetsuo and Dov, though. Talking to yourself never does any good; and there wasn't any more point in talking to Zuchelli than there would have been in talking to Elena.

The pistol kicked hard against his hand.

PART FOUR

STAFF

CHAPTER 19

Hero

Ari turned over command to Paulo Stuarti—Captain Paulo Stuarti, thanks to High Colonel Giacometti—a few hours later.

"A bit of free advice, Paulo, if you don't mind," he said as they walked down the street, past the rows of battered buildings, shattered windows open to the dust and air. The bodies of two Freiheimers lay in a dark puddle on the ground over by a doorway, the larger of the two reaching out toward the smaller, as though trying to protect him even in death.

"I'll take any advice I can get, Ari." Stuarti's hand reached for his shirt pocket, then clenched itself into a fist and dropped down to his side.

"Assume they're going to counterattack, and be more ready for them than they were for us."

Elena was dead, and that death was a sharp coldness inside him, but a real commander didn't wear his emotions on his face, so Ari Hanavi didn't wear his emotions on his face either.

"Nobody's ready for Company F." Paulo Stuarti grinned. The big blond man was stone cold sober now, and there was something of a strut in his walk.

Ari chuckled. He wasn't amused, not really, but a real officer would have chuckled.

Matteotti and Rienzi kept a discrete ten paces behind them while, ahead, a pair of fireteams from Romano's platoon kept watch. The bandage covering the right side of Rienzi's head was brown with caked blood, but he seemed alert. There were probably no Freiheimers left, at least along the eastern edge of Anchorville, but taking chances wasn't the order of the day.

What Ari Hanavi felt simply didn't matter. Fake it, Tetsuo had said, and it was that simple. A real commander would say something about taking care of the company.

"They're good men, Paulo. Not too long until the cease-fire—you take care of them, understood?"

He eyed Stuarti levelly, while the Casa decided whether or not to take offense at that. That didn't matter, either. Not a damn thing mattered.

"Of course." Stuarti's expression softened. "Understood, Ari."

"Good."

He looked down the street, at the rubble and the bodies, the shattered homes and lives. "You know," Ari said, "there's something I never thought to ask—what the hell is this war all about?"

Stuarti stopped. "You mean you don't know?"

"Nah." He shrugged. "It's never a big deal to Metzada."

"Well, it started when. . . ." Stuarti stopped himself. "Shit, Ari, do you care?"

Ari thought about it for a moment. "Not really. We do it for money, like all the other whores. How about you?"

"Well, yes, I do." Stuarti caught himself. "Well, no, I don't. Not at the moment. All I care about is getting the company through the next two weeks."

"Good answer."

Two skimmers were waiting up ahead, engines idling;

as they approached, the first of the skimmers—Giacometti's—lifted up on its skirts and slid away in a cloud of dust.

"This soldiering stuff pays you people real well, I take it," Stuarti said.

"That's not my department," Ari said. "Covers the bills, so they tell me."

Tetsuo stood in the door of the other skimmer. "Let's *move* it, little brother."

"Take care, Paulo." Ari turned to Matteotti and Rienzi. "Goodbye, the two of you."

"Take care of yourself, Captain," Rienzi said, clasping his hand for a moment.

"Damn mean trick, sir," Matteotti said, still smiling. His grip was firm.

"Well, I'm away." Ari turned and returned the salutes of Stuarti, Rienzi and Matteotti. "Well done, Company F," he said in a measured sort of way, the way a real commander would have.

He stepped into the passenger compartment and the door closed behind him, leaving him alone with Tetsuo, Dov and Shimon. Ari staggered to a seat and belted himself in as the skimmer lifted.

Beyond the dirty glass, he could see Stuarti waving goodbye, then beckoning to Matteotti, but then the skimmer turned and moved away and he couldn't see them anymore.

Ari looked over at Dov Ginsberg. The big, ugly man didn't look any different. Maybe he didn't know what it was like to love somebody, or maybe he didn't care.

Shimon Bar-El was eyeing him curiously over a lit tabstick. "There's all kinds of warrior's reflex," he said without any preamble. "Seems you got one, eh? Trouble is, that I don't quite know what to do with you. I can't read you out after this—you played it just right and took the town. Can't fault you for that.

"On the other hand," he went on, flicking ashes onto the floor, "you fucked up twice as an enlisted striker, so even if your head *is* on straight, you've got a problem reputation. Can't put you back in the ranks."

Tetsuo lit a tabstick and picked up the theme. "He sure as hell can't let you keep your commission and give you a company, or even a platoon—same reason. An officer has to have earned his command, and the consensus among Metzadans is that you haven't." Tetsuo smiled. It wasn't a pleasant smile, and it wasn't a report. "You would have made it easier on all of us if you'd gotten yourself killed, you know."

Ari looked from Tetsuo to Dov. "I suppose that still could be arranged." His hands were loose and empty on his lap, but if Shimon ordered Dov to kill him now, just maybe Ari could get his gun out and a bullet into the bastard. He would surely try.

"That's always a possibility." Shimon considered the glowing coal of his tabstick. "There's another choice. Since Avram Stein was killed, I find myself minus an aide-de-camp. The TO calls for a captain in that slot. Now," he said, holding up a hand, "don't speak too soon. You'll be on probation; all this will mean is just another chance.

"Or chances. Operation Triumphant is still running, and Generale Prezzolini has a real interesting job for the regiment. In another forty-eight hours, you'll be back in combat, right beside me. And Dov.

"Now, assuming you do get through the next couple of weeks alive, and we get our asses off this dirtball, you're still not safe. Next time we get an opportunity, you'll be presented as our specialist in commanding foreign troops, and get another chance to either build up a reputation. . . ."

"Or get killed," Ari said.

"Or get killed." Shimon shrugged. "One or the other will happen eventually, I bet."

"Or both," Tetsuo said.

Shimon waved him to silence. "Do we have a deal?"

Ari looked at him long and hard. It wasn't that he had any choice, but a real officer would have made the three of them sweat for a while, and Ari was going to spend the rest of his life impersonating a real officer.

"Deal," he said.

Yes, he was a spare part, newly machined, and put into a place where he would never quite fit. But if you had a part that didn't quite fit, you could always force it into place.

"You've got yourself an aide, General."

Shimon and Tetsuo visibly relaxed. Dov didn't look any different. Dov never looked any different.

They rode in silence for a while, then Tetsuo spoke up. "Ari? I'm sorry about the girl. I take it she meant something to you."

Yes, he wanted to say, she did, I loved her, and she's dead now. But that wasn't what the role called for.

"No big deal," Ari Hanavi said, feeling colder inside. "Doesn't matter."

"One more thing."

"What *is* it?"

"You going to tell Benyamin the whole story?"

Ari nodded. "I won't lie to Benyamin. Yes, I'll tell him everything."

"And what do you think Benyamin will say?"

Ari shrugged. "I don't think he'll say anything. I think he'll just smile."

He suddenly felt very old. He shut his eyes, leaned back, and tried to sleep.

Glossary

The following military terms may be of some interest and use. Some are standard terms, some are exclusively Metzadan, and some are standard terms that have been changed for the exigencies of the Metzadan situation.

[-]: Map notation for a tank, or a group of tanks.

1LT: Abbreviation for First Lieutenant, the middle-level company grade officer. The Metzadan insignia is two silver bars, worn on each shoulder or at the collar points. First lieutenants serve in low-level staff positions, command platoons, or are company commanders or execs.

2LT: Abbreviation for second lieutenant, the lowest-level commissioned officer grade in the MMC. The Metzadan insignia is a single silver bar. In many armies, a second lieutenant wears a single *gold* bar, proportioned (and colored) about like a stick of butter, hence the colloquial term "goddamn butter-bar" for a second lieutenant. Second lieutenants generally command platoons, although they may be company execs or the lowest-level staff officers.

administrative: The opposite of operational. The condition in which soldiers are not expected to shoot anybody, and will be disciplined for flourishing weapons about. Safety rules—involving loading of weapons, speed or altitude of flight, pre-emptive assault on innocent bystanders—are enforced.

aide-de-camp: General officers have the opportunity to name relatively junior officers as aides. An aide can act as a liaison, personal attendant, secretary, bodyguard and so on—varying quite a bit with the style of the general officer involved. The only common thread is that the aide is an assistant to the general, and not a deputy; he has no authority of his own, but may pass along orders from the general.

APC: Armored personnel carrier. Anything from a bus with reinforced sides to something that looks more like a tank, complete with main gun. An APC can run on wheels, tracks or fans. The main purpose of an APC is to move soldiers from point A to point B with some protection from fire, particularly small arms fire. One trouble with APCs is that, when there's shooting going on, infantrymen instinctively feel safer inside than outside. They're not.

arty: Slang for artillery. Also tubes, pipes, cocks.

Barak: Hebrew for "lightning." The standard Metzadan assault rifle, generally remanufactured to handle local ammunition.

basic training: The introductory course, designed to turn a civilian into a green soldier. *Not* a Metzadan usage; the Metzadan term is "school."

bat: Short for battalion. Never used for battery.

battalion: In an artillery unit, a group of three or more batteries under the same command. In an infantry unit, a group of three or more companies under the same command; a military organization of anywhere from about 700 to about 1200 officers and enlisted men.

battery: A group of artillery pieces, of the same type

and caliber, under the same command. Generally, a battery consists of six artillery pieces, operated by about fifty officers and enlisted men.

battery three: An order for each piece in an artillery battery to fire three times at the same target.

battle shock: Either quickly or slowly, getting shot at wears people down. You can figure an average of about 150 days of combat for most citizen soldiers before they're burned out and used up. Even if they're the good guys.

beaten fire zone: The territory that a weapon actually hits when fired. An autogun is usually the piece under consideration; the beaten fire zone tends to be elongated along the range axis (as opposed to the traversing axis) for reasons that are left as an exercise for the student. Cover is by definition not in a beaten fire zone, though concealment may be.

bounding overwatch: A sensible sounding maneuver which calls for two units to move by leapfrogging each other, usually at each other's flanks, separated by some distance perpendicular to the axis of travel. The lead elements take up hasty positions, signaling the trailing element to go forward and find their own hasty positions, and then switching off. Not really a good idea in relatively settled circumstances, but not bad when you expect that the enemy is on the run and won't have the time or inclination to set up a decent ambush. Other major problems are in maintaining control of the units, signaling accurately without arousing the enemy's suspicions, and making sure that when and if contact is made, the heroes to the rear at that time do *not* shoot at their teammates. (See *friendly fire.*)

brevet: A temporary promotion (or, in the MMC, possibly a demotion), used to make the promoted senior to officers who would otherwise be senior to him. If you want Second Lieutenant Shwartz to be able to order First Lieutenant Silverstein around, one easy way is to temporarily make him Captain Shwartz. Metzadan liaison officers, and frequently their enlisted assistants, are almost always brevetted to at least the same grade as their contacts in the hiring force. (See *negative brevet* and *French brevet*).

cadre: The permanent personnel at an installation or training unit, not expected to lead their trainees into combat. More colloquially, soldiers engaged in training other soldiers.

call sign: A tag name used, particularly during radio communication, which unambiguously identifies the parties to the conversation to each other. Ideally, the call sign is *not* intrinsically meaningful, in order to deny the enemy any information from intercepts or taps, and all requests and reports are encoded. "This is Fragrant Flower Four for Dustbin Three. Armadillo. Turnip. Eat my shorts," could be a request from a squad for more ammunition, an order from the commander-in-chief to attack at dawn, or a report from S4 on the number of condoms in stock. In practice, encoding is widely disregarded, as the convenience of simple communication is allowed to take precedence over the possible negative effects of the intercepts . . . until a disaster happens. Standard Metzadan practice is to keep much real-time communications in clear Hebrew, with a minimum of code, relying on encrypted communication (see *squash radio*) for sensitive matters.

captain (CPT): The highest company-grade officer rank. The Metzadan insignia is three silver bars, worn on the shoulder or collar points. Captains serve as staff officers or command companies.

captive of war: A legal term for a war prisoner of the lowest status possible.

Casalingpaesesercito (abbreviation, CPE): The army of Casalingpeasa, a nation-state on Nueva Terra.

chief of staff: The officer responsible for the coordination of the staff work of a major unit—usually a division or larger. A chief of staff of a brigade or smaller can be suspected of being in a makework post; small units usually just have the operations officer, with or without additional people working for him. In most armies, the chief of staff is the number three in the chain of command, after the commander and the deputy commander. The Metzadan policy is that the chief of staff is not in the chain of command.

claymore: Generic term for a remote-controlled anti-personnel mine, deployed above ground. The original claymore amounted to a curved piece of high explosive with several hundred ball bearings embedded in the convex face, with a well for inserting a detonator, wired to a remote triggering device. When the explosive was triggered by the operator, the ball bearings amounted to a very large and rather scattered group of buckshot. Claymores can also be used in booby traps as opposed to being actively triggered by an observer.

CO: Commanding officer. The guy in charge.

Colonel: The highest rank of field-grade officer. Insignia are three silver oak leaves, worn on the shoulder or collar points. Colonels command battalions and larger organizations, under the direction of a general, or serve in staff positions.

comm, commo: Communications. One of the three major parts of an army unit's mission: move, shoot, communicate. Communications are generally a two-edged sword: the better the commo, the easier it is to tap or intercept. Metzadan communication, being fairly sophisticated (and with real-time being done in Hebrew, a language familiar to few outside of Metzada) is relatively, but only relatively, secure.

CP: Command post. Normally set up behind the line, as opposed to the listening posts or forward observation posts, set up in front of the line.

CPE: See *Casalingpaesesercito*.

daisho: The traditional Nipponese paired swords, one long, one short.

deputy commander: The second in command. He has limited staff duties, and mainly serves as a second, subordinate commander. He's also the *spare* commander, in case the boss gets himself killed or cut off. Generally, he has pretty much unlimited authority to tell subordinate commanders "yes, sure, go ahead" but only limited authority to tell them "no, don't."

dogrobber: Colloquial for aide-de-camp.

Il Distacamento de la Fedeltà (abbreviation, DF): The overgrown Casalingpaeasan military police, which has judicial powers.

Exec: Second in command of a military unit, with staff duties. A combination of deputy commander and chief of staff. Colloquially, the deputy commander.

exit-pill: A suicide pill.

exsuit: A one-way waterproof exposure suit, designed to keep a man reasonably warm, and reasonably dry, in subarctic conditions.

Fairbairn dagger: A long, double-edged knife, designed solely for close combat, developed by Bruce Fairbairn, formerly Chief of Police of Hong Kong.

firefight: A small unit encounter with another small unit, when both are interested in closing with and destroying the enemy and neither has much interest in conserving ammunition. The opposite of an ambush, although a poorly executed ambush can turn into a firefight.

forward observer: The poor slob who gets to sneak up near the enemy and report corrections for artillery fire. He'd better keep his head down; he's the number one priority target of soldiers receiving artillery fire. He is also one of the lads who is religious about using correct radio procedures, and passionately devoted to commo security—because if he says he's on top of Old Smokey, instead of at Point Gimel, he's the fellow who is likely to get a quick cure in the form of enemy reconnaissance by fire.

freak: A radio frequency, either actual or (typically) virtual.

French brevet: A fictitious promotion.

friendly fire: Fire from supposedly friendly forces. Every bit as deadly as enemy fire. Bat Masterson once killed his deputy, quite by accident—and he wasn't the only one to have done it. "Friendly fire isn't."

Fundamentale: The Casalingpaesesercito basic training course.

G1, or adjutant: The personnel officer or department of a brigade or larger military unit.

G2: The intelligence officer or department of a brigade or larger military unit.

G3: The operations and training officer or department of a brigade or larger military unit.

G4: The logistics and supply officer or department of a military unit larger than a brigade. Probably the single most unappreciated specialty.

garrison: Opposite of "field." Garrison duty is that done out of fixed and more or less permanent positions, such as military bases or airfields.

general: The sole general officer rank in the MMC; a general is the only officer authorized to run an offworld contract. Insignia is a single star.

groceries: Colloquial for supplies.

green light: Authorization and direction to shoot someone or something, immediately. "You've got a green light on that asshole" means "Please shoot that person right now."

helo: Rotary wing aircraft; a helicopter.

herrenvolk: German for "master race." An archaic, sarcastic and unaffectionate term for humans of German descent.

integral: Part of, as opposed to attached. Mechanized infantry have trucks as an integral part of their organization, but would attach armor if they needed some.

khaki: 1. A dull, yellowish brown color. 2. Any Metzadan uniform other than mess dress, regardless of its color.

liaison officer: When you've got two different organizations trying to work together, you've got a problem. It's the job of the liaison officer to keep those problems to a minimum.

light colonel: Lieutenant Colonel

lieutenant colonel (LTC): The middle rank of field-grade officer. Lieutenant colonels are the commanders or execs of battalions, or serve as staff officers at the higher levels.

logistics: The art and science of getting the stuff—food, petrol, medical supplies, blankets, ammunition, and spare parts, including spare soldiers—to the right place at the right time.

loose deuce platoon: A two-tank tank platoon. The trouble is that it can too easily become a one-tank tank platoon.

maresciallo: A senior warrant officer rank in the Casalingpaesesercito, roughly equivalent to a chief warrant officer.

major (MAJ): The lowest level field-grade officer. Most majors serve as staff officers. The Metzadan insignia is a single silver oak leaf, worn on shoulder or collar points.

medic: A soldier, generally an NCO although sometimes an officer, who is also trained and detailed to provide first-aid and perform minor battlefield surgery.

medician: A battlefield surgeon/internist, although not a physician. He may be an NCO or an officer. In a medical context, a medician is senior to a medic in the way that a physician is senior to a nurse.

Mercenary's Toast: "Everybody comes back."

merkava: 1. Hebrew for "chariot." In general use throughout the Thousand Worlds to mean an armed military hovercraft mounting small-caliber automatic weapons and/or rockets. The usual plural is merkavas; the Metzadan plural is merkavot. 2. (Archaic): The main battle tank of the Israel Defense Force, circa 1990. Probably the most survivable tank of its time.

mortar: A small cannon, very short in proportion to its bore, which throws shells at high angles. Mortars are the infantryman's light artillery. The smaller ones are carried by infantrymen, and the larger ones are mounted on tanks, or hauled about by merkavas and jeeps.

moving overwatch: "You go first . . . I'll cover you from right behind. When you get to the limit of me covering you, stop. I'll go forward until I'm right behind you again, and then we'll do the same thing again." Faster than the bounding overwatch, as the folks behind can often both move and provide support at the same time.

NCO: Non-commissioned officer. Corporals and sergeants: enlisted men who command under the authority of an officer.

negative brevet, or Dutch brevet: A temporary demotion in rank, accompanied by a temporary increase of one-half step in pay grade for each rank demoted. The purpose is to give a critical job to the right person, who may be of the wrong rank. Personnel officers hate Dutch brevets, as it gives them major bookkeeping headaches, particularly with regard to the disposition of war loot.

nightgoggles: Active (bad) or passive (good) night vision devices. Infrared devices attract attention, and bullets, but are cheaper to manufacture. Devices that amplify ambient light rather than providing their own are more expensive, and require a higher level of technology, but better for those who don't like getting shot at.

OD: 1. Olive drab. An ugly green color, much beloved of some armies. 2. Officer of the day. An officer who is in charge of something—usually an installation of some sort—per order of the CO.

OP: Observation post, a place from which an enemy may be observed, and from where reports will be sent to a higher authority. It may be either overt or covert. The trouble with overt OPs is that the enemy tends to shoot at them.

operational: The opposite of "administrative," a state in which there is some serious expectation that there may be combat, and in which standard administrative rules—speed limits, loading of weapons, pre-emptive shooting of possible innocent bystanders—are ignored.

opcon: Operational control. The temporary placement of a resource under the authority of a local commander.

perp: Slang for perpendicular. Never used, even by Military Police, as a contraction for "perpetrator."

phut gun: A small-caliber pistol, equipped with a noise suppressor, shooting a subsonic bullet. Primarily used for assassination and as a backup weapon on reconnaissance.

pour encourager les autres: An old French expression meaning, literally, "to encourage the others," but more colloquially, "to discourage the others from screwing up." Generally, the reason you give for hanging slackers and cowards.

pravda: The official truth, presumptively different from the actual truth.

range card: The list of possible targets and traverse angles made by an autogun crew when emplaced. Primary purpose is to allow the relief crew, coming in at night, to be able to cope with a night attack before they've actually seen the territory. A secondary purpose is to keep everybody aware of areas that the autogun can't get at.

red light: Direction *not* to shoot someone or something, at least for the time being. E.g., "You've got a red light on the guy in the green uniform." Opposite of green light.

S1, or adjutant: The personnel officer or department of a military unit smaller than a brigade.

S2: The intelligence officer or department of a military unit smaller than a brigade.

S3: The operations and training officer or department of a military unit smaller than a brigade. When the unit doesn't have an exec, the S3 officer is generally third in line of command; in the smaller units the S3 generally is the exec. The S3 is the guy who gets to figure out how the battle is going to be fought, and—generally, Shimon Bar-El has always preferred to do it himself—writes up the orders. In a Metzadan regiment, the S3 is third in the chain of command.

S4: The logistics and supply officer or department of a military unit smaller than a brigade. The logistics officer is the fellow who makes sure that when the soldiers pull the trigger, not only is there ammunition for them to shoot, but there's been food for them to eat, and that they've had as recent a bath and change of clothes as is feasible.

sniper: A rifleman whose business it is to kill or wound enemy troops, primarily expecting success through better than average to superb marksmanship skills. He'd also better be real good at concealment: snipers are very much sought after targets.

stabsunderoffizier: A senior Freiheimer NCO rank, roughly equivalent to a staff sergeant.

squash radio: A device that will record transmissions, compress, encode and then transmit them on an assigned frequency or "freak," all of which is designed to minimize the possibility of interception.

stag: A work shift.

Ten: Metzadan communications designator for the second in command of a unit. If a company's call sign is Safed, the company exec's call sign will be Safed Ten. (See *call signs, Twenty*.)

TTD (Troop Training Detachment): A loose organization of approximately 250 Metzadan officers and men, which can be expected to train a foreign infantry force ranging in size from a battalion to a brigade.

Twenty: Metzadan communications code for commander of a unit. If C Company's call sign is Safed, C Company commander's call sign will be Safed Twenty. (See *Ten*.) If the first platoon of C Company's call sign is Safed One, the platoon leader will have Safed One Twenty as his call sign. More colloquially, the commander of a unit. ("Since when are you the Twenty around here?")

tube: The barrel of an artillery piece. Colloquially, the artillery piece itself.

Virgin: Somebody who has not been involved in combat.

VCP: Vehicle check point. Also known as a roadblock.

warrant: 1. Mild colloquialism for a warrant officer. 2. In Metzadan usage, a lateral promotion, particularly for combat specialists. This doesn't confer additional rank, but does nice things to one's pay voucher: a senior private with enough service time gets paid as much as his platoon leader. Warrants are also used to discourage people who are particularly competent at their jobs from seeking linear advancement for the sake of pay.

warrant officer: Not a Metzadan usage, but in other armies, a system of rank squeezed in between the highest level of noncommissioned officer rank, and the lowest level of commissioned officer ranks. Generally speaking, a man is promoted to warrant officer as a way of either giving him rank over senior NCOs *without* turning him into a goddamn butterbar, or so that an enlisted man can be required to perform functions usually restricted to the officer class, like flying helos.

weapons release: An authorization to fire at one's own discretion.

ROC BRINGS THE FUTURE TO YOU